PESTILENCE

(BREATHE IF YOU DARE)

BRIAN L PORTER

This work is dedicated to the memory of my mother, Enid Ann Porter (1914 – 2004). Her love and support never failed me, and to my wife Juliet, who supplies those commodities in our everyday lives together.

ACKNOWLEDGMENTS

Pestilence was originally published in January 2010. Recently, the book's original publisher sadly ceased trading and the book was left alone and bereft in the big wide world, together with my Jack the Ripper trilogy also published by the same company. As the majority of my books since those early days have been published by Next Chapter, (formerly Creativia) Publishing, I approached Miika Hanilla at Next Chapter, and he was delighted to accept *Pestilence* and my Jack the Ripper trilogy for publication by Next Chapter. I therefore owe him a big thank you for publishing this new, improved edition of *Pestilence,* complete with the superb new cover design, which differentiates it easily from the original.

My thanks also go to my researcher and proof-reader, Debbie Poole, who has worked extremely hard in going through and checking the original manuscript, page by page, eliminating a few errors which had crept past the book's original editor. It's a time-consuming and difficult task which requires meticulous attention to detail, and I can't thank her enough for her efforts in this regard.

As usual, I have to say thankyou to my dear wife, Juliet, who has exhibited inordinate patience while I've been at work on updating the book, which seems to have a special significance as the world currently finds itself in the grip of the deadly Coronavirus pandemic. To those who may have read the original edition of Pestilence, I hope you enjoy this new, updated edition, and for those coming to the book for the first time, I wish you the same.

INTRODUCTION

The English countryside is never typified more than by the beauty of many of the tiny villages and hamlets that lie dotted in the midst of its agricultural heartlands. Those villages, many dating back to the time of William the Conqueror or earlier times form that extraordinarily special backbone to the very 'Englishness' of the countryside. In many cases unaffected by progress and unchanging over the years these islands of peace within an otherwise frantically industrialised and heavy-industry driven economy often hark back to an era when life was lived at a slower pace, when neighbours could leave their doors open without fear of being robbed, and when everyone knew everyone else and the community cared for itself and each other as though the village itself were a living, breathing entity.

Every so often however, an event may take place that upsets and dislocates the unchanging equilibrium of even such idyllic locations. It may be fire, flood or pestilence, but it goes without saying that when such upheaval strikes life in those beautiful and tranquil havens may never ever be quite the same again.

What follows is the story of one such village, and of one such upheaval, and so we must take a short journey back in time to the year nineteen fifty eight, back to when it all began, to when death wore a new cloak, walked a new course, and the terror of a bygone age reached out to chill the hearts of those who crossed its path.

Author's note

The timing of the release of this edition of Pestilence is purely coincidental to the fact the world is currently in the grip of the Global Coronavirus pandemic. Hundreds of thousands of people have succumbed to this terrible illness and there are certainly some similarities between the reality and the fiction as presented in a small way in this book. Some of my associates have almost called the book prophetic, written as it was over ten years before the current pandemic. Any such similarity between the fictional events told of within these pages is entirely coincidental, though it cannot be denied that the feelings and emotions of the people of my fictional town of Olney St. Mary do without doubt chillingly mirror the reality as reported in the national and international press as we watch the horrors of the reality unfold. If this book carries a message it is simply...Stay safe, and happy reading!

CHAPTER 1

THE QUAINT AND PEACEFUL VILLAGE OF OLNEY ST. MARY HAD stood in its rural location for almost nine hundred years. Set in the tranquil Kent countryside, surrounded by vast swathes of hop fields that grew the crop for the beer that would quench a thousand thirsts, it had watched over the comings and goings of the centuries virtually untouched by time. The people of Olney had always lavished care on their village, isolated as it was by its pastoral surroundings. The nearest settlement to the village was the tiny hamlet of Bywater some twenty-five miles to the east, the nearest town, Ashford being nearly forty miles away. The coast lay to the south, a distance of just over forty-five miles as the crow flies.

It had been a Royalist stronghold during the long-ago days of the English Civil War when Cromwell had for a brief period of history established his Puritan Commonwealth in England's realm. As far as was known, however, no battles or even light skirmishes took place within fifty miles of the village.

Centuries later, a memorial was erected to commemorate and remember the lives of the fifteen men from the village who sacrificed their lives for their country during the great World conflagration of 1914-1918.

Later, during the Second World War Olney had been witness to an aerial dogfight during the Battle of Britain and a Messerschmitt Bf110 had been shot down by a defending Spitfire in the skies above the village, eventually crashing to the ground in flames just beyond the northern boundary of Olney in a field owned by Mr. Simon Parkes. The aircraft had been flying as an escort to a formation of German Heinkel bombers en route for London, and a great cheer went up from the local residents as they saw the aircraft hit the ground. The elation of those first on the scene was quickly tempered when they witnessed the fruitless struggles of the two unfortunate aircrew as they tried desperately to escape from the burning pyre that their aircraft had become. The remains of the German aircrew were later buried with due respect and reverence in the graveyard at St. Mary's church. German or not, they had been human beings, and the people of Olney were decent, God-fearing folk, who bore their fallen enemies no further malice. After all, the dead couldn't hurt them, could they? After that the village remained relatively untouched by the savagery of war, though rationing took its toll on the local businesses, and after the war another twenty names were added to the local war memorial. The sons of Olney St. Mary had once again stood tall and proud and given their all for King and Country.

As the nineteen fifties saw the world entering a new and relatively peaceful age the village regained its previous air of tranquillity, and little happened that could be described as newsworthy in the village of Olney. The remains of the crashed Luftwaffe Messerschmitt had been removed from Farmer Parkes' field by the RAF at the end of hostilities to be displayed in a museum and the field had been sold to the Parish council, where it had been turned into a playground for the local children. The fifties heralded the new consumer age, with washing machines, televisions and motor cars becoming the norm, rather than being the preserve of the wealthy or the middle classes. Work was plentiful, and though small, Olney St. Mary prospered. The majority of its working population were involved in one of the two main local industries; farming, or barrel making. A team of coopers still produced hand-made barrels for the brewery industry according to the methods laid down centuries earlier. Indeed, there would be little to distinguish between a twentieth century Olney-made barrel and one produced in the days of Cromwell's Parliament.

The tiny school, the church and the local pub, The Beekeepers Arms were the focal points of village life, and Sam Bradley's garage was the only place from which the locals could obtain cars, tractors and the spare parts for both. His was also the only petrol pump to be found for miles around, the profits from the sale of said petrol making Bradley one of the wealthier men in Olney.

Bradley had been excused war service due to his having been born with a club foot, though this didn't prevent him from growing up to be a tall and handsome young man who had no problem in his relationships with the opposite sex. He'd married during the war, and his wife Emily had given birth to their first child, a son, in 1944. David Bradley took after his father; he was a good-looking boy, taller than most of his contemporaries, and the child always seemed happy, the smile seemingly painted upon his cheery face. Two years later, a daughter followed whom the couple named Christine, and for the Bradleys, life was good. Sam's business prospered and the children were both healthy and strong, and popular amongst the other children of the village.

Young David spent much of his time in the company of his best friend Evan Parkes, one year his senior. Evan was the grandson of Simon Parkes and lived with his grandparents on the farm. Evan's father Michael had been one of the unfortunate sons of Olney who had perished fighting for his country during the conflagration of World War Two, being cut down by enemy mortar fire as he played his part in the battle to free France from the yoke of Hitler's tyranny. Michael's was one of the twenty names that were freshly engraved on the war memorial when peace returned to Europe and the world. Evan's mother Deirdre, never the strongest of women had become pregnant with Evan during one of her husband's last leave periods before his death and Michael had died in action without ever having seen his baby son. Deirdre had found life unbearable after the reported death of her husband, and she died in 1946 from what the locals described to each other as a broken heart. In fact, Deirdre had contracted viral influenza, and her body had been unable to cope with the ravages of the disease, thus leaving her young son in the care of his grandparents Simon and Ellen Parkes.

David and Evan played together almost every day and were seen together so often that a casual visitor might have mistaken them for brothers. Football, cricket, games of make-believe, of cowboys and Indians, the imagination of the two youngsters took them on a roller-coaster ride through childhood, and they became two of the most popular children at the tiny village school, where their teacher Eileen Devenish was always delighted with their schoolwork and good behaviour. As they moved into their teens, their education became the responsibility of Mr. Eric Padley who taught Olney's children of secondary school age. Both boys continued to be the best of friends, and to excel at their studies.

As the boys and their peers grew towards adulthood life in Olney thus proceeded in its usual idyllic fashion for those fortunate enough to live within its boundaries.

In 1958 the usual calm of Olney was disturbed by the death of the village's long serving general practitioner, Doctor Harold Meddings at the age of seventy. Meddings had been the doctor in the village for as long as most people could remember and the whole village turned out to attend his funeral in the tiny church, the service being conducted by Timothy Grafton, vicar of St. Mary's. Three weeks after the funeral the new doctor arrived to take over the deceased Meddings' duties. Sent at the request of the parish council by the local health authority based in Ashford, Doctor Hilary Newton's arrival set tongues whispering in Olney from her first day in the village. Doctor Newton was young, female, and pretty, a combination guaranteed to ruffle a few feathers in the previously staid village. With her long hair styled in the fashion of forties movie pin-up Veronica Lake the new doctor instantly became the object of any number of schoolboy crushes, not to mention raising the blood pressure of most of the adult population of Olney. Many of the older residents of the village passed less than complimentary comments on the appointment of a woman as their new doctor and for many weeks Hilary Newton's daily surgery was marked by a distinct lack of the elderly patients who had made up the bulk of old Doctor Meddings' regular clients. The young doctor was painfully aware that she would have a real job on her hands in gaining the respect and the trust of her new patients. Time of course would play a part, as eventually even the elderly residents of Olney would need the care of a qualified medical practitioner. They couldn't treat themselves with aspirin and old-wives remedies for ever.

Unfortunately for the new incumbent in the post of general practitioner to the people of Olney St. Mary that time was rapidly running out. Her services, and her medical knowledge were about to be tested to the full and she would have to work more than extremely hard if she were not to be found wanting!

CHAPTER 2

THE FIRST HINT OF THE TROUBLE THAT WAS YET TO COME IN Olney St. Mary came by way of a telephone call from Sam Bradley to the new doctor one sunny Tuesday evening. Hilary Newton was just filing the last of her patient record cards away after a particularly quiet evening surgery. Two sore throats, a newly diagnosed pregnancy and a strained back made up the sum total of the calls on her medical training that day.

She reached out to lift the jangling telephone receiver, never realising that that one call was about to change the lives of everyone in the village.

"Doctor Newton," she announced to the as yet unknown caller.

"Doctor, we haven't met yet but my name's Bradley, Sam Bradley. I own the garage in the village."

"I know who you are Mr. Bradley. I've seen you around and someone told me who you were in case I needed my car repaired in the future. What can I do for you?"

"It's my son doctor, young David. He came home from school complaining of feeling unwell and he seems to be running a temperature. He's complaining of feeling cold despite his body heat and he's coughing a lot and seems short of breath."

"Hmm, sounds like he could have a dose of the 'flu Mr. Bradley. Listen, you keep him warm and give him plenty of fluids to drink and I'll be over to see him in a few minutes. I've just a couple of things to clear away here at the surgery and I'll be right over. You live in the house behind the garage, don't you?"

"That's right Doctor, and thanks."

"Don't worry Mr. Bradley. I'm sure David will be just fine."

Five minutes later Hilary Newton picked up her ubiquitous black 'doctor's bag', locked the surgery door and got behind the wheel of her Ford Prefect. The little beige car wasn't quite as imposing as the old Austin Princess that Meddings had driven but it suited her. Though it was only half a mile from the surgery to the Bradley house she thought it would appear more professional if she appeared on call in her car rather than on foot.

Sam Bradley met her at the door to his home. His wife Emily, he explained, was upstairs sitting with David in his bedroom. Bradley informed the doctor that in the last few minutes David had begun to complain of pain in the muscles of his arms and legs, and that he felt as weak as a kitten. Hilary asked the man to show her to his son's bedroom.

Young David Bradley looked awful! It was evident to the doctor that the boy was in some discomfort from the pains that he'd been complaining of. He seemed to be trying to lift his aching arms and legs from the bed, as though being in contact with the soft mattress was in itself a cause of agony to the boy.

"Here's the doctor David, you'll soon feel better now, son" came the consoling words from his mother. A little overweight and with a shock of mousey brown hair that desperately needed a perm, Emily Bradley looked as though she were about to burst into tears at any moment. Her son was ill, and she wore the worried and anxious look of mothers all around the world when they think their child is in danger from some unknown source.

Moving right up to the boy's bedside Hilary placed a thermometer under the boy's tongue with her right hand while placing her left hand on his forehead. She barely needed to wait for the mercury to rise in the thermometer to ascertain that the boy had a high fever. When she removed the thermometer and took a reading, she was appalled to find that the boy's temperature was a hundred and two degrees. This was one very poorly young man. David shivered despite his temperature.

"I feel really cold, Doctor," he said through gritted teeth. "I hurt all over."

"Don't you worry David. We'll soon get you sorted out."

"Is it influenza then, Doctor?" asked the boy's mother.

"Quite probably, Mrs. Bradley. I'll give David something to help bring his temperature down and you must make sure he takes on plenty of fluids to prevent dehydration." She passed a small supply of white tablets to the boy's mother.

"Panadol," said the doctor. They contain paracetamol, a new drug that helps to reduce fever. David is old enough to take it. Give him two tablets now, two more at bedtime, and repeat the dose when he wakes in the morning. I'll be back to see him tomorrow. Try to keep him calm, Mrs. Bradley. You might try wiping his brow with a cool wet towel to give him some relief from the fever symptoms as well."

"Right then, Doctor and thank you. You see David; it's just a dose of 'flu. You'll be right as rain when the doctor's tablets start to work. Isn't that right Doctor?"

"Let's just hope that David is feeling much better by the time I come to see him tomorrow."

As she was about to leave the house Sam Bradley approached her and asked

"What did you say those pills are called, doctor?"

"They contain Paracetamol Mr. Bradley. It's relatively new and was introduced three years ago. It's been clinically trialled and tested and believe me it's much kinder to the stomach than aspirin, which can cause all sorts of problems in someone as young as David."

"Well, you're the doctor. I must say we don't hold with all these new-fangled things here in this part of the world, Doctor Newton."

"It's a simple pain killer Mr. Bradley, what we call an analgesic. It's also the best drug on the market to help reduce his temperature. I promise you it won't harm David in any way. Now, why don't you go and see your son? You and your wife should take it in turns to sit with him through the night, just in case his temperature rises any further. If it does you must send for me right away, do you understand?"

Sam Bradley appeared to be mollified by the doctor's words and allowed himself to relax a little.

"Right then, if you're sure Doctor. We can call you at any time if he takes a turn for the worse?"

"Any time at all Mr. Bradley, I mean it. Now, I'll bid you goodnight. As I said I'll be back to see David in the morning, right after surgery."

"Yes, okay. Goodnight, Doctor Newton."

It took Hilary less than five minutes to drive the half mile to her home. During those minutes she reflected on the state of her latest patient. That David Bradley was ill she was in no doubt about. That it was influenza she was reasonably sure about, though she had the terrible feeling that she might be witnessing the manifestation of a new strain of the killer bug. Influenza had been responsible for millions of deaths throughout the history of mankind and the 'flu virus had developed an uncanny means of mutating from time to time, developing new and more powerful biological weapons in its global war against the human race. Hilary knew that if this was indeed a new strain that had found its way to Olney, then she would need help from outside. Of course, she knew that it was early days and that the last thing she should do was panic. Tomorrow was another day, and she would see how David Bradley was as soon as her morning surgery was over.

As she unlocked her front door and pushed it open, she could hear the incessant ringing of the telephone from within.

Rushing to answer it in case it was Sam Bradley with news of a sudden rise in David's temperature she snatched the phone from its cradle.

"Hello?"

"Is that the doctor?" asked an anxious and unknown voice.

"Yes, this is Doctor Newton. Who's speaking please?"

"Doctor Newton. This is Simon Parkes at Birtles Farm. Can you come to see my grandson right now, please Doctor? He's very ill, boiling up he is, and shivering at the same time and..."

"It's alright Mr Parkes. Listen, keep him warm and I'll be there in just a few minutes. I've just visited the Bradley boy and he has the same symptoms. I think we're looking at a case of influenza. I'm sure it looks much worse that it really is. Don't worry, please, I won't be long."

"David Bradley?" asked the farmer. "He and Evan are best friends, doctor. Do you think they've both picked up the same bug?"

"I'll know better when I get there Mr. Parkes. Now, if we can get off the phone?"

"Oh yes, sorry Doctor. We'll be waiting."

The drive to Birtles Farm took a little longer than the one to the garage. It took Hilary Newton almost ten minutes to reach the farm gate, and another three minutes to slowly navigate her way along the long dirt track that led up to the farmhouse. Simon Parkes was waiting on the step that led into his home when Hilary pulled her Ford Prefect to a halt and stepped from the car.

The next few minutes were a virtual repeat of her earlier visit to the Bradley home. Ellen Parkes was made of sterner stuff than Emily Bradley. Perhaps being a farmer's wife and being used to the occasional illness amongst the animals on the farm, she was a little more hardened and able to cope with her grandson's sickness.

"Right Doctor, what do you think?" she asked after Hilary had spent five minutes closely examining young Evan Parkes.

"I can't say for certain, Mrs. Parkes, but I think it's influenza. He's showing the same symptoms as David Bradley and your husband says that they're best friends. They could have picked up the influenza virus from the same source if they've spent a lot of time together recently."

"A lot of time together? Those two boys are virtually inseparable Doctor, always have been."

"That would certainly explain them both succumbing to the virus at the same time Mrs. Parkes. Now, I'm going to give you some tablets that should help to bring Evan's temperature down and ease the pains in his muscles. I'm going to call back and see him in the morning, as soon as I've been back to see the Bradley boy. Don't you worry; we'll soon have Evan on his feet again."

Ellen Parkes nodded at the doctor and turned towards her grandson.

"Thanks Doctor. Now you be a good boy and do as the doctor tells you, Evan. You must rest and take these tablets she's prescribed for you."

"Yes Nan," said the boy. His voice seemed quite feeble and it was evident that he was struggling to speak, perhaps because of the soreness in his throat.

As she sank into a chair in her house soon afterwards Hilary Newton looked up at the clock on the wall. It was ten o'clock. Between the two house calls she'd spent three hours ministering to her two young patients. She was exhausted after a long day in the first place, now she was ready for a hot drink and bed.

After a cup of cocoa Hilary Newton made her way upstairs to the bathroom, where she washed and changed into her favourite pink nightie, which was hanging on a hook behind the door, and then to her bedroom. As she lay in bed she tried to think if she'd missed anything that might have helped her in her diagnosis of the two young boys that evening. In her last few seconds of cognitive thought, before she was overtaken by the dark and welcome blanket of sleep Hilary decided that she'd done all she could for the boys. If it was influenza, and she was relatively certain of her diagnosis, then she was comforted by the thought that the disease was admirably treatable. Medical science had moved by leaps and bounds since the 1918 influenza pandemic which had swept around the world like one of the four horsemen of the apocalypse, leaving millions dead in its wake. No, the two boys would soon be up and running again. She was sure of that.

The events that were to follow over the next few days were to prove Hilary Newton catastrophically and tragically wrong.

CHAPTER 3

HILARY ROSE AT SIX A.M. HER NIGHT HAD BEEN UNDISTURBED by further telephone calls, so she assumed that the two boys she'd treated the previous night were either improving, or at least their symptoms had grown no worse during the hours of darkness. She washed her hair and was grateful that she'd bought the new electric hairdryer from a department store in Ashford before moving to Olney. There were no such luxuries available in the Olney St. Mary general store, the only retail establishment in the village apart from a small newsagent which was located adjacent to Bradley's garage. The dryer was noisy but effective, and her hair was dry in minutes.

Downstairs, she filled the kettle and placed it on the gas hob in the kitchen. While it boiled, she prepared her usual bowl of cornflakes, sprinkled with a dusting of sugar. She sat down to her breakfast and had almost finished the cornflakes when the kettle began its cheery whistle on the stove to inform her that the water had boiled. Hilary poured the boiling water onto the tea leaves which were waiting in the bottom of the tea pot, and two minutes later she poured herself a delicious cup of her favourite morning tea.

She made her way back upstairs to her bedroom, pausing long enough on the upstairs landing to peep into her spare bedroom, which currently acted as a repository for her as yet unpacked belongings, still stored in boxes on the floor. The room also contained the remaining items that had belonged to the late Dr. Meddings. They would be collected by his niece at some date in the near future, or so Hilary had been informed. She made a mental note to start sorting out her things very soon. She had yet to totally personalise the cottage which housed her surgery. It was of a decent size, with two bedrooms, a kitchen and three living rooms downstairs, one of which acted as her waiting room, another doubling as the consulting room which contained all the medical paraphernalia associated with a doctor's place of work, down to the skeleton hanging on a metal frame in one corner of the room. Hilary had noticed that the skeleton was positioned in such a way that it appeared to be 'looking' at the eye test chart which was tacked to the wall directly opposite its location. More than anything, the rent on the cottage surgery was cheap by the standards of the day, just five pounds a week, and Hilary had been only too pleased to accept the position of general practitioner in the village of Olney. Where better to begin one's solo career as a G.P.?

In her room once more she dressed for the day ahead. Knowing that she would soon be visiting Birtles Farm once more, she decided to forego her usual formal attire for the morning surgery. Leaving her dress and jacket on their hangers in the wardrobe, she instead selected a beige polo necked sweater and a pair of tan trousers and topped the ensemble off with a pale brown cardigan. She extracted a pair of as yet unused green wellington boots from the bottom of her wardrobe. She'd change into them at the farm. She applied a hint of eye shadow and lipstick and checked her appearance in the mirror which stood on a swivelling stand on the dressing table. She'd do!

Morning surgery began at eight thirty, and when Hilary peered into the waiting room, she saw that she had only two patients waiting to take advantage of her professional services. Seventy-year-old Mrs. Eileen Docherty had been to see Hilary the previous week. Doubtless she required further reassurance that her arthritis wasn't about to lead her sudden demise. The second person waiting was equally as old as Mrs. Docherty, but the lady was unknown to Hilary. She'd soon find out her name of course once surgery began.

Hilary nodded and said a cheerful "Good morning" to her patients and went through the waiting room into her consulting room. She'd barely sat down in her chair behind the old mahogany desk when the phone began its infernal jangling.

"Doctor Newton," she answered.

"It's Sam Bradley, Doctor Newton. I know you said you'd be calling after your surgery finished but I think you should come right now if possible."

"Is David worse, Mr. Bradley?"

"Yes Doctor, he is. He seemed OK all through the night, and then this morning he started to complain that the pains in his muscles were getting worse. He can't stop shivering, though his body is red hot to the touch, and he's developed a cough that sounds as though his lungs are full of liquid. We're very worried; please can you come straight away? His mother is frantic with fear."

The mother wasn't the only one, thought Hilary. She could sense the man's fear as she listened to him describing the boy's symptoms.

"I'll be right there Mr. Bradley. Tell your wife not to panic. I'm sure we'll soon have David stabilised. It might just be a case of his fever breaking, a crisis point after which his temperature will begin to fall, and he'll start his recovery."

Even as she spoke the words, Hilary herself feared that she may have been wrong in her initial diagnosis of young David Bradley, but if she had been, then what could be causing his symptoms? He'd shown all the classic hallmarks of a bad case of influenza the night before, but the cough and strange sounds coming from his lungs worried her more she dared let on to the boy's father.

"OK Doctor, and thank you." said the garage owner as he hung up the phone on her. Whether he trusted her or not Hilary couldn't be sure, but Sam Bradley knew that at that point in time Hilary Newton was the only option open to him in his efforts to make his son well again.

"I'm sorry ladies, but I have to leave to attend an emergency. Can I ask you to come back and attend the evening surgery?"

The two elderly ladies in the waiting room looked aghast as Hilary breezed into the room with her black bag in hand.

"But, what about my arthritis?" asked old Mrs. Docherty, "And Mrs. Henshaw here is having terrible trouble with her varicose veins."

At least Hilary now knew the name of the mystery patient.

"Look ladies, I really am deeply sorry, but I have a very sick young boy to attend to and I must go, now! Please come back later."

Hilary Newton didn't look back as she exited the surgery door. She knew that she'd probably done irreparable damage to her relationship with two of her elderly patients, but varicose veins and arthritis could wait. By the sound of his father's phone call, David Bradley's problems couldn't. After she'd gone the two old ladies sat dumbfounded in the waiting room for a few minutes before rising to leave. Nothing like this had ever happened to them before. Eileen Docherty remarked to her lifelong friend Polly Henshaw that.

"This would never have happened if they'd sent us a man to replace Doctor Meddings. You just can't trust these young girls to be as professional as a man, that's what I say."

"Quite right, Eileen. Who ever let women become doctors anyway? Doctoring is man's work, that's what it is. So much for the bloody National Health Service."

It quite escaped the two women that they both shared the same gender as the young woman they were so intent on maligning. Mind you, they would have probably said "That's different", if pressed on the matter; such was the mindset of their generation.

As the two walked down the street towards their respective homes Eileen Docherty shouted to her friend as they parted.

"It was the war, Polly, that's what did it. Not enough men, so they let these slips of girls do a bit of training and now they can call themselves doctors."

Her friend nodded and waved, and the two women were soon ensconced in their cosy cottages brewing tea and bemoaning the fact that of all things, they had a woman doctor to contend with in Olney St. Mary.

When she arrived at the Bradley house, Hilary was shown straight up to David's sick room by his worried looking father. One look at the patient was enough to tell Hilary that she was now dealing with a terribly ailing young man. Beads of sweat were dotted on his brow, though the boy was shivering as though chilled to the bone. When she took his temperature, she found it had risen by one degree from the previous night, but the thing that worried Hilary most of all was the cough. It was as his father had described on the phone. The boy had developed a 'liquid' cough that spoke of massive lung congestion.

"Look, Doctor."

The boy's mother held a towel out in Hilary's direction. She could see flecks of blood on it.

"He started to cough it up a few minutes ago, and he says he feels dizzy."

The young doctor was now seriously worried about her patient. His rapid deterioration indicated to Hilary that the boy was suffering from something rather more serious than influenza, though what it could be she felt unable to decipher at the time. She could discount bronchitis, pneumonia and a whole raft of other diseases or infections affecting the lungs and the bronchial tract as his symptoms were far more radical than would be found in any of those. Being able to eliminate the things that it couldn't be was all very well, but none of that helped her in diagnosing the true nature of what ailed young David Bradley.

As she watched it became obvious that the boy's breathing was becoming more laboured. He coughed again, and blood spattered the bedclothes. Hilary needed to think quickly. Her options were extremely limited. Should she continue to treat the boy 'blind' in the hope that she could discover the cause of his illness and apply a cure, or should she call for an ambulance and have David admitted to hospital in Ashford forty miles away? At least there the doctors could administer the necessary clinical and pathological tests to determine the nature of David's illness.

"May I use your telephone please, Mr. Bradley?" she asked. "I'd like to speak to someone at the hospital in Ashford to determine whether we should admit David for tests."

"Do you really think that's necessary Doctor, to admit him to hospital I mean?"

"It may be the best thing for David, Mr. Bradley, and until I can be absolutely certain what it is we're dealing with here I'd rather not take any chances with your son's health."

Emily Bradley, sitting in a chair beside her son's bed looked imploringly at her husband.

"Sam, let the doctor send him to hospital if she thinks it's for the best. We just want David to get well again, don't we, son?" she directed her last words to young David as she clutched the boy's hand reassuringly.

David appeared almost too feeble to speak, and merely nodded weakly at his mother.

"Do whatever you think necessary, Doctor," said Bradley.

Five minutes later Hilary was connected to Doctor Paul Trent, a consultant and a specialist in respiratory diseases at the Ashford General Hospital.

"I don't like the sound of it, Hilary," said Trent, who'd known Hilary from her days as a junior house doctor at the hospital, after hearing her full description of David Bradley's symptoms.

"It sounds too virulent and far too fast in its physical attack on the boy's system to be a simple case of the flu. Listen, I'll arrange for an ambulance to get over to Olney St. Mary right away. You have the boy ready when it gets there, and we'll have him admitted for in depth tests to try to ascertain what's causing this."

"I forgot to mention that I have a second case Paul."

"What?"

"Yes, another boy, similar age, the two patients are best friends, rarely apart apparently. I'm going to visit him as soon as I can make David comfortable here. I'm hoping that he hasn't deteriorated in the night as well."

"Look Hilary, whatever this is, I think you ought to prepare the other boy's parents as well. Tell them that we might need to have their son transferred here to Ashford along with the other boy. Do the second patient's parents have a telephone?"

"Yes, and it's the grandparents actually."

"Very good. Here's what I want you to do. If the second boy is as poorly as the first one when you get there, you ring the Bradley house and tell them to direct the ambulance to wherever the second patient is. I'll make sure the ambulance crew are aware that they might have a second pick up to make."

"Thanks Paul, I appreciate your help."

"Don't give it another thought Hilary. If you've got something nasty in the air around that picturesque little village of yours then we'd best find out and deal with it sooner rather than later, don't you think?"

"Of course. I don't want to start losing patients when I've hardly got my feet under the table in the village, do I?"

"Exactly. Now, off with you and attend to your patients, Doctor. I'm going to get that ambulance on its way to you."

"OK, Paul. Like I said, thank you."

Evan Parkes was, if anything, in a far worse condition than David Bradley when Hilary arrived at the farm. It took her less than a minute to decide that he too should be sent to the hospital in Ashford. She used the Parkes' telephone to call the Bradley house and instructed Sam Bradley to direct the ambulance crew to Birtles Farm after they had safely loaded David into the ambulance.

Two hours later Hilary waved the ambulance away from the farm with her two young patients aboard. She hoped that it wouldn't take Paul Trent too long to isolate and identify the cause of the two boy's illness. Unfortunately, events were about to take a turn for the worse.

When the telephone rang in her office ninety minutes later, she rushed to answer it, assuming it to be Doctor Trent with an initial report on the boy's arrival at the hospital. It was indeed Trent on the phone, but the news he had to relate to her was of the worst possible kind.

"Hilary, I'm sorry," he said, "but Even Parkes died in the ambulance on the way here. David Bradley is hanging on, but I must warn you, it doesn't look good for him either. I need to work fast to try to find out what the hell this is, so please, I need to go. I'll call you when I have more news."

"Yes, right Paul. Thank you," Hilary spoke into the mouthpiece, but Trent was already gone.

She sat in her chair for over twenty minutes, unable to comprehend what had happened. Two young boys, healthy and fit up until a couple of days ago had suddenly been struck down by something she had been unable to identify or treat. Now, one was dead and another close to death if Trent's words were accurate.

Eventually, Hilary Newton rose from her chair and took a deep breath. Whether she liked it or not, and with no real idea of what she was going to say, she made her way to the door. She had a terrible and unwanted visit to make.

CHAPTER 4

"BUT I THOUGHT YOU SAID IT WAS ONLY THE FLU," CRIED
Ellen Parkes, her earlier veneer of stoical acceptance of Evan's
illness having totally evaporated with the news of her grandson's
death.

Her husband stood by her side, one arm around his wife and a
look of shock etched deeply into his rugged features. Hilary had
driven straight to their house after receiving the phone call from
Paul Trent and there had been no easy way for her to inform the
couple that their beloved grandson had died en route to the
hospital. Now she had to cope with the consequences of the
grief her news had generated.

"That's what I thought initially, Mrs. Parkes, and it might still
prove to be influenza."

"I didn't think people still died from that," said Simon Parkes,
speaking very quietly.

"For the most part they don't, Mr. Parkes but there are some
strains of the 'flu virus that are more virulent than others, and
we're only now discovering that there are new variants evolving
all the time. We just don't know if this could be one of them.

We'll know more when the doctors at Ashford have had a chance to do tests on David Bradley and on..."

"On Evan's body? That's what you were about to say wasn't it, Doctor?"

"Yes, Mr. Parkes. I'm afraid it'll be necessary to conduct a post-mortem examination. It's the law in the case of a sudden and unexplained death. Without it the doctors can't issue a death certificate you see."

Ellen Parkes was sobbing almost uncontrollably by then. Hilary realised that this woman had lost her son and daughter-in-law to the ravages of war, and now their legacy to her and her husband in the form of their son had also been wrenched away from her by the as yet unknown disease that had come upon him so suddenly. She felt an enormous sympathy for Ellen and her husband, in addition to a heavy burden of responsibility for what had happened to Evan.

Had she missed something in her original diagnosis? Could she have been more thorough in her evaluation of his condition? Should she have known what it was that ailed the boy? All of these questions were running through her mind whilst at the same time she tried to find the right words with which to console the grieving couple, if indeed there were such things as the 'right words' to use on such occasions.

"He was so young, so fit." This came from Simon Parkes.

"He had everything to live for, Doctor," added his wife.

"I know," Hilary said quietly, trying to keep the couple as calm as she could.

"I also know that there's nothing I can say at the moment that will help you, but the important thing is to try and find out what caused this dreadful thing to happen to Evan and to poor David, and hope that we can find a way to stop it happening to anyone else."

Simon Parkes was ready to speak, but at that moment Hilary noticed a shudder run through his body as though the emotion was proving too much for his usual 'stiff upper lip' façade. He might be a rugged and tough farmer of the land, but he was human after all. Fighting back tears that had suddenly welled up in his eyes he tried his best to respond to Hilary's last words.

"We know you're right, Doctor, but whatever it was that killed our Evan, finding out about it won't bring him back will it? I'm sorry that David is suffering as well, don't get me wrong, but I can't think past Evan right now, and neither can my wife. If you don't mind, I think we'd prefer it if you left now. We'd like to be on our own."

"Yes, please Doctor, we don't blame you. You did your best I know that, but it wasn't enough was it?"

Ellen Parkes words struck deep into Hilary's heart. *It wasn't enough, was it?*

She could think of no appropriate response to that grief laden accusation, though she realised that it hadn't been meant unkindly. The thing she'd learned very quickly about these country folk was that they spoke pretty much as they thought and often the use of diplomacy was an alien concept to their mentality. No, Ellen Parkes wasn't being hurtful in her remarks, she was simply being truthful according to the way she saw things.

"Right, well, I'll go then," Hilary said after a pause. "I'll be in touch as soon as the hospital let me know anything about the results of the tests."

"The results of the post-mortem don't you mean Doctor?" asked Simon Parkes.

"Well, yes."

"I should have gone with him in the ambulance," Ellen sobbed as her husband showed Hilary to the door. As she walked the few yards to her car she looked back to see the farmer holding his sobbing wife in his great, strong arms, and from the movement of his shoulders it was clear that he had waited only until Hilary had left the house before allowing his own emotional floodgates to open.

Thinking it was impossible to feel more wretched than she did at that moment, Hilary drove slowly back to her surgery. Almost fearing the consequences of what she might hear she nevertheless felt compelled to phone Ashford General as soon as he got back into the house. Paul Trent wasn't optimistic.

"The boy is barely hanging on Hilary. We've run a whole battery of tests and I've asked for the results to be rushed through as fast as possible, but at the moment nothing seems to be slowing down the progression of the disease. If it is 'flu then it's the most destructive and virulent strain of the disease I've ever seen in my life. I've asked Malcolm Davidson, head of my department to take a look at young David. He's just finishing his daily rounds and then he'll be joining me. I have a wild theory about this, but I'd rather not discuss it until I'm sure."

"What sort of wild theory Paul? You can't just throw that at me and then expect me not to want to know what you're thinking."

"Listen Hilary, let's just say that if I'm right, and I hope to God I'm not, then you've got a *very* serious problem on your hands down there. If I'm wrong, then I'm the only one who'll have egg on his face. Davidson will help me confirm or deny my theory when he sees the boy, then I'll get back to you."

"Paul, you can't do this to me!"

"Davidson will be here soon, Hilary. In the meantime get your textbooks out. Look up the symptoms in detail, particularly the rapid onset and progression of the disease. You might get some idea of how I'm thinking that way. I'll be in touch again soon, I promise."

Before Hilary could protest further, Paul Trent replaced the receiver and the line went dead.

"Damn you, Paul Trent," she shouted aloud into her empty consulting room, before reaching behind her to the bookshelf where her medical dictionaries and textbooks waited invitingly for her to explore this strange medical phenomenon that had struck at the young men of Olney St. Mary, and which Paul Trent seemed reluctant, or perhaps afraid to mention by name. Hilary Newton began to read...

CHAPTER 5

DOCTOR MALCOLM DAVIDSON STOOD BY THE BEDSIDE OF David Bradley. At the age of fifty-six, he was ten years the senior of Paul Trent, though in appearance they looked almost the same age. This wasn't because Trent had aged considerably, more that Davidson had kept himself in good physical trim all of his life, and the man didn't look a day over forty-five. Perhaps that was why many of the nurses on the wards at Ashford General had something akin to a schoolgirl crush on the Head of the Department of Chest and Respiratory Diseases.

Now though, he, like Trent and the two nurses gathered at David's bedside in the isolation ward was swathed in a shapeless green gown and he wore a surgical mask to protect him from... from what? He had been intrigued by Doctor Trent's request, passed via his secretary, to attend at the bedside of David Bradley. Trent's preliminary diagnosis, if confirmed, could prove to be the precursor to a situation that would have been unimaginable when Davidson had risen from his bed that morning.

Davidson gazed down at the young patient. David Bradley was struggling to breathe, and his respiration was being aided by the oxygen mask that was placed over his lower face. A saline drip was attached to his left forearm ensuring the boy received sufficient fluids to keep his body adequately hydrated. Sweat peppered the boy's exposed areas of skin and young David Bradley hovered on the edges of consciousness, barley knowing where he was or who was with him. Davidson asked for the boy's chart and one of the nurses quickly unhooked it from its place at the end of the bed and placed it in the doctor's waiting hand. After studying it for a minute the senior consultant moved closer to the boy. With his hands covered by surgical gloves he began to examine the patient, who betrayed little sign of even being aware that he was being touched.

Davidson stood back from the bed, and Trent followed him. Speaking in hushed tones, Davidson addressed his colleague.

"You were right to send for me Paul. All your test results back up what you initially thought, and my own examination unfortunately confirms it. How many people know about this so far?"

"Only you and I, sir," Trent replied. "The nurses only know that they're looking after a boy with an as yet unknown condition, and of course your secretary would have read my message."

"What about the doctor who referred him to us?"

"Hilary Newton sir, she used to work here. She's the new G.P in Olney St. Mary; she's only been there a few weeks. She thinks she's dealing with a particularly virulent strain of influenza, though I have hinted that it may be something more serious."

"Well, I think Doctor Newton might soon be regretting taking up the post of General Practitioner in that out of the way outpost of humanity. I went there once years ago. Nice place to visit, even better place to leave behind. She'll have to be told Paul, and she'll need help. I very much doubt that this boy and the one who died on the way here will be the only cases she has to deal with. She can't possibly handle a potential epidemic on her own. I'll have to report this to the Health Ministry of course. We're talking about a serious communicable disease and they'll want to take steps to stop it spreading. Good God, Paul, if this gets out amongst the general population it could wipe out half the country in a few weeks."

"I know sir. That's why I wanted your confirmation before I informed anyone of my diagnosis. What about that help you mentioned for Doctor Newton?"

"I'm sure the Ministry will send a team of specialists to the village as soon as they get my call. In the meantime, I'd appreciate it if you yourself would drive to Olney and take a couple of trusted nurses with you, if you can find any who'll volunteer. Be honest with them though Paul, tell them the risks, let them decide for themselves. I'll need you to be my eyes and ears in the village until the Ministry decides what to do. Whether we like it or not, Olney St. Mary is covered by our authority and we must do what we can to help. I just hope we can isolate the source and halt the spread before it claims too many lives."

"Don't worry sir; I'm sure I'll find a couple of reliable nurses who'll go with me. Those who work in the communicable disease unit will be well aware of what they're walking into and I'm sure they won't back out of trying to help the people of Olney."

Davidson looked as though he had hardly heard Trent's last comment.

"I just hope we're in time."

"Time, sir?"

"To prevent a national or perhaps international epidemic, Doctor Trent. Good Lord, Man. The prospect of such a thing happening in our lifetime just shouldn't exist. How the hell did it start and in particular in a God-forsaken place like Olney?"

Paul Trent had never seen the head of his department so visibly shaken. By their very nature, doctors are always calm and outwardly in control of themselves and their emotions. To be otherwise would be to have a disquieting and unsettling effect on the patients who daily placed their lives in the care of the medical practitioners. This was different, however. Few doctors in the latter half of the twentieth century and certainly none in the western world of the nineteen-fifties had been faced with such a diagnosis as this.

As Paul Trent took his leave of his superior and went to find the nurses who would accompany him to Olney St. Mary, Malcolm Davidson, suddenly looking his age, sat down heavily behind his desk in the privacy of his office and made the telephone call that would change the lives of the people of Olney for all time.

As soon as he was connected to the most senior member of staff on duty at the Ministry of Health in London, Malcolm Davidson wasted no time on pleasantries, preferring to come straight to the point. He knew that he and the people of Olney, and England as a whole, didn't have the luxury that the usual pleasantries demanded.

"Yes sir, it's confirmed I'm afraid. One dead and one on death's door so far. There are bound to be other cases."

At the other end of the line a silence was followed by another question. Davidson answered immediately, with the slightest of a tremor in his voice betraying his own anxiety.

"I'm sorry to have to say that of the three variants of the disease the worst one by far is the one we're dealing with. It's Pneumonic Plague sir, the deadliest form of the disease. We thought it had been eradicated in this country, but it seems we were wrong."

As the medical authorities and other concerned government departments slowly limbered into action and the wheels of officialdom turned slowly in their efforts to assemble the necessary people and equipment to deal with this new and wholly unexpected and unprepared for emergency, Hilary Newton and the residents of Olney things were about to see their situation lurch from bad to so very much worse.

CHAPTER 6

IN RESPONSE TO MALCOLM DAVIDSON'S REQUEST, PAUL TRENT soon had his team of volunteers in place. There had been no shortage of nurses bravely stepping forward to take a leap into the unknown with Trent. Plague after all was unknown in their lifetimes and they were all aware of the risks they ran in joining him on his mission of mercy to Olney St. Mary.

In the end, he'd selected two unmarried nurses, Patricia Knowles and Christine Rigby for the task. Trent thought that their single status would make their visit to Olney less traumatic for their families. After all, he'd have hated it if anything happened to the nurses under his command anyway, but if they had husbands or children then it would have made matters much worse, especially in terms of his own conscience. Patricia, known to everyone as Pat, and Christine were both experienced nurses and very level-headed girls. He had no worries about their commitment and reliability.

After giving them two hours to go home and pack whatever they needed for the trip to Olney, Trent picked up the telephone. It was time to let Hilary know that he was on his way, and why.

"But it can't be, Paul. Not in this day and age," Hilary spluttered down the telephone when Trent broke the news to her.

"I'm sorry Hilary, but there's no doubt. It's a confirmed outbreak of pneumonic plague. We must take every possible step to confine it and prevent any spread of the disease. I'm leaving for Olney myself to assist you in a couple of hours with two specialist nurses to help, and The Ministry of Health will have a team assembled and down to the village as soon as they can, probably in the next day or two. Now tell me, have you had any further cases since we spoke earlier?"

"None that have been reported to me. No. Paul, I can't believe that plague has struck here, and I diagnosed it as influenza. I feel so inept."

"It's not your fault Hilary. You weren't on the lookout for anything as serious as plague, and the early symptoms do mirror those of the flu to some extent."

"But I'm a bloody doctor, Paul. I should have known!"

"Hilary, calm down. It's not the time for self-recriminations. We have a job to do. You've two patients, so far, now we have to try and make sure you don't lose any more. Do you understand?"

"Yes, I know Paul, I'm sorry. Look, when you and the nurses get here, you'll need somewhere to stay won't you?"

"I hadn't really thought of it."

"I think the best place would be here at the surgery. I can make some room in the spare bedroom for the girls and there's a camp bed I can put up for you downstairs if you don't mind roughing it a bit."

"That'll be fine, thanks. It might set a few tongues wagging in your little village but what the hell. Now, I must get going. The sooner I'm with you the sooner we can start trying to find the source of the outbreak and eradicating any chance of further cases."

"Yes, right, well I'll see you when you get here, Paul, and thanks."

"Thank me when this is all over Hilary. We may have a tough few days ahead of us before this thing goes away."

"I know, but thanks anyway. I know you're all taking a risk just by coming here."

"All part of the job, I'm afraid, Doctor Newton. It's all part of the job. Now, I'm going. See you soon."

"Yes right, see you soon," said Hilary, and the phone went dead in her hand. Trent was gone.

After the call ended, Hilary felt the weight of a palpable burden of silence that seemed to descend upon the room. The only interruption to that silence was the ticking of the clock on the wall, which now appeared to be grossly amplified by the very silence that hung like a pall and enveloped the young doctor.

Pneumonic plague! Hilary couldn't have imagined that anything quite so terrifying would be visited upon her so soon into her tenure as a village G.P. She needed to find something to occupy her mind until Trent and the nurses arrived. In the absence of any further cases so far, she decided to read up on the history and treatment of the plague that had struck her new home. Most of her textbooks were still in packing boxes in the spare room and Hilary spent a good half hour rooting out the volumes she required.

At last, armed with two thick tomes that she thought appropriate to her research, she made her way downstairs. After making herself a pot of tea she settled down in her consulting room and was soon lost in the pages of text that detailed the horrendous past record of pneumonic plague outbreaks, and went on to describe the treatments, both ancient and modern, that had been applied in an attempt to at first control, and eventually eradicate the disease.

The clock continued its interminable ticking on the wall, the hands creeping slowly round the face until Hilary at last looked up and realised that she'd been reading for over an hour. Trent and the nurses should arrive within the next sixty minutes, she estimated, and she put the heavy book down and rose from her chair. Returning upstairs, she foraged around for a few minutes until she found what she was looking for. She had enough sheets and blankets for the nurses and for Paul Trent, and now she took them all outside and hung them on the washing line to give them a decent airing.

Next, she trekked back up the stairs, carrying the heavy Hoover vacuum cleaner, a can of furniture polish and a large yellow duster. She soon had the spare bedroom looking habitable. Most of the boxes containing her books and bed linen she simply pushed to the sides of the room, against the walls, and the clothes that lay strewn on the spare bed, still on their hangers were soon carried through to her bedroom, where she hung them on the outside of her wardrobe. She needed a second one and hadn't yet had time to go shopping for it. Having not been in the village for too long, she'd put off driving all the way to Ashford just to look at wardrobes, thinking she'd have plenty of time to settle in to her new home. She realised now that maybe she should have ordered one before she'd left town and had it delivered in advance of her move to Olney. Then again, hindsight wasn't about to help her domestic situation now. After twenty minutes of determined dusting, polishing and vacuuming, Hilary stood back to admire her handiwork. The room smelled of fresh polish and now presented a far more habitable environment than it had a few minutes before. Though far from perfect, it would certainly suffice as a temporary base of operations for the two nurses who'd be arriving shortly.

As if on cue, of a car horn sounded outside the house. Hilary walked through to her bedroom, located at the front of the house, and looked out of the window. Paul Trent and the two nurses were exiting from Trent's car. Hilary saw that he still drove the same car he'd owned since she'd first known him, a blue Ford Zephyr. She opened the window and shouted a greeting to the three new arrivals and made her way quickly down the stairs to welcome them to her home. Their arrival certainly hadn't been planned for. It definitely came in the light of terrible circumstances, but in the light of what may lie ahead; Hilary was grateful and very happy to see the new arrivals her doorstep.

CHAPTER 7

JUST AS HILARY WAS HELPING PAUL TRENT AND NURSES Knowles and Rigby carry their luggage and equipment into her home, over at St. Mary's Church the Reverend Timothy Grafton was busy working alongside two of the parish's elderly ladies. Emily Jones and Mabel Thorndyke had been staunch supporters of the church since long before both became widowed some years previously. The two women now felt it part of their everyday lives to decorate the little church with flowers each week in readiness for the two services held by Reverend Grafton every Sunday. Now, as always on a Friday, they were busily arranging fresh displays in the six wall hanging baskets that adorned the walls of St. Mary's, having already decorated the floor standing urns that greeted the congregation as they entered through the front doors. Later, they'd attend to the two matching urns that stood to the right and left of the altar. Finally they'd move on to the one that stood directly in front of the pulpit from where Grafton would deliver his regular Sunday sermon. It was a ritual in the art of logical progression. They followed the same rigorous order of arrangements each week, and the Reverend would always accompany them, not interfering, but just being there to offer his help and assistance in reaching some of the higher wall baskets.

So far, word of the death of Evan Parkes hadn't filtered through to the villagers. The Bradley and Parkes families were keeping their own counsel so far, their grief a very private affair. David Bradley still clung to life, albeit by a thread, and his family would be praying for a miracle. That being said, they hadn't felt the need to consult their local vicar. Timothy Grafton knew no more than the two old women whom he now worked beside.

"Fearful sick, I heard they were," said Mabel Thorndyke.

"Took them away in an ambulance they did," replied her friend, Emily. "I saw them take young David Bradley away and the ambulance headed off in the direction of the farm, so I expect they picked young Evan up at the same time."

"What d'you think it is that ails them, Reverend?" asked Mabel.

"I don't think we should speculate too much on the subject ladies. After all, the boys' health is the concern of their families and themselves alone. We shouldn't be gossiping about things that don't concern us."

"Things will concern us soon enough if they've caught something contagious," Emily Jones prophesied.

"Then perhaps a prayer for the recovery of the youngsters would be in order, ladies?"

Knowing that the vicar had them cornered, the two women bent their heads as Grafton delivered a short prayer for the boys' recovery. As their 'amens' echoed up towards the roof of the near empty church, Mabel Thorndyke returned to her previous thread of conversation, undaunted by Reverend Grafton's plea for a lack of gossip on the subject.

"I saw them both a few days ago. They're good boys they are. They offered to help clear the fallen leaves from my garden. That tree of mine is so beautiful in spring and summer, but at this time of year it just produces a veritable carpet of leaves all over my garden. Them boys were really helpful and cleared the lot in an hour."

"I thought I saw them when I walked past your house," said Emily.

"Yes, and d'you know the nicest thing? They wouldn't take a penny from me for doing it. They both just said that it were a pleasure to help and asked for a glass of lemonade each before they tripped off back to doing whatever they were up to before they came along."

"I hope you washed out the glasses well afterward," warned Emily Jones. "You never know what germs they might have been carrying. You might be the next one to be carted off in an ambulance. You mark my words Mabel Thorndyke."

Timothy Grafton had heard enough.

"Now ladies, I'm sorry, but that's really quite enough. I'll have no more of this gossip and tittle-tattle in the church thank you. As for you Emily, I'm surprised at you. There's no need to go frightening poor Mabel by assuming such things. I must insist that we return to the matter in hand and forget all this nonsense and speculation."

"Yes Vicar."

"Sorry Reverend."

Both women fell silent, feeling suitably chastised by the Reverend, and the little group returned to the business of flower arranging. Work continued in what Grafton considered a blessed silence. A half hour later they completed the last of the arrangements, a beautiful and heady mix of colours and scents directly in front of the pulpit.

After gathering their hats and coats from where they'd left them hanging in the vestry, the two ladies of the parish bade Timothy

Grafton a fond if slightly chastened farewell and headed off to their respective homes.

Unfortunately, for the prophetic Emily Jones and the Reverend Timothy Grafton, and tragically for the widow Mabel Thorndyke, it would be the last time either of them would see her alive.

CHAPTER 8

"I THINK THAT'S ABOUT EVERYTHING HILARY," SAID PAUL Trent as he heaved the last of the nurses' suitcases up the stairs and into the spare room. It had taken half an hour to unpack the Zephyr, as all the medical equipment had been offloaded first and placed carefully in Hilary's surgery downstairs. Finally, Trent had brought his and the nurses' luggage into the house, first depositing his own cases in the sitting room and then attending to the girls' belongings.

"Well done Paul. Now, come and take a seat for ten minutes while I make us all a cup of tea."

Christine Rigby and Patricia Knowles were already in the kitchen and had taken it upon themselves to attend to the business of making tea. Hilary was surprised to find herself redundant as the two girls shooed her from her own kitchen and made her sit down. Soon the four of them were seated comfortably and Paul Trent made the formal introductions. Outside he'd simply introduced the girls by name. Now, he wanted Hilary to know exactly who he'd brought with him from Ashford to live under her roof for however long the current crisis lasted.

"Nurse Knowles, Patricia is a specialist in the care of patients with tropical and communicable diseases. She's been at the hospital for about five years, is that right, Nurse Knowles?"

"Yes, Doctor Trent," the girl replied. It was of course nineteen fifty-eight, and a degree of formality still existed within the various echelons of the National Health Service that some feel is sadly lacking in the modern age.

"And Nurse Rigby has similar qualifications but has been with us for over eight years I believe?"

"It'll be nine years next month, Doctor."

"Of course, you both know that Doctor Newton was employed at Ashford until recently before taking up the post as G.P. here in Olney St. Mary."

The two nurses nodded in unison.

"It will be up to us to do what we can to both treat any new cases and to attempt to contain this outbreak until such times as the Health Ministry sends a team down here to back us up."

"Do we know how long that will be, Paul?" asked Hilary.

"At the moment I'm afraid the answer is no. Until I make a preliminary report on the likely extent of the outbreak, I believe the Ministry will hold off on sending in a team of specialists."

"But that's madness, surely! This thing could spread like wildfire through the village overnight and we're supposed to just sit here and wait for the Ministry of Health to decide when it's become serious enough to warrant them sending in help?"

"You have to see it from their point of view Hilary. You've had two incidents so far, with one death. They may prove to have been quite isolated cases. If there are no more cases within the next forty-eight hours, I think we can safely report that the outbreak is contained and that there is no imminent danger to the village or the general population."

"You're spouting government propaganda there Paul. If you truly believed what you've just said there would be no need for you or the girls to be here, would there?"

"I'm simply passing on what I've been told Hilary. We're not going to achieve anything by bickering amongst ourselves, so I suggest we get on with the job."

"In the light of there being no current cases, what do you suggest we do, Doctor Trent?" asked Hilary, quite formally, and attempting to contain her frustration.

"Look, we need to find out just how those two boys contracted the disease in the first place. It's likely that they both picked it up from the same infection source. We must find out where it is, or was, and ensure that no-one else is exposed to the contaminant. I suggest that you and Nurse Rigby visit the Bradley home to search for clues and Nurse Knowles can accompany me to visit the Parkes' if you'll provide me with directions."

Just as Hilary was about to reply the telephone began to ring. The four people present in her surgery all looked at each other expectantly. It took Hilary a full five seconds to pluck up the courage to walk across the room and lift the heavy bakelite phone from its cradle.

"Doctor Newton," she said softly, and then listened intently to the voice at the other end of the line. She remained silent for over a minute and then simply replied 'Thank you' to whoever was speaking to her.

Replacing the telephone on its resting place, she turned to face Paul Trent and the two nurses. Ashen faced, she addressed them gravely.

"That was Malcolm Davidson in Ashford. You can make it two out of two dead now, Paul. David Bradley died twenty minutes ago."

A dreadful stillness greeted her words. It felt as though someone, or something had sucked the air from the room. Everyone seemed to hold their breath, waiting for somebody to speak. At length it was Paul Trent who shattered the awful pall of silence.

"Perhaps we should forego the visit to the Parkes' farm. It might be an idea if I accompany you to the Bradley house Hilary."

"No Paul. You should go to the farm. It's important that we start to track the source down as soon as possible. I've already broken the news of the Parkes boy's death to his grandparents, I'm sure I can do the same with the Bradleys. Nurse Rigby can still accompany me to the Bradley's though. She'll be a great help, both with the parents and with beginning our search."

"I wasn't suggesting you couldn't handle it, Hilary."

"I know you weren't Paul, and I appreciate the offer of your support, but it's important that you go to the farm. You know that as well as I do. I don't care what the men from The Ministry say, this thing is not contained, and these were not isolated cases. I doubt we've seen the last case of this outbreak, and it won't be long before we have more cases on our hands, perhaps too many for the four of us to cope with."

"Look Hilary, I'll make you a promise. If we find just one more case that is not connected to the Bradley or the Parkes families, then I'll phone Davidson and ask him to apply whatever pressure he can on the Ministry. If we can show that the disease is free amongst the general population of Olney, then there's a chance it could soon spread across the countryside and infect thousands, possibly."

"I'll hold you to that, Paul," said Hilary as she pulled her coat on and beckoned for Christine Rigby to follow her.

"Hilary," Trent called as she ushered Nurse Rigby through the front door.

"Yes?"

"I need the directions to the farm."

"Oh yes of course, do forgive me."

She quickly gave Trent the simple directions to the Parkes' farm and remembered to give him a spare key to the front door in case he and Nurse Knowles should return before she did.

With that, she waved goodbye to her colleagues and she and Christine Rigby were soon driving the short distance to the Bradley home. For the second time in less than twenty-four hours Doctor Hilary Newton was about to be the harbinger of bad news in the village where she'd hoped to do so much good.

CHAPTER 9

SAM BRADLEY LOOKED TERRIBLE AS HE OPENED THE DOOR TO admit Hilary and Christine Rigby. Clearly, something apart from his son's illness was bothering him. As soon as he saw his visitors, he made an almost telepathic connection with Hilary Newton, and he knew without her saying a word exactly what she'd come to tell him.

"He's gone hasn't he Doctor Newton? We've lost our boy."

Bradley's face was ashen, almost ghostly in appearance.

"I'm sorry Mr. Bradley. The hospital did all they could, but ..."

"It's alright Doctor, you don't need to tell me. I'm sure they did all they could for the lad. I'm just glad his sister isn't here to see this."

Hilary wracked her brain for a minute, and then remembered seeing a reference to a girl in the family in her surgery records.

"Sister? Of course, you have a daughter too don't you? Where is she, Mr. Bradley?"

"Carol is a very clever girl Doctor. She won a scholarship to Kent Ladies College when she was eleven. She's not due home until the end of the school term. She'd doing really well. Perhaps it's a blessing she wasn't here when David caught this thing. Now his mother's going down with it too, and I daresay it won't be long before I'm next on the list."

Ignoring the subject of Carol Bradley for the time being Hilary focussed instead on Sam Bradley's last words.

"Are you telling me that Mrs. Bradley is ill now?"

"She's been poorly for the last hour or so. It came on real sudden. She just seemed to collapse all at once. She's lying down upstairs. I was about to call you in fact, then I saw your car coming and I knew you were bringing me bad news. How can I tell her about David when she's feeling so ill?"

"Look, first things first, Mr. Bradley. We need to see your wife. This is Nurse Rigby by the way."

"Hello Nurse," said Bradley almost mechanically, barely noticing the short, pretty, dark haired girl who stood beside the doctor. He looked like a man who'd had the life sucked out of him. His son was dead, his wife possibly had the same disease that had killed him, and Hilary suspected that Bradley had been correct in his earlier statement. He could be next."

Sam Bradley escorted Hilary and the nurse up the stairs to the master bedroom, where his wife Emily lay on the bed. Hilary could see that the room was well furnished, with two double wardrobes in real mahogany and a matching dressing table. The carpet was a thick pile, woven Axminster in a floral design, of obvious good quality. Right now though, all Sam Bradley's money couldn't bring his son back, and could do little to help his wife.

"Emily, the doctors here, my love," said Bradley to the woman on the bed.

Emily Bradley looked up, the movement apparently causing her some degree of pain.

"That was quick. I didn't know you'd made the call yet, Sam."

Hilary had no choice. She needed to get the bad news out of the way before she could continue.

"Your husband didn't call me Mrs. Bradley. I came with Nurse Rigby here to tell you the news about David."

"Oh, how is he Doctor Newton? Is he getting better?"

Hilary's silence in response to the question told Emily Bradley all she needed to know.

"No, please God no," was all she said, and her face dissolved into a mask of tears. The poor woman, already ill, buried her head in her pillow and sobbed uncontrollably."

Sam Bradley walked across to the bed, sat down beside his prostrate wife and placed a soothing hand on her shoulder. His trouser leg rode up and Hilary saw for the first time the heavily built up special shoe that Bradley wore to help compensate for his club foot. She knew of his problem from reading his records, but she'd thought he handled his disability very well. In every other respect he gave off an aura of strength and dependability. It seemed a little strange to see the evidence of his incapacity so close to hand.

"She was too hot to lie under the blankets," he said to Hilary, as if to explain Emily's place on top of the bed rather than under the bedclothes.

Hilary could sense that Sam was about to go into shock. She needed to get him to focus on something else for a few minutes while she examined his wife. She realised that he hadn't even asked what had killed his son. Then again, would giving the disease a name help Sam Bradley at this time? She thought not.

"Mr. Bradley. Would you mind going downstairs and putting the kettle on. I'm sure a cup of tea would help us all right now, you and Mrs. Bradley especially. I'm sure Nurse Rigby will be happy to help won't you, Nurse?"

"Of course, Doctor. Come on Mr. Bradley, you'll have to show me where things are."

Experienced nurse that she was, Christine Rigby had virtually read Hilary's mind. She knew exactly what the doctor was trying to do, and she now switched on her years of experience to ensure that she kept Sam busy.

"Yes, right, I suppose so," Bradley stuttered, unsure of himself for the first time since Hilary had met him.

He allowed Christine Rigby to usher him gently from the bedroom and down the stairs where he and the nurse soon began the ritual of making a large pot of steaming hot tea. As the bedroom door quietly closed behind the exiting pair, Hilary turned her attention to Emily Bradley.

She placed a reassuring hand on the top of the weeping woman's shoulder. Emily continued to cry quietly into her pillow, her head turned away from the doctor, away from the cruelty of the world around her.

"Mrs. Bradley, I'm so sorry about David, really I am, but I need to examine you now. Your husband says you suddenly felt weak and hot and on the verge of collapse. Is that right?"

Through her tears the woman seemed to find the will to nod her head almost imperceptibly, but enough for Hilary to glean an affirmative answer to her question.

"Please Mrs. Bradley, I need you to turn over so that I can see and examine you properly. Can you do that for me, please?"

Slowly, the grieving mother of David Bradley turned over until she could see the figure of Doctor Newton by the side of the bed. When she saw that Hilary had donned a protective green face mask her face collapsed into another bout of uncontrollable tears. After a minute of sobbing Emily Bradley pulled herself together and took a very deep breath. The tears subsided, and Hilary began her examination.

———

Paul Trent and Patricia Knowles were getting very dirty indeed. Simon and Ellen Parkes, though deeply grieving over the death of their grandson Evan had been most co-operative so far. Parkes and his wife hadn't yet made the long trek to Ashford to view the body of Evan. Showing both sense and fortitude, Parkes had informed Trent that he thought it best to leave such a visit until the next day, when both he and his wife might be better equipped to deal with such a trial. Paul Trent was impressed by Simon Parkes. His stoicism in the face of tragedy spoke volumes for the ruggedness of the people of this tiny outpost of English village life. Though both he and his wife were deeply grieving for the loss of Evan, the pair had readily agreed to Tent's request to search the farm for a possible source of the infection that had struck the two boys down. They were shocked, though hardly surprised to learn of David Bradley's death. They had almost thought it inevitable after being informed of Evan's death en-route to Ashford.

Now, Simon Parkes was busy giving Trent and Patricia Knowles a tour of the farm, pointing out the places where he knew the boys had spent a lot time. They'd searched the barn, the shed where Parkes kept his tractor, plough and other mechanical equipment necessary for the day to day running of his farm, and were now almost up to their ankles in sticky wet mud as Parkes showed them the pond at the bottom of his 'number two field', where the boys would often fish for sticklebacks with a home made net.

This was the field where he kept his small herd of six dairy cows. The Friesians provided not only Parkes, but many of the villagers with a supply of fresh milk. Parkes had assured Simon Trent that his milking parlour was clean and of the highest standards. After the field it would be the next stop on their tour. The presence of the cows had also meant that several cow pats lay like land mines, dotted around the field. No-one had so far escaped placing at least one foot in one of the dung heaps, which clung to their shoes as they trudged around the pond.

"Is it rats you'll be searching for?" Parkes had asked when Trent explained that they needed to search his farm. "You can't ever be totally rid of rats on a farm, Doctor Trent."

Trent proceeded to give Parkes a brief run down on the disease and its causes.

"It may be rats, which is the generally held belief, but there could be other sources of infection Mr. Parkes. Plague is transmitted by a little beast of a bacterium called Yersinia Pestis. The bacillus is carried by the fleas that infest the rats, and the fleas can jump onto a human being, bite the host and infect them with the disease. With this being a farm, it maybe that the fleas have managed to bite or infect other rodents that may be present on your property, perhaps mice, voles or such like. Wherever the boys played they could have come into contact with a flea-carrying rodent and become infected that way."

"You mentioned other sources Doctor?"

"Yes. We must consider the possibility that a stranger came to your village, perhaps just passing through, and that he or she was a carrier of the disease. It's possible that the carrier can harbour the infection without displaying any symptoms themselves, although they can infect anyone they come into contact with. A cough, a sneeze or breathing in the close vicinity of another person can be responsible for the onward transmission of the disease. Do you know of any strangers having been in Olney in the last week or two? They might have just stopped to ask the boys for directions, or to fill up their car with petrol, anything like that?"

"I rarely leave the farm Doctor, except to visit the village shop, and once a month to go into Ashford for supplies. As for someone stopping for petrol, you should ask Sam Bradley. He owns the filling station after all, and the boys spent almost as much time together over there as they did here."

"I'm sure Doctor Newton will ask the question of Mr. Bradley. She's over there now. In the meantime, it would help if we could find a dead rat or rodent of some description. We can then send it to the laboratory in Ashford for testing."

Search as they might however, Paul Trent and Patricia Knowles found nothing at the farm to indicate a source of the infection that had struck the two boys down. Two hours later, they left the farm and drove back to Hilary's surgery, where the young GP and Christine Rigby were waiting for them, having returned from the Bradley's house a half hour earlier.

Leaving their muddy and rather smelly shoes on the mat outside Hilary's front door, Trent and Knowles walked through to the surgery where Hilary and Christine greeted them with grim faces.

"Did they take it badly?" Trent asked.

"Worse than that, we've got another case," Hilary replied. "Mrs. Bradley is infected now. She exhibited the first symptoms shortly before we arrived. I've treated her with Streptomycin, her husband too, and hopefully we've caught it in time in her case."

Discovered in Nineteen-Forty-Three, streptomycin had proved effective in the treatment of both bubonic and pneumonic plague. The two doctors and the nurses had taken prophylactic doses of the drug before leaving for their visits to the Parkes and the Bradleys in the hope that it would provide them with protection against the disease.

"I hope so too," Trent replied to Hilary's news. I left a supply with the Parkes as well. We may have to dose the whole village Hilary. Even then we can't totally assume immunity. The infection may already have taken hold and any number of people could be incubating the disease as we speak. We found nothing at the farm, incidentally."

"Nor at the Bradley's. I asked Mr. Bradley if he remembered any strangers passing through recently and he's seen no-one he doesn't know for over a month. Only locals have patronised his garage and filling station lately. Listen Paul, if we need to give antibiotics to the whole population of Olney, we'll have to tell them why, and that could just cause something of a panic don't you think?"

"You're right. We may need to enlist the help of the police."

Hilary hesitated for a moment before replying. Then, with a wry look, she explained to Paul Trent.

"Look Paul. Your theory is sound enough and I agree that the police should, under normal circumstances, be able to help us. Unfortunately, Olney St. Mary, not being a hotbed of crime, has just one village constable assigned to look after matters of law and order. I've met Constable Greaves a couple of times He's about fifty-five, nearing retirement and is probably still a constable because of a distinct lack of ambition early in his career. I think he sees his posting at Olney as a nice cushy way of seeing out his days until retirement. I doubt he's the best man in the world to deal with a village-wide panic. We might need reinforcements."

"Which at this point we can't rely upon receiving, Hilary. Until I can convince someone that we need more resources, we're it, as far as Olney is concerned."

"But I thought you said that if there was another case..."

"Yes, another case outside of the original infected families. So far, that hasn't happened. As far as the Ministry is concerned, it remains a local and isolated outbreak. There's been no spread to the rest of the village."

"I hope for everyone's sake it stays like that Paul. What about the antibiotics though? We should distribute them to everyone."

"Agreed. Whether we like it or not Constable Greaves is our only option for help at present. I suggest we go and see him and try to call an emergency meeting of the residents. Is there a village hall or something we could commandeer for the purpose?"

"Behind the church. We'd have to get the vicar's permission."

"Okay then. Let's go see the Constable. He can help explain the urgency to the minister.

You ladies can start to prepare individual doses of streptomycin while we're gone," Trent instructed the two nurses. "It's a good job we came prepared."

Christine Rigby and Patricia Knowles began unlocking two of the metal cases they'd offloaded from Trent's Zephyr earlier in the day. The cases contained enough of the antibiotic to treat everyone in Olney. Malcolm Davidson had made sure that they carried a week's supply of the antibiotic for everyone. He'd promised more if it became necessary.

Leaving Christine and Patricia to their task, Hilary Newton and Paul Trent exited through the front door and began the short walk to the local police house where they hoped to find

Constable Greaves at home. They were about to place a large responsibility on the shoulders of the constable.

To his credit, and the ultimate relief of everyone in the room, when the situation in Olney St. Mary eventually reached boiling point P.C. Keith Greaves would not be found wanting.

CHAPTER 10

IN HIS OFFICE IN A QUIET ANNEXE OF THE MINISTRY OF Health, just behind Whitehall in London, Douglas Ryan sat behind his massive oak desk, surrounded by the material giveaways that identified him as a medical man. The oak-panelled walls were hung with oil paintings depicting such greats in the field of medical research as Edward Jenner, Marie Curie, and Louis Pasteur. On his desk sat several items of antique medical paraphernalia, many of which should and probably one day would grace the halls of a museum. Pride of place went to a Victorian Microscope that had once belonged to the great Victorian, Walter Reed, the man who originally discovered the link between mosquitoes and the spread of yellow fever. That one single piece of equipment testified to Ryan's own field of expertise. As chief virologist to the Ministry of Health it had fallen to sixty-year old Ryan to investigate the reported outbreak of pneumonic plague in Olney St. Mary, and to prepare a plan of action that would work to first contain the disease, and then prevent any spread of the outbreak.

Sat in comfortable leather chairs across from Ryan were the two men he'd chosen to help formulate his plan. In his smart navy-blue pin-striped suit, Charles Macklin looked every inch 'the man from the ministry'. As Ryan's number two, he was exactly that. The second man wore the uniform of the Royal Air Force. Group Captain Donald Forbes held a senior position at the Ministry of Defence's primary biological and chemical research establishment at Porton Down, in Wiltshire. Between them, the three men in Ryan's office probably knew more about viruses in general, and plague in particular, than any other trio of brains in England.

Douglas Ryan looked up from the papers he'd been perusing for a minute or two. His face was grave, reflecting the seriousness of the situation.

"Gentlemen, we have a potentially serious situation on our hands. Doctor Malcolm Davidson, whom I happen to know personally, has sent me this report from the hospital where he is currently employed, in Ashford, Kent. Two cases of pneumonic plague have been confirmed. Both victims were teenage boys and they hailed from a village in the midst of the Kent countryside called Olney St. Mary."

"Never heard of it," said Forbes.

"Neither had I until today," Ryan went on.

"It appears that the place is as rural as it's possible to get. That in itself could prove our salvation, as its very isolation from the surrounding towns and villages should make containment that much easier."

"Do we know how or where the two boys contracted the infection?" asked Macklin.

"No we do not. The local GP, a Doctor Hilary Newton is a former member of Davidson's staff in Ashford. She only recently took up General Practice in the village, and she originally suspected a highly virulent strain of influenza to be the cause of the boys' maladies. When they exhibited further symptoms she called for an ambulance. One boy subsequently died en-route to hospital in Ashford, the other died soon after being admitted. Davidson and one of his senior men, Paul Trent, jointly confirmed the plague diagnosis and as we speak Trent and two specialist nurses are with Doctor Newton in Olney St. Mary, trying to offer help in containing the situation. The reason I've called you gentlemen here this evening is so that we may decide what courses of action are available to us if the situation in this little village escalates and gets out of hand."

The faces of the two men seated across from Ryan both reflected his grave look. They were well aware of the potential for a national disaster if pneumonic plague were to break out into the general population. Even with the antibiotics available in nineteen fifty-eight, the mortality rate from an outbreak of pneumonic plague could be as high as ninety percent. In short, such an outbreak, if allowed to go nationwide could potentially devastate the country, killing millions. Clearly, all three men in the room knew that they could never allow such a thing to happen. Steps would have to be taken to eradicate the outbreak at its source.

"First thing we need to do is establish the original source of the infection," said Forbes. "Then, we must act to isolate the village from the outside world as much as is humanly possible. Only medical staff and any civilians tasked with playing a role in the containment operation should be allowed to enter Olney St. Mary. We need to set up a perimeter of, say, ten miles around the village, and establish an exclusion zone. Nothing and no-one goes in, or comes out without the express permission of the medical authorities."

"That sounds reasonable Donald," said Charles Macklin.

"Most certainly," Ryan agreed. "Next, we need to put together a treatment plan, for those already infected. I'm going to brief Malcolm Davidson to put his man Trent in charge on the spot. He can direct the situation from within for now and place any orders for drugs through Davidson. That way we should be able to keep a lid on it as much as possible and avoid any sort of general panic. I do not want the radio or newspapers getting their hands on this information at present. After all, we don't know the extent of the outbreak so there's no need to start a general panic."

"What about the television people sir? They're getting more and more aggressive with their news reporting of late. The BBC is always looking for bigger and better stories. If someone from this village gets news out by telephone for instance we could end up with cameramen from the BBC trying to get into the village and they wouldn't react well to it being cut off from the rest of the country."

"Good point Charles. I've given some thought to that one. We can't cut the telephone lines to the village because that would also cut off the medical people already on the ground there. We need to be able to keep in constant contact with them as this thing progresses."

"What's the population of Olney St. Mary?" asked the Group Captain.

"About a hundred and fifty," Ryan replied.

"Assuming that that total includes husbands, wives and children we can safely assume that there are not many telephones in the village," Forbes went on. "It shouldn't be too hard to get the G.P.O. to cut off the individual telephone lines to all the private houses and businesses in the village except the ones we specify."

"Of course," said Ryan. "Charles, be good enough to telephone the GPO, (General Post Office) and make the necessary arrangements. Tell them we only want the local doctor's number to remain active, and perhaps the local police station, if they have one. We may need to enlist the help of the local constabulary before this is over. This will effectively seal off the village. No-one will be able to telephone the radio or the television people."

"I'll get right on to it sir, as soon as we finish here."

The meeting continued for another five minutes, with the three men agreeing on the decisions which would soon affect the lives of all the people of Olney. As he brought the meeting to a close Douglas Ryan once again assumed his previous grave expression as he addressed Forbes and Macklin.

"Gentlemen, it is only just over a decade ago that this great nation of ours emerged bruised and battered from a world war which wrought untold havoc on our people. That conflagration was more than enough for a generation to have to endure. I will not, repeat *not*, see this country ravaged by a plague when it is within our hands to eradicate it at an early stage. We will take whatever steps are necessary to help the people of Olney St. Mary to survive this outbreak. We will do whatever it takes to wipe out the plague from within the borders of the village, but I will not let it escape into the country at large. In the end gentlemen, if the health of this great nation of ours seems at risk from a catastrophic epidemic of pneumonic plague then I would rather see the inhabitants of one small village isolated in a secure hospital facility where they can be cared for or allowed to die, away from the glare of publicity. The people of the Middle Ages had a healthy respect for the plague gentlemen, and though they were unaware of the true cause of the disease they had a drastic means of ensuring its eradication from a town or village. Purification by fire was a radical but effective means of destroying the vermin and the infection they carried. If we have to, we will institute a scorched earth policy that will see every building in the village razed to the ground. Do I make myself clear?"

"Perfectly sir," said Charles Macklin.

"Absolutely," replied the Group Captain.

"May I ask just one question, sir?"

Ryan could see that Group Captain Forbes had something on his mind.

"Of course. Ask away."

"Does this plan have Ministerial approval, Doctor Ryan?"

Ryan had expected that either Forbes or Macklin would ask just such a question. His money would have been on Forbes. Macklin, as his assistant would have been less likely to query his boss's strategy.

"The Minister for Health has been informed that a small and insignificant outbreak of pneumonic plague has been discovered in an isolated village. I will continue to update him on the situation but I've told him that at present there's no cause for immediate concern and that we have every hope of containing the situation without any fear of the disease spreading outside the confines of Olney St. Mary."

"And if it does spread, sir?"

"Then, Group Captain, I'm sure the Minister will inform the Prime Minister if he deems it necessary. We all hope that such an eventuality will never come to pass of course. This is simply a matter for the medical authorities of the country, of whom we are the appointed representatives in the handling of this outbreak. Does that answer your question?"

"Yes, of course sir."

"Good, then I suggest we draw this meeting to a close. It's getting late and I'm sure we all have homes to go to. I thank you for your time gentlemen. We shall meet again very soon. I suggest we meet again here at five pm tomorrow."

Ryan picked up the papers on his desk, tapped them into a neat pile and placed them within a brown manila folder. The meeting was at an end.

Within two minutes Macklin and Forbes had donned their coats and left the office, bidding the government's chief virologist goodnight. Alone with his thoughts, Douglas Ryan reached across to the elegant Waterford Crystal decanter and matching whisky tumblers that adorned the centre of his desk and poured himself a large glass of Teachers finest Scotch whisky. Sighing quietly, he allowed himself to sink back into the luxury of his well used leather chair. The meeting had gone well. Both Forbes and Macklin would not hesitate to do what must be done. For the people of Olney St. Mary, the die had been cast. There could be no turning back from the inevitable. They would live or die, but the plague would never leave the village, on that fact alone Ryan was determined.

As the traffic around Central London eased with the end of the evening rush hour, Ryan eventually rose from his desk, gathered his overcoat from the hat stand that stood in the corner of his office and descended the four flights of stairs to the underground car park reserved for senior staff members at the Ministry of Health. There, he unlocked the gleaming black Humber saloon that he'd recently acquired and drove the fifteen miles to his home in a quiet leafy suburb of the great metropolis. Soon he was sitting down to a meal prepared by his wife of thirty years, Margaret. The game pie with roasted vegetables was just what he needed after a long day at the office. The bottle of claret that accompanied it was superb. After a pleasant hour engaged in conversation with Margaret, Ryan yawned. He was tired. Before long, the couple left the comfort of their sitting room and made their way to bed. Margaret wasn't as tired as her husband and decided to read a little by the light of her bedside lamp. Ryan's head barely touched the pillow however before he drifted into a deep and peaceful sleep. That night, Douglas Ryan slept unusually well.

CHAPTER 11

IF THERE WAS ONE THING THAT POLICE CONSTABLE KEITH
Greaves enjoyed, a hearty breakfast sat firmly at the top of his
list. This morning, his wife, Tilly, had provided him with a feast
fit for a king. Bacon, sausages, eggs, mushrooms, grilled
tomatoes and fried bread adorned the plate that she'd placed in
front of him. As a mark of respect to his wife, and because he
loved his food, he proceeded to devour the lot with gusto. Tilly,
who had been christened Mathilda, but had always hated the
name, had been married to Greaves for over thirty years. It was
Keith, who in the early days of their courtship had first called
her the name by which she was now universally known. Tilly, she
thought, had a far friendlier sound to it than her given name.

Her appearance was in sharp contrast to that of her husband.
Whereas Keith had grown heavier over the years thanks to an
expanding waistline, and as his hair had grown thinner and
begun to turn grey, Tilly had kept the slim figure of her youth.
Her hair had retained the same burnished auburn sheen that had
first attracted Keith to her when he'd set eyes on her across the
dance floor at the Hackney Emporium all those years ago. In
truth, Tilly looked at least ten years younger than her forty-eight
years.

As was usual, she'd sat watching the man she loved eating his breakfast as she herself enjoyed a simpler affair comprising two boiled eggs, two rounds of toast and a cup of tea. They spoke little. They felt comfortable with each other and both rather enjoyed the companionable silence that usually hung over the breakfast table. There would be plenty of time to talk after clearing away, when they'd finished.

The silence left Keith Greaves free to reflect on his thoughts. He'd been surprised to find the new doctor on his doorstep the previous afternoon, accompanied by a stranger, whom she'd introduced as another doctor from the hospital in Ashford. When they'd explained the reason for their visit, he'd shown little surprise and none of the panic that they might have expected at the mention of the word, 'plague'. Greaves had been a copper for a long time, and it would take more than that to scare him. After all, he'd lost his own father to the great Spanish flu pandemic in 1918, had served as a constable in London during some of the worst bombing of the Blitz, and had seen his fair share of horrific sights in life. He might not have made much progress up the promotion ladder, but he was a steady and enduring member of his profession, just what was needed at a time like this. He'd instantly agreed to do whatever Doctor Newton and Doctor Trent required of him in respect of helping to control both the spread of the plague, and any potential panic among the residents of Olney.

He'd accompanied them to visit the Reverend Grafton and had helped secure the use of the village hall for a meeting to be held at five p.m. the next day. This was that day of course and his next job was to visit every house and farm in and around the village and ensure that everyone attended. They'd taken the vicar into their confidence, and he'd promised to say nothing until the doctors had informed the people of Olney of the situation in their village. Sam Bradley and the Parkes had agreed not to reveal the cause of the boys' deaths to anyone for now. They would say that they were awaiting the results of 'tests'. Doctor Newton had given him a supply of tablets for himself and his wife with orders to take one twice a day to help fight off any potential infection. She'd explained that there was no actual serum available to immunize against the plague. The tablets by themselves wouldn't necessarily protect them from catching the disease but may help to prevent them dying as a result if they did become infected. It wasn't the best scenario available but, in the circumstances, Greaves thought it better than nothing.

As he mopped up the last of the juice from his tomatoes with a slice of fried bread, the constable smiled across the table at his wife.

"You've done me proud this morning, Tilly girl. That was excellent my love."

"Well, from what you told me last night, I thought you'd need fillin' up before you go out this mornin'. I've a feelin' you'll be doing a fair bit of cyclin' today."

"Too right I will Tilly. I've got to see everyone in the village and make sure they get to the hall this evening."

"I hope those tablets she gave us work, Keith. It was terrible what's happened to those poor young boys. I just hope and pray it doesn't affect anyone else, you and me especially."

"Now then, don't you go worryin' your head about that my girl. We'll be fine. Just remember what the doctor said. If you meet anyone while you're out today you're not to breathe a word of what tonight's about, or what killed the boys. The doctor wants to be the one to inform everyone, and that's as it should be."

"Keith Greaves!" Tilly admonished her husband. "Now when have I ever broken a confidence that's come my way because of your work? I'd never say a word to anyone, and you should know that."

"I do know that Tilly. I just had to say it, that's all. This is a very serious matter after all."

"Well, you just go about your business and don't you worry about me shootin' my mouth off. My lips are sealed."

"I know my dear. I'd never doubt you for a minute. Now, I'd best be makin' tracks."

It took Keith Graves just two minutes to put on his tie, his jacket and duty armband, after which he strode to the back door of the house, provided by the police force for its village constable. His bicycle was parked in the garden, resting against Keith's potting shed. He guessed correctly that he wouldn't have much time for gardening in the next few days.

Tilly kissed her husband goodbye as she held the back-garden gate open for him, and Keith Graves set off on his cycle trek around the village and its surrounding farms. As he disappeared down the lane towards the nearest house to his own, that of Emily Jones, he turned his head to look back and waved cheerfully to his wife. Tilly waved back, trying to mirror his happy and optimistic manner. In truth however, she was worried. She'd tried not to show it to Keith but, well, just the word plague had been enough to frighten the wits out of Tilly Greaves. With a heavy heart and a mind full of worry Tilly walked back into the house where she hoped the business of the day's housework would keep her mind occupied until her husband arrived home for lunch.

———

Having been disturbed from her dusting of the piano in the sitting room by someone knocking on her door, Emily Jones was surprised to find the village constable on her doorstep.

"Hello Keith," she said, having been on first name terms with her close neighbour and his wife for many years.

"Good mornin', Emily. I've somethin' important to tell you. D'you mind if I come in for a minute?"

Emily Jones was intrigued by the story Keith Greaves related to her. She couldn't however get him to reveal the nature of the special meeting that evening. He made her promise to be there, and in truth, her inquisitive nature would never have permitted her to miss it. In an attempt to be helpful, and perhaps give her the chance to pass on a bit of gossip, she asked if the constable would like her to inform her friend Mabel Thorndyke of the meeting. It would, she assured him, be no trouble at all and would save him one call from the list of many he had to make that day. Keith Greaves thanked Emily and readily agreed. He was soon on his way, refusing her offer of a cup of tea. He had many stops to make and wanted to get on his way. Leaving Mrs Jones to deliver the news of the meeting to her friend, Greaves took his leave and was soon out of sight, pedalling down the lane towards his next port of call.

Less than an hour after Keith Greaves left the home of Emily Jones, the widow knocked loudly on the door of the constable's house. Tilly Greaves found a distraught and worried woman standing outside her home. Emily had knocked and knocked, she said to Tilly, but couldn't raise a reply from her friend Mabel Thorndyke. The front and back doors were both locked and Emily couldn't get in to see if her friend was alright. She was a genuinely concerned and anxious lady. Mabel didn't have a telephone so there was nothing she could do. Perhaps, she'd asked, Keith could go and check on Mabel?

Unfortunately, by the time Emily arrived at his house, Keith Graves was two miles from the village proper, at the farmhouse belonging to George Askew. It would be another three hours before Greaves returned to his home to be informed of the problem at Mabel's house, and a further half hour before he finally battered the front door down and gained entry, only to find the body of Mabel Thorndyke in her bed, where she'd died, alone and unable to call for help.

When he related the news to Emily Jones who had waited outside on his orders, the poor woman became beside herself with grief for her friend. Keith Greaves walked the sobbing widow to his own home and left Emily in the care of his wife as he went to try and find Doctor Newton. He was no expert, but he doubted that Emily's death was totally unconnected with the previous deaths of the two boys, especially when Emily had mentioned the lemonade that Mabel had given the boys when they'd cleared the leaves from her garden. That was a connection that surely couldn't be ignored!

CHAPTER 12

MICHAEL SWEENEY WAS A MAN OF MANY TALENTS AND multiple occupations. In a village the size of Olney that was often a necessity, and even more so in Sweeney's case. As the village undertaker his services were not exactly in constant demand, so he also earned a living as a stonemason, and as a gardener and part-time florist. Therefore, when it came to funerals Michael Sweeney pretty much had the market cornered in many respects. His gardening enterprise brought in a steady enough income, as many of the elderly residents of the village were only too happy to pay a reasonable regular sum to keep their cottage gardens looking good, and Sweeney was naturally green-fingered. At the age of forty, life tasted good to Michael Sweeney and he enjoyed the slow pace of life in Olney, having lived in the village for most of his life. He'd left the village only to serve his country during the war, and even now he rarely spoke of his service during those dark days. In fact, the residents of the village would have been surprised to hear that their local undertaker had received the Conspicuous Gallantry Medal for courage under fire during the D-Day landings. He'd saved his platoon from certain death, when, as a corporal in the Royal Engineers, he'd single-handedly charged at and destroyed a German machine gun post that had pinned him and his men down. Michael was unmarried and his parents had died before the war. Modestly, he'd decided that the medal would mean nothing to anyone at home, so he simply never mentioned it to his friends or neighbours after he was demobbed.

Even the usually unflappable Sweeney was a trifle surprised however when he found the local constable and the new doctor at his door with a strange request. Keith Greaves had already been to his home once that morning with news of the meeting in the Village Hall.

Now he was told that he was to call and collect the body of Mabel Thorndyke from her cottage. Nothing odd in that, but he was to wear a gown and protective gloves as provided by the doctor when he did so. He was told that the old lady may have died from a highly contagious disease and that there was a chance he could become infected through the transmission of any sort of body fluids. The thing he found the strangest though was that the doctor informed him that she and a colleague would need to perform an emergency post-mortem on the old lady and would need to use his laying out room for the purpose of carrying out the procedure.

"They usually take the bodies into Ashford if they need to do a post-mortem," he replied when the doctor finished speaking.

"I know that Mr Sweeney, but this is an emergency. My colleague Doctor Trent will be here soon to carry out the procedure. We have to know what caused Mrs Thorndyke's death. In the meantime we'll order an ambulance to come and take the body as soon as we've finished. I'll want you to store it in your cold room until it's picked up. You must keep it securely locked away until the pick-up is made. Do you understand?"

"I see, and yes, I understand. Tell me Doctor, is this anything to do with the meeting tonight and what's happened to the Parkes and the Bradley boys. The whole village knows about them passing away."

"It may be connected Mr. Sweeney. That's why we need to do the emergency postmortem. Now, can we count on your discretion in the matter? We don't want it blabbing around all over the village."

"No one'll hear a word from me, Doctor."

"Good. The constable here will escort you to the cottage and make sure you're not disturbed."

Greaves and Sweeney left and made their way to the Thorndyke residence. Hilary Newton went home, spoke to Patricia Knowles and then quickly drove over to the Bradley house where Paul Trent and Christine Rigby were paying a house call on Mrs Bradley.

"She's responding well to the antibiotics," said Trent when Hilary walked into the Bradley's bedroom. "Hello Mrs Bradley."

Emily Bradley smiled wanly at her from her position in the bed. Trent took Hilary to one side and spoke quietly to her.

"I can't say that she'll pull through yet, but there's been no further deterioration. She's definitely holding her own."

"Good. Mrs Thorndyke's body should be ready for you in about half an hour, Paul. I've asked Nurse Knowles to get everything necessary together and she'll meet us at the undertakers. And one more thing Paul, you remember what you promised if we had an unconnected death?"

"Already done, Hilary. I used Bradley's phone to call Malcolm Davidson as soon as you phoned here with the news. The strange thing is that he's already notified the chief virologist at the Ministry and he's apparently 'taking steps' to assist. Davidson couldn't tell what those steps were unfortunately but, in the meantime, he's going to despatch another doctor and nurse to help us until the Ministry's people get here. They should arrive later this afternoon. He's asked if we sort out accommodation for them."

"Accommodation? Hell Paul, this is a tiny village. We're not exactly overrun with hotels you know. In fact we don't even have one! We'll have to try the pub. They may have a room to let."

Five minutes later, after ensuring that Emily Bradley was comfortable the two doctors descended the stairs and found Sam Bradley in his kitchen.

"How is she, Doctor?" he asked Paul Trent.

"Holding her own, Mr Bradley. If she doesn't get any worse in the next twelve hours, I think your wife will stand a good chance of making a full recovery."

Bradley visibly breathed a massive sigh of relief.

"Thanks, Doctor. What about poor Mrs Thorndyke? Do you think it was the same thing as killed David and Evan that did for her too?"

"We'll soon know Mr Bradley. We're leaving now to conduct a post-mortem on Mrs Thorndyke. Please let us know if there's any change in your wife's condition."

"Of course I will. Please, if you see her, give my condolences to Mrs Jones."

"Mrs Jones?" asked Hilary.

"Yes, Emily Jones. She was Mrs Thorndyke's best friend. Those two old ladies were almost inseparable. She has the same name as my wife you know. Emily Jones and Emily Bradley the two Emilys. Mrs Jones and Mrs Thorndyke both had a bit of a soft spot for the boys, and Mrs Jones and my wife have always got on well, probably because they share the name. Mrs Jones would always stop and have a chat in the street if she saw my Emily."

"Yes, well, if we see her, we'll be sure to pass on your sympathy Mr Bradley. Now, really, Doctor Newton and I must be going."

Paul Trent was growing impatient. He knew that, with this latest case, he and Hilary, and indeed everyone in Olney St. Mary was facing a race against time. The disease was on the march, and they had to do all they could to halt it before it took a decisive hold on the population of the village. The longer they delayed, the longer would grow the odds on a successful eradication of the infection.

They drove to the premises of Michael Sweeney in Hilary's car. She'd drop him off at Bradley's later to pick up the Zephyr. As they drove the short distance Paul Trent voiced a major concern, something that was bothering him greatly about the whole scenario in Olney.

"Do you know what I find terribly strange, Hilary?"

"No, but you're about to tell me."

"Yes, I am. Between us you and I and the two girls have searched the homes and the properties of the two dead boys and failed to find any sign of a source of infection."

"Surely, all that means is that they picked up the infection somewhere else in or around the village."

"That's true Hilary, and it also means that we could be in for a whole string of cases before much longer if we don't find out where they did become infected. But it's not just that. It was something at the Parkes' farm."

"Go on, Paul. You've got me intrigued."

"OK. Well, it's not so much a matter of what we *did* find, as being more a case of what we *didn't* find, if you know what I mean."

"Paul, you've lost me. Drop the riddles and tell me what you're talking about, please."

"It's a farm Hilary, alright? Well, when you search a farm the way we did, the one thing you expect to come across, alive or dead, is rodents; mice, rats, you know what I mean. The thing is, and I'm sure it must be significant, though I haven't worked out how, is that we didn't find one single rat or mouse, at that farm, not even in the barn. I've been looking around today and for a country village it seems a little short on wildlife. I haven't seen a mouse scurrying across the road, or a squirrel running up a tree or anything like that."

"That is odd, I grant you, though I don't see how it helps us." Hilary replied.

Unfortunately, there was no time to continue the conversation. Hilary applied the brakes and switched off the engine. They'd arrived at Sweeney's, and the post-mortem examination of Mabel Thorndyke was about to begin.

CHAPTER 13

"It's confirmed I'm afraid. She must have felt terrible and gone to bed, where she probably lay until the end, unable to summon any help, poor woman."

Paul Trent had just completed the rudimentary post-mortem on Mabel Thorndyke's remains. He'd seen enough to reveal the cause of the old lady's death. Hilary Newton stared at the open chest cavity of the woman who must have died in a state of fear and bewilderment, not to mention the pain she must have endured. As a doctor, Hilary had seen death on many occasions, but something about the way Mabel had met her end seemed to Hilary to be more than cruel. There she'd lain in bed in her home, within yards of people walking and cycling, or driving past her front door, and yet she'd been so ill that she'd been unable to call out or even to rise from her bed and perhaps stagger out into the open. Her best friend Emily hadn't seen her for a day and a half, but that hadn't been unusual according to Emily. They were close but didn't necessarily live in one another's pockets.

"The progression of the disease must have been exceedingly rapid in her case," said Hilary, at last returning from the inner world of her thoughts.

"Very fast, I think," Trent replied. "It was probably helped along by her age. Her body, and her respiratory system in particular just couldn't cope with the massive infection and the disease just ran rampant through her system. She would have been reduced to total immobility within hours of the onset of the fever."

"A ghastly death, Paul."

"Very. The poor woman must have been terrified, and I just hope she fell into unconsciousness long before the end."

"Even so, it was still very quick. From my own research I'd have thought that from onset of the disease to the terminal phase should have taken at least three to four days. From what Emily Jones told us, Mabel was healthy enough the last time she saw her. She hadn't complained of any aches or pains or of feeling in any way unwell. If that's the case Paul, we're looking at a period of no more than forty-eight hours from onset to death. That's frighteningly quick."

"You're right Hilary, and that raises the spectre of something else I've been thinking of."

"Which is?"

"What if the disease has mutated?"

"Mutated? But how?"

"I don't know, Hilary. It's just a thought so far. Look, even the two boys died too quickly from my point of view. They exhibited the first signs and died within little more than the time it appears Mrs Thorndyke withstood the ravages of the plague."

"But, how could it mutate? Has there ever been any sign that the plague bacillus has the ability to do so?"

"Certainly, nothing that I've heard of, and I'm sure I'd have seen it if it had been written up in any medical journals or papers."

"Then how could it...?"

"I don't know if it has Hilary. Like I said, it's just a thought, but it would explain the speed at which the disease is moving once it hits its victims."

"Then do you think you should speak to Davidson about your theory?"

"I don't have anything to back it up with, or in truth even anything to base it on apart from a gut feeling. It may just be that the people here have an exceptionally low tolerance to the infection. After all, pneumonic plague hasn't been seen around here for many, many years. It would be hard to imagine that anyone in Olney carries any natural antibodies to help fight off the disease. It's almost like introducing the common cold virus to an alien world. It would probably wipe out the whole population in no time due to a lack of natural built-in resistance to the virus."

"So, what do we do Paul?"

"We do the best we can, until help arrives. We need to make sure that everyone in the village, or at last the vast majority, are at the meeting tonight. If we can distribute enough prophylactic antibiotics, we might at least be able to stave off a wholesale outbreak. That would at least minimise the overall infection rate."

"Unless it really has mutated, in which case the antibiotics could prove useless."

"We might know more when I go back to the Bradley's house. If Mrs Bradley shows signs of improvement, then we can assume that the drugs are helping."

"Or, that she has some natural resistance; or that, as expected, the disease doesn't kill everyone who contracts it. You did say the rate of fatality allowed for the possibility of an automatic number of survivors."

"Yes, well, that's also a possibility. I'd prefer to think that the drugs are helping though."

"I know Paul, but don't you see? We're not going to know either way. If Mrs Bradley survives it may or may not be because of the streptomycin."

"Either way, we have to treat the people of Olney as if the drug will help. If the rate of fatality rises far beyond the expected rate, then we will have an indication that the drugs aren't working. Until then, we have to have faith in what we're doing."

"You said that as if you're expecting a lot more cases Paul."

"Unfortunately, Hilary, that's exactly what I'm expecting. Now come on, let's close this lady up and get her on ice. We should get back to the Bradley's house. We have to concentrate on the living and try to keep them all that way if we can."

After Paul Trent finished sewing up the chest cavity of the late Mabel Thorndyke, Hilary went to fetch Michael Sweeney from his office. He'd waited patiently for the doctors to complete their work and would now be needed in order to place the body in storage pending the arrival of the ambulance, which Hilary ordered using his phone before leaving the office.

Trent gave Sweeney instructions to seal the body in a plastic sheet, and then to lock it in a temporary coffin, which would normally be used to house bodies awaiting embalming. The coffin would then be placed to one side of Sweeney's cold room where he was to leave it undisturbed until the ambulance arrived from Ashford in about two hours. He was instructed to wear protective clothing and a mask whilst handling the body, and to disinfect himself and dispose of the gown and mask after completing his task. The ambulance crew would of course remove the coffin with the body when they arrived. Trent urged Sweeney to then disinfect the room as well. He'd already applied a strong disinfectant to the mortuary slab on which he'd carried out the postmortem, but he urged Sweeney to do it again when the ambulance left with the body.

Sweeney, unflappable as ever, listened intently to Trent's instructions and assured the doctor that his instructions would be carried out to the letter. Somehow, Trent knew that Sweeney would do just that. Something in the man engendered confidence and Paul Trent thought that Sweeney would be a good man to have by his side in a crisis. He couldn't have known it at the time, but Paul Trent's analysis of the character of Michael Sweeney was indeed correct, as would be proved by future events. For now though, he and Hilary Newton bade Sweeney goodbye and were soon back in Hilary's car, headed to the home of the Bradleys.

CHAPTER 14

THE PASTEL SALMON COLOURED AUSTIN A40 SOMERSET trundled along the narrow country lanes that wound through the heart of the Kent countryside, bound for Olney St. Mary. Built in nineteen fifty-three, the Somerset was intended to resemble the transatlantic designs of the U.S. automobile market, though most thought it a little too frumpy to ever hold its own against the Packards and the Chevrolets of Britain's close wartime allies.

At the wheel of the Somerset, Doctor Guy Dearborn looked across at his passenger and smiled at the pretty girl by his side. Edith Kinnaird had proved to be a cheerful travelling companion, even if he'd struggled to understand her heavily accented brand of the English language from time to time. Originally from a village just outside Aberdeen, Edith had never lost the slightly guttural dialect of her homeland, though Guy thought that added to her charm.

Malcolm Davidson had had no qualms about selecting Dearborn for the role of assistant to Trent and Newton in Olney. Aged just twenty-eight, Dearborn was employed at Ashford as a Senior House Officer. Though possessing a grandiose sounding title, an SHO was in fact nothing more than a newly qualified doctor, who would learn his trade 'on the job' in the hospital for two or three years before graduating to bigger and better things. Dearborn however was a little different from the majority of his colleagues. Firstly, he descended from a long line of doctors, his father Miles having at one time worked closely with Davidson. Secondly, young Guy was a rising star in his profession, and had already been noted as having the potential to achieve great things in whatever field of medicine he eventually decided to specialise in. All those who'd worked with him at Ashford agreed that Guy Dearborn had a brilliant, incisive mind, and an in-built instinct for the art of diagnosis. He always appeared calm and unflappable and possessed a flair for logical thinking and deduction. He had gained a reputation for thoroughness in his work and application to detail, exactly what was required in the current situation in Olney. Finally, Guy Dearborn owned a car. In an age when most junior doctors could be seen either walking or perhaps cycling to the hospital from their accommodations, or at best powering through the streets on motor scooters or motorbikes, Guy's natural wealth though not prodigious, proved sufficient to place him on a rather more secure financial footing than most of his peers. The fact that Dearborn could transport both himself and the nurse allocated to accompany him, plus a large amount of medical supplies to Olney served as a big plus in favour of his selection for the appointment.

As for Edith Kinnaird, the pretty Scottish nurse had volunteered at the same time as Patricia Knowles and Christine Rigby, was equally well-qualified, and shared the other girls' single status. Davidson would have liked to send more people, but the manpower resources at his disposal were limited, and he had to think of his responsibilities to the hospital.

So it was that the duo drew closer to Olney with each passing mile. Both Dearborn and Kinnaird had enjoyed the journey, the Kent countryside remaining green and pleasant despite the time of year. Perhaps due to an unusually warm and extended summer, most of the trees retained their leaves, with only a few beginning to show signs of autumn. Soon, the green would turn to shades of brown and russet as the seasons changed and the fields and hedgerows would be decorated with a carpet of rustling fallen leaves. The sky was clear azure blue. Hardly a cloud in sight marred the vista that unfolded before their eyes as the Somerset crested the top of a long rising stretch of road, flanked on either side by those very hedgerows that held such a plethora of bird and wildlife. As the car levelled off at the top of the hill a breathtaking panorama opened up before them. Dearborn slowed the car's speed to a mere twenty miles per hour and, seeing a lay-by just ahead he pulled the Somerset to a halt.

"A good place to stretch our legs I think," he said, smiling at the highly attractive Edith Kinnaird. "We might as well take five minutes to enjoy the view. I doubt we'll have much chance later."

"A good idea, I'm sure," Edith replied, as Dearborn quickly got out of the car and moved around to the passenger side, opening the door and holding out his hand in gentlemanly fashion to assist her from the vehicle.

"Just look at that view," he exclaimed as they stood together looking out towards the horizon.

"Beautiful isn't it?" Edith replied.

As far as the eye could see the rolling countryside of Kent stretched out before their eyes. A patchwork of varied hues of greens and browns marked the innumerable fields belonging to the many farms that made up this beautiful 'Garden of England'.

Here and there, small clusters of trees stood like silent sentinels of the land, guarding the fields that housed them. Farmhouses and their surrounding outbuildings could be seen, appearing like miniatures on a model landscape, their solid reality only betrayed by the wisps of smoke that told of the fires burning in the hearths of their kitchens. Tiny sheep and cows moved as though in slow motion in the far distance, where the occasional livestock farm intruded upon the predominantly arable landscape. In the midst of the swathes of colour, a dark grey asphalt snake seemed to be slithering across the scene. It wound around and apparently through the farms and fields until it entered a large cluster of homes and solid structures, exiting at the far end and continuing its journey on toward apparent infinity as it stretched away to the far horizon.

Guy Dearborn pointed to the little village that had but one road leading in and another one leading out.

"Look there," he said, indicating the settlement to Kinnaird. "That has to be Olney St. Mary. There isn't another village for miles. We should be there in about twenty minutes I think."

"It looks idyllic, doesn't it, Doctor?"

"I'm sure it is, Nurse, under normal circumstances. Unfortunately, these are not normal circumstances as we both know."

"True, doctor. Do you think we'll be able to do much to help?"

"That's why we're here, Nurse. We'll do what we can because that's our job isn't it?"

"Of course. I never thought I'd ever see a case of pneumonic plague close up, I must admit."

"That's the thing with our profession Nurse. We never know what to expect from one day to the next. As for the plague, I'm like you in thinking that I'd never see it up close, but it looks like we were both wrong in our estimations. It looks as if we're going to see not just one case, but maybe a whole village infected with the bacillus."

"Doesn't it frighten you, Doctor Dearborn, not even just a little bit?"

"It doesn't frighten me, but I'll tell you now that we'd all better have a healthy respect for the disease we're fighting, or it could just turn around and bite us all when we least expect it to."

On that note of sombre warning, Guy Dearborn and Edith Kinnaird climbed back into the Somerset. Dearborn started the car, slipped her into gear and began a slow descent of the hill, down into the valley, and onto the snake of a road that led to the village of Olney, *into the jaws of death,* thought Dearborn as they approached their destination.

CHAPTER 15

"EVERYTHING'S IN PLACE SIR," SAID GROUP CAPTAIN DONALD Forbes.

He and Charles Macklin were once again seated across the desk from Douglas Ryan, who'd asked Forbes for an update on the plan they'd devised the previous night. Forbes went on:

"You just need to say the word, and I can have a team of Infantrymen in place within two hours. They'll seal off the only roads in and out of the village and institute constant patrols of the village boundaries to prevent unauthorised entry into Olney. A second team will maintain the ten-mile exclusion zone you specified, giving us a double barrier against possible external penetration of our designated perimeter. I also have a medical team standing by who can be flown by helicopter to the village and could be in the field within an hour of being called for."

"Good. And what have you to report, Charles?"

"The people at the GPO were very co-operative sir. We only have to give them the numbers of the telephones we wish to remain active in Olney St. Mary, and they will ensure that every other line in the village is disconnected as soon we give the order. I can have the village isolated from outside communication at the drop of a hat. You just have to give the word."

"Excellent, gentlemen. You've done a good day's work. I've spoken with Malcolm Davidson and he tells me that there's been another death in the village. An old woman died alone without having an opportunity to call for help, so we don't know how long she'd been infected, or where and how she became contaminated. She could have been exposed to the same contaminant as the two boys or may have caught the disease through contact with them. Another woman, the mother of one of the boys, has the disease but is so far holding her own, thanks to high doses of streptomycin. We've still no idea of the source of infection. Davidson has sent another doctor and a nurse to the village to assist the medics already in place."

"So, do we move to isolate the village yet sir?" asked Forbes.

"Yes, we do. Doctor Trent is apparently holding a meeting of the village residents tonight, even as we speak, to inform them of the situation, so we need to move fast to prevent any spread of damaging information. Charles, would you be so kind as to telephone your contact at the General Post Office and arrange for the immediate disconnection of all telephones in Olney with the exception of Doctor Newton's and the Police House?"

"I will sir." Macklin rose to leave, then hesitated.

"You have a problem, Charles?"

"Just a couple of things, sir. Does the doctor in the village and the police constable know we're about to cut off the telephones? Also we must be aware that if the phones are cut, then people will lose the ability to telephone the doctor for assistance. Also, there's the local post office to consider. People could still send telegrams."

"Charles, we must act swiftly. I'm sure I can get Davidson to call Doctor Trent after the village meeting to explain the necessity of what we've done. The post office in Olney is apparently a sub-post office within the village stores. They have to telephone any telegrams through to Ashford, and of course their telephone will be cut off too. As for the villagers, it's a tiny place, and they will just have to send for help in person if they need the doctor."

"But, the outlying farms sir?"

"Charles, go and make that call, now please."

"Yes sir, of course," Macklin replied, and he rose and left the room to retire to his own office where he would make the telephone call that would effectively seal Olney St. Mary off from the outside world until the plague outbreak could be resolved. While he was out of the office Forbes filled Ryan in on the military options available to resolve the situation if the current plague outbreak became an epidemic.

When Charles Macklin returned to Ryan's office some five minutes later to report the success of his call to the GPO, Ryan ordered that the village should be sealed off by the following morning. Forbes would make the arrangements, and have the medical personnel flown in at 0930 hours. Even as the people of Olney retired to their beds that night, moves would be afoot to ensure the complete and total isolation of their village. The draconian measures discussed just twenty-four hours previously by the three men at the Ministry had been set in motion and there would now be no turning back.

———

In Olney's tiny village hall the emergency meeting was becoming heated

"Plague?" a voice from the middle of the hall shouted. "You say they died of plague, but how could they Doctor, in this day and age?"

"Plague is not and never has been totally eradicated from the world," Paul Trent replied to the question. "We're doing all we can to find out where and how the boys and Mrs Thorndyke became infected. We have high hopes that we can contain the spread of the disease before it attacks too many of the people here in the village."

"So you're saying that there will be other victims, no matter what we do?" This came from a young woman sitting near the front with a young girl of about five years old sitting beside her.

"Isn't there a vaccine?" came from another disembodied voice at the back.

" Why can't we be evacuated until it's safe to return?" came from another.

Trent went on to explain that there was no plague vaccine yet available, and that evacuation would only lead to a potential risk of spreading the disease over a wider area. To the young woman with the child he tried to be as reassuring as he could.

"It's true that there will probably be other cases before the outbreak is finally eradicated, but we can minimise the extent and the severity of any such infections by administering you all with what we call prophylactic doses of an antibiotic that is proven to work against the plague. The nurses at the table at the back of the hall with Doctor Dearborn and Doctor Newton will distribute the medicine to each of you, sufficient for all of your families, as you leave the hall."

Every eye in the room turned to stare at the back of the village hall, where Hilary, the newly arrived Guy Dearborn and the three nurses waited for the meeting to conclude. Hilary had decided to let Paul Trent deliver the message to the residents, as he was the senior physician and also, as an outsider, his words might be considered to bear more weight than the local GP's.

The meeting broke up soon afterwards, and Hilary, Guy and the nurses soon had their supply of streptomycin distributed to the anxious villagers. When a couple of the residents tried to bully Hilary and Guy into giving them a few extra tablets 'just in case', they were quickly rebuffed by the intervention of Police Constable Greaves, who was, to Hilary's surprise, aided in his efforts by none other than Michael Sweeney, who quickly threw his weight behind that of Greaves in helping to maintain order. It wouldn't be the last time that Hilary Newton would have cause to thank Michael Sweeney over the next few days.

That evening, several worried residents of Olney St. Mary tried to telephone friends and relatives in other towns and villages to inform them of the dreadful news that pneumonic plague had broken out in their village. They were each surprised and frustrated to find that on top of the terrible news of the disease in their midst, the telephones were now out of order as well. Had it been daytime, when people would have been going about their daily lives around the village, the loss of the telephone service would soon have been discovered to be village wide. As it was, the night-time disconnection served to delay that knowledge until the following day, by which time Douglas Ryan's isolation zone would be in place and the Ministry's medical personnel would already be in the village.

As the concerned, fearful and apprehensive residents of Olney St. Mary took to their beds that night, their exclusion from the mainstream of society had already begun. No-one knew it at the time, but the lives of the people of the peaceful little village would never be the same again.

CHAPTER 16

HILARY NEWTON WAS AWAKENED AT SIX-THIRTY A.M. BY THE incessant ringing of the telephone, downstairs in the surgery. Shaking the sleep from her eyes, she pulled on her warm woollen dressing gown and hurried to answer the call, thinking that another of the residents of Olney might have contracted the disease and needed her services. Instead she was surprised to hear the voice of a man who identified himself as Charles Macklin, assistant to Douglas Ryan, the government's chief virologist at the Ministry of Health. Macklin wouldn't tell Hilary the reason for his call, insisting instead on speaking to Paul Trent. Leaving Macklin hanging on, Hilary walked across the hall to the sitting room, knocked and entered the room and found Trent awake, obviously woken, like her, by the ringing telephone.

Ten minutes later Tent completed his conversation with Macklin and turned towards Hilary with look of mild shock on his face.

"Paul, what is it? What's wrong? What did that man say?"

"All the phones in the village, with the exception of yours and the one in the police house have been disconnected."

"Why? What for?"

"Because the Ministry of Health doesn't want anyone in Olney contacting the outside world and revealing that we have a plague outbreak in the village."

"But that's crazy, surely. They can't keep it covered up Paul. Anyway, we could have it all under control before long. Why the panic?"

"It appears that the chief virologist is anxious to avoid a panic. He takes the view that it's only a decade since the country was ravaged by war, then there was Korea, and it's only a couple of years since rationing ended for good, and the last thing the people of this country need is to be told that a potentially lethal plague epidemic is about to strike at them. He thinks that a little inconvenience to the people of a small village like Olney St. Mary is a price worth paying to maintain the equilibrium of the nature's psyche."

"But how will people call us if they need us?"

"I asked the same question. Macklin says they'll have to do what people did in the days before telephones and get a message to us in person."

"How ridiculous! Don't they realise that the delay in us learning of new cases could prove fatal to some of our potential patients."

"I got the feeling that they don't care if we lose a substantial number of patients Hilary, as long as the disease isn't allowed to break out of Olney. There was something else as well."

"Go on, what now?"

"In a few hours they're sending in a team of medics from the Ministry. They'll be arriving by helicopter. In the meantime the Army are setting up a ten-mile exclusion zone around the village to prevent anyone getting in or out. It will stay in place until the infection is controlled and eradicated."

"Bloody hell, Paul! It's like something out of a nightmare. They're treating us and the people of the village like lepers in Biblical times. What if these people need hospitalisation?"

"Apparently there'll be helicopters on standby if we need them. Any serious cases can be airlifted to a military hospital that's been designated to receive them by the Ministry. They'll be placed in a secure isolation ward and treated by specialists from the Ministry's own crisis management team."

"I don't like the sound of any of this Paul."

"To be truthful, neither do I Hilary, but we have no choice. We're just going to have to do the best we can in the given circumstances."

Just then a gentle knock on the surgery door signalled the arrival of Patricia Knowles and Christine Rigby. The two nurses looked tired and bleary-eyed.

"We heard the telephone ringing," said Christine. "Is there something wrong?"

The two nurses were soon given the news of the call from Macklin, and Paul Trent decided to walk the short distance to the Beekeepers Arms where Guy Dearborn and Edith Kinnaird had managed to find rooms for the duration of their stay. He wanted to inform Dearborn and the nurse of the impending arrival of the Health Ministry's team, and of the apparent segregation of the village from the rest of the country. He quickly washed and shaved before setting off for the pub, while Hilary and the girls began cooking breakfast. Though nobody really felt like eating after Macklin's news, Trent had insisted that they all eat a hearty breakfast. They would need all their energy for the day ahead, he'd said. Despite their collective lack of appetite the three women knew he was right.

———

Guy Dearborn reacted with predictable calmness when Paul Trent knocked loudly on the back door of The Beekeepers Arms. Always an early riser, he was already up and about when Trent arrived, and answered the door himself. Charlie Peace and his wife Peg were busy cleaning the pub ready for the day's business and Edith Kinnaird was in the bathroom, preparing herself for the day's work.

"Well, that's a turn up for the books," said the unflappable Dearborn. "I suppose we should get ready and come and join you and the others at the surgery. We ought to be ready for them when the Ministry's people arrive."

"Thanks Guy. We'll expect you for breakfast at the surgery in a few minutes then, ok?"

"Ten minutes should do it," Dearborn replied. "Edith and I, well, Nurse Kinnaird that is, have already eaten one of Mrs Peace's finest breakfasts. Superb!"

Ignoring the brief slip of familiarity shown by Dearborn towards the pretty Edith Kinnaird, Trent left the young doctor to interrupt her morning ablutions and get the two of them over to Hilary Newton's surgery at the double. True to his word, barely ten minutes had passed before Dearborn and Kinnaird joined the others and began preparing for the arrival of the airborne medical team.

Before they arrived, Hilary and Christine would visit the Bradleys to check on the progress of Emily Bradley, while Paul Trent and Nurse Knowles would prepare an inventory of their equipment and supplies. Guy Dearborn would stand in for Hilary in the surgery and treat any patients who cared to turn up that morning, with Edith Kinnaird to assist should any female patients arrive requiring intimate examinations.

All went well until Guy received his second patient of the morning. Gareth Potts was the local butcher. A single man, like many in Olney, due to the lack of eligible females, he had been feeling unwell all night, he reported. He'd been at the meeting the previous evening and had taken the tablets given to him by Doctor Newton and thought he might be suffering a reaction to them. Within a few seconds of examining the man, Guy Dearborn knew that this was no reaction to the medication. Another case of pneumonic plague had just presented itself in Olney St. Mary. Lacking the means to contact his more senior colleagues Guy Dearborn showed just why he was so highly regarded. In the absence of any designated medical facility in the village, he sent Potts straight home, accompanied by Nurse Kinnaird who would make him comfortable and administer a further dose of antibiotics. Dearborn promised to join them as soon as he could close the surgery. Ten minutes later he'd departed, leaving a note on the surgery door to the effect that the doctor was 'on call'. Instead of going directly to the Potts house however, he stopped off at the vicarage, where he asked for, and received, the vicar's permission to use the village hall as an emergency treatment centre if the number of cases of plague were to suddenly escalate. He was sure that Trent and Hilary Newton wouldn't mind his having used his initiative, and in truth, when they arrived back some time later, they were delighted that he'd shown such resourcefulness. Trent did however have one question for Dearborn. Having the use of the hall was one thing, but where would they find the beds to fill it if they had to quarantine a substantial number of the village population?

Guy readily confessed that he 'hadn't quite worked that one out yet,' and for the first time that day, Paul Trent and Hilary Newton allowed themselves to laugh a little at the young doctor's obvious lack of forethought for the overall effectiveness of his idea. Unfazed by the apparent problem of the beds, Dearborn promised that he'd work on it. Without quite knowing why, Trent and Newton had every faith in him to solve the problem.

With Emily Bradley still making progress, albeit slowly, in her fight against the plague, and with Gareth Potts being ministered to by Edith Kinnaird, the rest of the team had little to do but wait for the arrival of the airborne medical team. They'd waited for less than half an hour before the steady throbbing and clacking of rotor blades announced the impending arrival of the 'men from the ministry'.

CHAPTER 17

THOSE AMONGST OLNEY'S RESIDENTS WHO WERE OUT IN THE open air couldn't help but see and hear the helicopters as they descended upon the village like a swarm of angry dragonflies, the thwack, thwack of their rotors growing louder as the choppers descended ever nearer to the ground. The noise was such that the headmaster of the little village school stared out of his office window and such was the rarity of such an occurrence that he quickly allowed the school's population to escape their lessons briefly so that they could go out and watch the surprise event of the day.

The four Bristol Type 171 'Sycamore' helicopters swung in a wide arc around the centre of the village before coming into land on the village green, the only place suitable for all four to touch down in the same location. All four had had hastily painted red crosses added to their usual camouflage paint scheme, and the presence of those symbols had an instant effect on the morale of the beleaguered villagers, who waved and cheered at the new arrivals as, one by one the pilots flared out and the skids of the helicopters made contact with terra firma. Built to carry the pilot plus three others, each of the four Sycamores quickly disgorged a dozen highly trained doctors and nurses from the

Ministry of Health's Crisis Response Team, plus a more than adequate supply of medicines and equipment.

First to deplane from the lead helicopter was a short bespectacled man in a brown pin-striped suit, with out of place leather patches applied to the elbows of the jacket. Bending low to avoid the wash of the spinning rotor blades he made his way quickly to where Paul Trent and his colleagues waited. They must have looked like doctors, as none of them recognised the new arrival that made a bee-line for them as though in no doubt as to their identity.

Above the sound of the helicopter engines and in the windblast from the still rotating blades the little man attempted to introduce himself.

"I'm Doctor Angus McKay," he shouted, "and I'll presume that you're Doctor Trent."

Paul Trent held out his right hand, shook that of the newcomer and replied,

"Yes, that's right, and this is Doctor Hilary Newton, and Doctor Guy Dearborn."

"Aye, well, we'll have time to get better acquainted once these whirlybird contraptions have left us in peace. I see my team have nearly unloaded everything, so I doubt the monstrosities will disturb us for much longer."

Paul looked towards the makeshift landing area where, sure enough, without any help from their leader, the remaining members of his party had quickly offloaded their equipment and supplies and were standing back, waving a goodbye to the pilots who had brought them to Olney. A loud roar spilt the air once again as the four Sycamore pilots increased the revolutions on their engines. In less than a minute the four helicopters rose into the air, circled the village just once, and then banked left and headed off in a westerly direction. In less than a minute the sounds of the departing helicopters receded into a distant thudding in the sky, until, as the aircraft themselves reduced to no more than tiny specks in the eyes of the watchers, the air became still and quiet once more. The only sign of their having been there were the eleven people who, with their assorted bags and cases, now stood on the village green, waiting for instructions from their boss, the balding, bespectacled Angus McKay.

After consulting with Trent and Hilary Newton, McKay instructed his team to carry their equipment the short distance to the village hall, where they would set up their base of operations. Guy Dearborn's original suggestion of using the hall as a treatment centre had been modified slightly, but he was pleased nonetheless that his idea of utilising the place had been accepted. McKay was reticent when asked by Trent exactly what he and his team intended to do apart from a short,

"Why, we're here to help, Doctor Trent, what else?"

Apart from that he seemed reluctant at that point to explain exactly what form that help would take. Not until all his team's equipment had been transferred to the village hall did McKay appear to relax a little and accept Hilary Newton's invitation to accompany her and the others to her surgery for an update on the situation in Olney, and a cup of tea or coffee, whichever he preferred. When asked about the accommodation needs of his team, he'd simply pointed to four very large bulbous green canvas sacks, which Trent identified as military eight-man tents. Obviously, the newcomers would be sleeping under canvas, though with space for thirty-two people in the four tents, they would have plenty of personal space.

"We have four doctors, including myself, six nurses and two epidemiologists in our party," McKay began as he sat sipping coffee in Hilary's surgery. Trent and Dearborn stood listening intently; Hilary Newton was seated behind her desk. He continued.

"My instructions are to ensure that the outbreak of pneumonic plague you have reported to the Health Ministry is not allowed to spread outwith the confines of Olney St. Mary."

His use of the Scottish 'outwith' sounded quaint and antiquated in the present situation. Then again, Hilary Newton thought that Angus McKay looked a little stuffy and antiquated himself.

"And just how do you propose to 'forbid' the disease to leave the village?" she asked, a little angry at his almost ludicrous pronouncement.

"As I'm sure you're all aware, steps have been taken to isolate and exclude Olney and its residents from the rest of the country until the situation is resolved. Troops are in place at strategic locations in the surrounding area. They will, I promise you, prevent anyone either entering or leaving the village until it is given the all clear. As to that matter, I am now, on the orders of the Minister for Health, in sole and complete charge of the medical initiative in Olney St. Mary. You will work directly under my control and in tandem with my own people. I hope you understand those orders and have no problem with them."

Trent, Newton and Dearborn nodded their assent. All three found the little Scotsman to be officious and overbearing and full of his own self-importance, but he had the authority of the government behind him and they had no choice but to comply. After all, they assumed that he, like the rest of them, had the health and welfare of the people of Olney St. Mary at heart. That, after all, had to be their number one priority. The truth of the matter was that the incumbent physicians all felt slightly overwhelmed by the speed of the actions taking place around them. Even as McKay sat explaining the draconian measures he intended to implement, which Hilary thought akin to declaring marshal law in the village, outside they could hear the sounds of activity as the Ministry's medical team hammered tent pegs into the ground. Soon, the miniature tent village would be assembled on the village green and McKay and his people would be ready to set to work. The little Scotsman then went on to inform them that another helicopter should arrive in less than an hour, carrying a large marquee which would be set up and used as an emergency field hospital if the number of cases of infection reached the expected proportions. Hilary wondered how he or his superiors had arrived at the 'expected number' of cases, though she didn't think it wise to ask. She doubted he'd provide her with a reply. In short, there was something about Doctor Angus McKay that Hilary found profoundly unsettling. She didn't like the man. When he left soon afterwards to supervise his people and to await the arrival of the incoming helicopter, she wasn't surprised to find that her colleagues felt exactly the same about McKay as she did.

"Repulsive little man," she exclaimed as soon as her front door closed as he left.

"I have to say I agree with you, Doctor Newton," said Guy Dearborn. As the junior doctor of the three he couldn't quite bring himself to use Hilary's first name, though she'd asked him to. "Why, he's almost reptilian."

Paul Trent added his input to the conversation by voicing his suspicions about McKay's motives. Trent was acutely aware that things were on the verge of getting out of hand in Olney. This wasn't the response he'd expected from those in authority at the Ministry of Health.

"That's a bit strong, Guy, but I have to say he doesn't come across as the most sympathetic of people. He's evasive as well. Did you notice he never actually explained what it is he and his people intend to do here? Surely if it were a simple case of providing help and assistance to the three of us, he'd have offered to do whatever we thought necessary, rather than pompously assuming command of the village the way he did? There's more to McKay than meets the eye, of that I'm sure. I want to know what the hell they intend to do now they're here. As for a military exclusion zone, that's a massive case of overkill in my book."

"That's the most frightening bi,t Paul. Why do they feel the need to cut us off like that?"

"I don't know Hilary. It's almost as if they fear that we're going to start an epidemic that will decimate the country, and they're prepared to do whatever is necessary to seal off what they see as the source of the infection."

As Trent's words sank in, Guy Dearborn was the first to respond with a verbal assessment of what he'd said.

"Bloody Hell! What you're saying, Doctor Trent, though not in so many words, is that by 'whatever is necessary' you think they'd be prepared to eliminate the whole of Olney if they thought it would stop the plague from spreading to the rest of the country, am I right?"

"I'm not sure if they'd go quite that far Guy, but I do think that McKay and his people, apart from helping to treat whatever cases we encounter over the next few days, just might have a secondary agenda that we as yet know nothing about."

Hilary looked aghast at the two men as she listened to the conversation.

"You can't possibly think that the government would sanction something as drastic as destroying a village just to contain a small outbreak of plague, Paul, surely?"

"I don't know Hilary; I just don't know."

Any further conversation was brought to a sudden halt by the thumping of rotor blades overhead. Trent rose and walked across to the window, looking up as he did so.

"Looks like our hospital is about to arrive," he said as another Sycamore, probably one of the earlier squadron that had returned to base to collect the marquee circled the village green before coming in to land, the downdraft from it's rotors throwing up a shower of dust and leaves from around the edges of the green.

Wondering what would happen next in the stricken village, and what they could do to maintain a calm and stable situation amongst the villagers, the three doctors stepped outside to watch the unloading of the large green canvas and tarpaulin bags that held the makeshift emergency hospital. Minutes later, in another crescendo of sound and dust, the Sycamore lifted off and in seconds silence returned to the village green. The residents of Olney watched the departing helicopter disappear into the distance, and a few remained to view the assembly of the marquee that slowly sprouted up on the village green. The remainder tried, as far as was possible to go on with the normal business of the day.

Trent, Newton and Dearborn joined Angus McKay to be introduced to the newly arrived doctors, nurses, and the two epidemiologists. Despite their dislike of the man, they were all impressed by the level of his professionalism and organisation. He quickly explained his plans for dealing with further cases of the plague, and for trying to locate and identify the primary infection source. Soon, McKay's nurses were being despatched to strategic locations around the village armed with printed posters that detailed the procedures to be followed over the next few days, as the doctors tried to help contain and eliminate the infection from their village. By then, some of the villagers had discovered that their telephones were inoperative, and as some of them began to meet and talk together and exchange such information, that and the arrival of the strangers in their midst began to have a disquieting effect on some of the residents. That disquiet would soon find itself growing as, by the end of the day, the first beds in the new emergency hospital began to be filled.

To the horror of the doctors and residents of Olney St. Mary alike, what had gone before had been merely a precursor to the real terror of the plague that was about to be released!

CHAPTER 18

GROUP CAPTAIN DONALD FORBES WAS A WORRIED MAN. Perturbed by what he'd seen as an overreaction by Douglas Ryan to the situation in Olney St. Mary, he'd requested a private meeting with the virologist. Now, he sat eye to eye with Ryan in the latter's office. Charles Macklin was nowhere to be seen.

"Just why did you ask to see me this morning, Group Captain? We have a meeting scheduled for this evening as you well know. Couldn't it have waited until then, whatever it is you're so keen to discuss?"

"No sir, it most certainly could not wait. I'm unhappy with the way this Olney situation is being handled. I spoke with my commander, Air Commodore Bright early this morning and he made a couple of telephone calls. It appears Mr Ryan that you are acting independent of government in this matter, and that places me, my people and everyone concerned with the management of the Olney St. Mary outbreak in a highly fragile position if things go wrong."

"Go wrong, Group Captain? What could go wrong? We're simply responding to an outbreak of a highly contagious disease upon our shores. It is my sole intention to prevent the spread of that disease by any means I can employ to do so. What, pray tell me, is so heinous about that?"

"The fact, sir, is that you are prepared to go to the extraordinary lengths that you've previously outlined. For God's sake, Doctor Ryan, you talked about destroying the whole village if we're unable to eradicate the source of the infection. This isn't the Middle Ages you know!"

"That, as you well know, is simply a last resort option. As for being 'extraordinary' I hardly need to remind you that the Great Fire of London was seen as the greatest single factor in ridding London of the Great Plague back in the seventeenth century. If we have to raze one small village to the ground in order to prevent a similar outbreak here and now in the twentieth century, then I'd have thought you'd realise that such an action would be a small price to pay to protect the population of Great Britain from a disastrous epidemic. Oh yes, and as for Government sanction, I hardly need remind you or Air Commodore Bright, that I work on the express instructions and directly under the auspices of the Minister of Health. Any action I take is undertaken on his authority, and I am answerable to him and him alone."

"That's as maybe Doctor, but why me? Please tell me why you asked for me and my people to become involved in this case. I'm sure you don't need reminding that I work at Porton Down, and that Porton is essentially a weapons research and testing facility. I'm laying my cards on the table when I say that I believe you are withholding information from me. Are we looking at a biological weapon here, something that I and my people are unaware of?"

Douglas Ryan leaned back in his chair, threw his head back and in an uncharacteristic show of emotion, he laughed out loud. The laughter continued for a mere ten seconds, but it was enough to unsettle the RAF officer. Ryan soon regained his composure and looked hard at the Group Captain.

"Really, Group Captain Forbes? What do you take me for? I'd have thought that if any biological weapons were involved, you and your people at Porton Down would have known about it long before me. The answer to your question is far simpler and much more logical than that I assure you. Charles Macklin and I aside, you are probably the most eminent virologist currently alive in this country. That made you an ideal and logical candidate for the relief operation. Secondly, because of your military background, you have a ready-made supply of both staff and materiel at your disposal. When I requested your secondment to this case, I was also aware that you would be able to organise the supply of the necessary military hardware in the form of helicopters and personnel, not to mention being capable of organising the troops required to cordon off the village if necessary. The Ministry of Health is primarily concerned with providing healthcare for the nation. We have neither the manpower nor resources at our disposal to provide the most excellent logistical support that you have been instrumental in arranging for the relief of Olney St. Mary. Now please, could you be gracious enough to accept that you were chosen for this task because you are the best man for the job, and forget this wildly insane theory of yours? Biological weapons indeed! Poppycock, I assure you, pure poppycock!"

There was little left for Forbes to say. Somehow, Ryan had shot his theories down in flames. The man appeared to have a perfectly logical answer to every one of his questions regarding the handling of the Olney affair. Finding It hard to push the man any further, Forbes had no choice but to agree to continue in his role as military liaison to the relief operation, and was soon ushered out of the office by Ryan, with a "See you this evening" being Ryan's parting words.

Forbes drove back to his own base feeling anything but satisfied by the meeting. He was still sure that Ryan was hiding something, but despite his and his own commander's reservations, he had no choice, as a serving officer, but to obey his orders. For now, he would continue to do as he was instructed, but he felt that Doctor Douglas Ryan would bear incredibly careful watching. Forbes promised himself that at the first sign of anything approaching irregularity he would raise his concerns once more. As a serving officer, he at least retained that right, but whether he could do anything to interrupt Ryan's plan, and he was sure that the man had such a plan, he wouldn't know until the time came.

For now though, the Group Captain had work to do. The next phase of the operation to contain and eliminate the plague was about to be set in motion, and on this occasion, he had no qualms or worries about the action required.

CHAPTER 19

HILARY NEWTON AND PAUL TRENT WERE SATISFIED THAT
Emily Bradley was making good progress. The antibiotics
appeared to have fought and won their battle with the plague,
and slowly at first, and now with greater rapidity, Emily had
begun her journey along the road to recovery. Sam Bradley had
expressed great relief at his wife's improved state of health, but
now had another worry on his mind. The loss of telephone
service had prevented him calling his daughter Carol's private
school. He had meant to call the previous day to make sure that
the school didn't send the girl home as planned at the weekend.
He had originally thought to have his daughter home in time for
the funeral of young David, but with his wife falling ill, Bradley
had forgotten to make the call. He was terrified that his
daughter might end up walking unknowingly into a plague
epidemic. He wisely hadn't revealed the cause of David's death
to the school, merely telling them that it had been a sudden
illness that had killed his son. Not wanting to give away the fact
that her telephone was still operational, Hilary said that the
newcomers from the ministry had a radio telephone with them,
which was true enough, and that she'd get a message to the
school on Sam's behalf.

Leaving a grateful Sam Bradley to nurse his gradually improving wife, Hilary and Trent took their leave of the garage owner and made the short journey back to the surgery. On their return, they were greeted by a worried looking Christine Rigby. She informed them that Guy Dearborn was at the hospital marquee with McKay and his people. Patricia Knowles had gone with Dearborn. Apparently, soon after Hilary and Trent had left for the Bradley house, a messenger had arrived from McKay to tell them that while they'd been pinning up McKay's 'guidelines' for the residents around the village some of his nurses had been approached by worried inhabitants. Husbands, wives and children were apparently falling sick all over Olney, and they wanted the nurses to tell them what to do. Following McKay's instructions, the nurses had told them all to wait in their homes, and that help would be sent.

Subsequently the nurses had reported back to McKay, who had despatched teams to each of the homes of those who had reported illnesses to the nurses. Of the eight teams to be sent out, six had returned with patients for the new hospital, the other two having returned with reports of minor ailments, unconnected with the plague. Since the initial influx, another four had arrived, including Gareth Potts, the butcher, making a total of ten cases so far in the space of a couple of hours.

Paul Trent was horrified to hear such news, as was Hilary, who again bemoaned the loss of the telephone service.

"If they hadn't cut off the damned phones, someone could have reached us at Sam Bradley's house and let us know what was happening," she protested to no-one in particular.

"I know Hilary. You're right of course, but it's no use moaning about it now. What's done is done. We'd better get over there and see what we can do to help. Nurse Rigby, you'd better stay here and man the fort in case anyone comes to the surgery looking for help."

"Yes of course, Doctor," Christine replied.

Leaving the nurse at the surgery, the two doctors hurried across to the hospital where they found an appalling sight awaiting them.

Shown by McKay into what he called the 'isolation' wing of the large marquee, they were confronted by the sight of the ten new patients, all of whom looked as though they'd suffered from the plague for days, rather than having only just contracted the disease, or at least, only just having exhibited the signs of infection.

"This is just terrible," said Hilary. "They look as though they're near to death, every one of them. Were they this bad when you had them brought in?"

"That's just it," McKay looked perplexed. "They were nowhere near this bad two hours ago. As soon as we got hem in here, they began a rapid deterioration and so far, massive doses of streptomycin have done little to slow the progression of the disease in any of them. I just cannot understand it."

"I had a thought yesterday Doctor McKay," said Trent, as a nagging thought came back to the forefront of his mind.

"Aye, and what would that be, Doctor Trent?"

"Well, what if, and I'm not saying it's definite of course, but..."

"Och, get on with it man," said the little Scotsman impatiently.

"Ok, well, what if the disease has mutated?"

"Mutated, how?"

"I don't know how. But, let's just say for the sake of argument that it has. Then we could be facing a strain of pneumonic plague that is resistant to our modern antibiotics."

"But Paul, Emily Bradley is getting better," Hilary protested.

"Yes, she is," Trent replied, "but as you know, in any epidemic, there will always be survivors. It may just be that Emily Bradley is one of the lucky ones who help to make up the survivors' quota of the equation."

"He's quite right you know, Doctor Newton," said McKay. "Even at the height of the Black Death in the seventeenth century, there were in fact more survivors than fatalities you know."

"But this isn't bubonic plague is it? It's pneumonic, and the death rate is usually far higher, around nine in ten. So far, we've lost three and saved one of the cases we know about. That in itself doesn't look too good, does it?"

"Aye, well, that's only one in four, indeed it is, but it's too small a sample to base any projections on at all. We'll have to wait and see how these latest cases fare after a day or so. Then we'll have a better idea. As for your mutation theory Doctor Trent, I don't think we have any evidence as yet to support such a wild idea, but I'll agree it can't be dismissed out of hand. Then again, I've never heard of the plague bacillus having the ability to change its genome, or to mutate in any way whatsoever. Let's go take close look at the patients shall we. Then you can both give me your opinions."

The three doctors donned gowns and masks from a portable wardrobe next to McKay's makeshift desk and made their way into the heart of the ward. As they approached the first bed, they identified a masked Guy Dearborn as he stood in attendance on the bedridden patient. To Hilary's shock, but perhaps not to her surprise the patient was none other than Emily Jones, the close friend of the late Mabel Thorndyke.

"Hello, Guy."

"Hello, Doctor Newton. Sorry I couldn't get a message to you sooner."

"That's alright. It wasn't your fault. Hello, Mrs Jones. How are you feeling?"

"Oh, Doctor Newton, I'm fair poorly I am. This is the thing what did for poor Mabel isn't it? I'm dying too aren't I?"

"Now, now, Mrs. Jones, let's not be so pessimistic," Hilary replied. "Your namesake Emily Bradley is doing fine and recovering nicely. There's every chance that you'll make a full recovery too. Just do as the doctors say, and we'll do everything we can for you. Please, just concentrate on getting well, and let us do the hard work."

"I didn't know Emily had it too, and yet you say she's getting better?"

Hilary nodded.

"Well then, I'd best do all I can to stay with you all then hadn't I?"

"That's the spirit, Mrs. Jones," said Dearborn.

McKay made a sort of 'harrumphing' noise in his throat which signalled that he wanted to move on. Ten minutes later, they'd completed their brief tour of the ward. Aside from Emily Jones, there were two children, girls who looked to be aged under ten years, four women, all under forty and three men, none of whom were personally known to Hilary, though Dearborn soon introduced her to Potts. All appeared to be in great distress as a result of their symptoms, and each was attended by either one of McKay's doctors or nurses, with Patricia Knowles being employed at the bedside of one of the children. Hilary and the others had yet to be introduced to some of the newcomers and had no way of telling if those at work were McKay's medical practitioners or the epidemiologists. At least the nurses were easily identified by their uniforms, which showed them to be members of the

Princess Mary's Royal Air Force Nursing Service, as opposed to regular nurses in the employ of the National Health Service. When Hilary commented on this fact to McKay the little man was quick to answer.

"Yes, Doctor Newton, they are indeed military nurses. The Ministry of Health requested assistance from certain sections of the armed forces in order to pull this operation together as fast as possible. That way, they thought we could organise relief for the people of this village far quicker than if we'd had to wait for volunteers from within the NHS. These good people here are all from the RAF Hospital at Wroughton and as such they are a ready-made team, used to working together under pressure, and ready to do whatever is necessary. We'd never have been able to get such a team here or managed to obtain the manpower and resources we have here today without assistance from the military. You have to understand that speed is of the essence in trying to eradicate this disease, and speed is what we have achieved thanks to these fine people."

Both Hilary and Paul Trent were aware of the RAF hospital at Wroughton, near Swindon in Wiltshire, and McKay's logic appeared sound enough.

"Yes, I see," said Hilary. "I'm sure we're all incredibly grateful, Doctor McKay. They all look very professional, I must say."

"The best, Doctor Newton, that's what they are, the very best nurses available, and they're ours for the duration of this emergency."

"In that case I'm sure that we're all very grateful for their being here."

Their conversation was cut short by the sound of yet another helicopter approaching the village. The unmistakeable sound of rotor blades slicing through the air and then the change of pitch as the aircraft hovered overhead intruded into the marquee, securing the attention of everyone inside, staff and patients alike.

"Ah, this'll be the searchers," said McKay, cryptically.

"Searchers?" The question came from Paul Trent.

"Aye, Doctor Trent, searchers. Somewhere in the vicinity there must be a source of this infection. We need to find it fast. Group Captain Forbes who is seconded to the Ministry has arranged for a party of RAF Regiment troops to comb the village and farms of Olney in order to trace the local rodent population. It's almost certain that there are infected rats around here, and we must find them soon, and destroy the lot of them."

That was the point at which Paul Trent remembered something he'd been told earlier by one of the villagers, though he couldn't remember who. What he did recall was that his search of Simon Parkes' farm had been remarkable in that it had singularly failed to locate even one rat, mouse, or in fact, any sign of rodent life whatsoever. He mentioned this to McKay as they walked outside to greet the landing helicopter.

"Is there a rat catcher?" asked the Scotsman.

"I beg your pardon?"

The cacophonous sound of the helicopter as it came down to land caused a brief lull in their conversation. Three men climbed down from the aircraft wearing RAF uniform, each of which bore the unmistakeable shoulder flashes of the RAF Regiment. One of McKay's doctors ran to meet them and inform them that he'd brief them personally in ten minutes. As soon as the three men had their feet and their kit bags on the ground the pilot lifted the Sycamore into the air once more and was quickly gone.

As silence returned to the makeshift landing field Trent turned once more to McKay.

"You were saying, Doctor McKay?"

"Was I? Saying what?"

"Something about a rat catcher?"

"Yes, that's right. Is there a rat catcher in the village? These wee places often have a man who does the rounds, ridding the village of unwanted rodents. If there's a nest of the little buggers around he'd be the man to ask where to find them. It would save our men a long and possibly time-consuming hunt if they knew at least where to begin their search."

"I'm afraid I can't tell you that, I've not been in the village long enough. I can ask Doctor Newton. She might have come across such a man since her arrival her in Olney."

"I would say, Doctor Trent, that the best person to ask is fortuitously heading in our direction right at this moment."

Paul Trent followed the direction of the pointing hand of Angus McKay, to see Police Constable Greaves approaching on his bicycle.

"As you say, a timely arrival," he commented to McKay, who stood looking pleased with himself, almost as though Greaves had appeared by divine response to his question concerning the rat catcher.

Greaves cycled as near to their position as he could before dismounting from his bicycle and propping it against one of the black and white painted bollards that formed a boundary around the village green. He bent down, removed the bicycle clips from his ankles and with them in hand he marched smartly across to where the doctors stood waiting for him.

"Afternoon everyone," he said cheerfully, displaying the stoical stiff upper lip strength of character typical of his tough East End upbringing and his experiences in the Blitz. There might be a plague loose in his village, but Keith Greaves wasn't going to allow it to get in the way of him being the cheery and helpful local bobby, no way!

"I thought I'd just pop along and see how you folks are gettin' along, and how them that are sick are fairin' with the illness."

"Well, Constable, you couldn't have appeared at a more opportune time as it happens. We're very well, thank you, and your fellow villagers are all receiving the best care and attention we can give them. What I want to know from you is whether there is a rat catcher here in the village."

"Now it's funny you should ask that, Doctor McKay. The thing is you see, the man you're obviously looking for is within a few yards of where we're standing."

McKay and Trent both turned their heads in both directions, expecting to see the man indicated as being close to them, but apart from the three RAF regiment men who were being escorted to the marquee by one of McKay's men, there was no-one else in sight.

"Could you explain that last remark, Constable?" asked McKay.

"What? Oh yes, I see. Well, the man you want is Nobby Clark, and right now as far as I know he's lyin' in one of them beds in that oversized tent you call a hospital."

"Eh? I've no record of a man with that occupation in my record of admissions, or that name. Wait a minute though, there is a Clark I believe, but his first name is..."

"Robert," said Greaves. "That's him Doctor. Robert 'Nobby' Clark."

"But I'm sure he listed himself as a handyman when he was admitted."

"That's right Doc. Handyman, chimney sweep, electrical repairs, and rat catcher; you name it, Nobby does it. A real Jack of all Trades he is."

"Please come with us Constable," said McKay, as he and Trent led Greaves into the hospital. Quickly masking up once more and ensuring that Greaves did the same, they moved into the isolation ward. One of McKay's staff moved to greet them, and McKay spoke quickly to the man as he drew near.

"Doctor Naylor," said McKay, "please show us to the bed of the man named Clark. It's important that we speak to him right away."

"I'm afraid that won't be possible sir," Naylor replied.

"Why the hell not, Naylor? It's vitally important. He may be able to help us find the source of the infection."

"He can't sir, not now or ever I'm afraid. I'm sorry, but Robert Clark died about ten minutes ago."

CHAPTER 20

"BLOODY HELL, DOC. POOR OLD NOBBY."

"Indeed Constable. It's also a case of 'poor old us' as well I'm afraid. I'd rather hoped that Mr Clark could have helped us locate the rats that could be the cause of this infection that is blighting your village."

It had been a good two minutes since Doctor Naylor had given them the shocking news about the death of the village rat catcher. Keith Greaves had been the first to break the silence that had followed that news. No-one seemed to have been able to say anything as the realisation sank in that they may have lost a great opportunity to locate the source of the infection. McKay's reply had thrown the whole thing into bleak perspective. Now, the RAF Regiment personnel would be searching 'blind' and much valuable time and effort could be spent looking in the wrong places. After all, the newcomers wouldn't have a real clue where to start their search.

Constable Greaves, however, didn't appear to share the Ministry man's pessimism.

"Oh, I wouldn't say it's quite that bad, Doc."

"No? Then just how bad would you suppose it is Constable?" asked McKay with a hint of sarcasm in his voice.

"Well, if I were you sir, I'd be knockin' on the door of Michael Sweeney if I were you."

"The undertaker?" Hilary joined in the conversation.

"That's right, Doctor," Greaves explained. "Whenever poor old Nobby found himself a bit busy like, he'd call on his good friend the undertaker to help him out. Michael Sweeney's a clever man and quite resourceful. He knew a thing or two about rodent infestation before he got together with Nobby. Seems he used to tag along with one of the local farmers when he was a boy and was quite a dab hand at layin' the traps and the poisons and so on. Anyway, if Nobby Clark sometimes appeared to folks to be in two places at once if we had a large infestation around the village; it was because good old Sweeney was helpin' him out. So there you are Doctor, all isn't yet lost to you in that regard, unless maybe Michael Sweeney is ill as well."

"He certainly isn't here, I'm sure of that," said McKay. "Do you know where this man Sweeney can be found?" He directed the question at Hilary Newton.

"Yes, of course I do," she replied. "He's keeping the body of an earlier victim on ice for us at his mortuary."

"Then I think you and Doctor Trent should get over there right away and bring this Sweeney character to see me. While you're at it you can organise the transfer of the body by helicopter to the hospital in Ashford. We must get it out of here as soon as we can and conduct a detailed postmortem."

"I did an emergency post to determine the cause of death," said Trent.

"Yes of course, but we need to obtain a more detailed report on the remains. We have to find out if the bacillus had changed in some way to make it more difficult to resist, and which allows it to kill so quickly."

"We're on our way," said Trent, grabbing Hilary by the arm and leading her away from the makeshift hospital, leaving McKay standing beside Keith Greaves, surprised at their rapid departure.

As they walked swiftly in the direction of Sweeney's mortuary, Hilary expressed her surprise to Paul Trent at his abrupt departure from McKay and Greaves.

"To be honest Hilary," said Trent, "I'm finding Angus McKay very much an acquired taste at the moment, and it's a taste I'm having difficulty acquiring. He's a good doctor to be sure, and he appears to know what he's doing, but he's also the most self opinionated, self-centred and egotistical little man I've ever met. I just can't bear to be in his company for too long. Even a few minutes communing with the dearly departed in Sweeney's cold room will be far more pleasurable than spending another ten minutes in McKay's presence."

"Looks like we'll have to try and make sure you only receive small doses of Angus McKay for the time being," she grinned at him.

"I know we have to work with him, Hilary, but there's nothing in the rule book that says I have to like him is there?"

"Nothing at all," she concurred.

———

Michael Sweeney was more than helpful when the two doctors explained their problem. After expressing his regret at the death of his friend Nobby Clark, he thought for a moment or two and then proceeded to provide them with the information they required, as best he could.

"It's funny you know. Nobby had quite a busy time of it up until recently. This being such a small village almost in the middle of nowhere there was always a large population of rats, mice, voles, moles and such around. They were most prevalent around the farms of course but they'd often encroach upon the village itself and then they'd invariably get in the way of us humans and our nice comfortable lives. That's when Nobby would be called in to get rid of the little buggers. Sometimes, if the infestation was a large one, he'd call on me to give him a hand, which I was always happy to do. Then, about, oh, I'd say three to four months ago, he told me that trade had fallen right off. Nobody seemed to have a rat problem, not even on the farms. He even went looking for them once or twice, but he told me that he'd failed to find a single rat anywhere, alive or dead. When I asked him what might have caused them to disappear, he couldn't say for sure. He thought that maybe something had killed them all, but then he said that he should have been able to find the bodies. Had something scared them away? Some predator, perhaps, a newcomer to the village? Nobby thought that unlikely. Rats might be vermin, but they're determined and brave vermin, that's what he always said, and he was right. Rats are bloody brave I'll tell you. they'll attack an enemy five or ten times their own size, and not give up until either they've won the fight or died trying. Then, about two weeks ago he found something that scared him, and scaring Nobby Clark took some doing I'll tell you."

The two doctors' ears pricked up at Sweeney's last comment. Trent asked the question.

"What was it Mr. Sweeney? What frightened a man like Nobby Clark?"

"Why, rats of course Doctor, that's what. But these were dead rats, dozens of 'em. He'd thought it strange that no bodies had turned up to explain why they'd all disappeared, and then he went and found a veritable rat graveyard, the way he explained it to me. You know, kind of like one of them places where the elephants go to die. I've read about them in books."

"Where was this graveyard?" Hilary Newton asked.

"Well, there's this old drainage ditch just across on the other side of the village. It runs right across the Eastern boundary of Olney, and once formed part of the irrigation system for a field that no longer exists. The field was once owned by Simon Parkes, but he sold it to the village after the war, and they built a playground there. Anyway, Nobby used to clear the ditch of debris under a contract from the parish council, just to make sure that it didn't get clogged up and flood the village in winter when the heavy rains sometimes cause it to fill up. This time, when he went along as usual to clear it out, he found the rats."

"Did he report it to the parish council?" The question came from Trent.

"No. He thought it might upset people to know they'd had all those dead rats just lying there so close to the kids playground and apart from me, I doubt there's another soul in the village that knows about it."

"What did he do with the bodies, do you know?"

"Yes, Doctor Trent, I know all right. He burned them. He packed all the little blighters' bodies into hessian sacks, and I helped him carry them to his back garden where he made a bloody great bonfire and got rid of the lot. He put petrol on the fire to help get rid of the smell of the burning rats, and anyway, Nobby's house is far enough away from anyone else's that it wouldn't have bothered anyone anyway."

"That's it?" asked Hilary. "He never found any more?"

"Not that he told me about," Sweeny replied. "Why? Should there have been more?"

"I don't know Mr. Sweeney. It's just a bit odd that all the rats in the village died in the same place. There could be other 'graveyards' that your friend Nobby didn't find. Also, there's the question of mice and the other smaller rodents. What happened to them?"

"Well Doctor Newton, I can't answer you for sure. The thing is, regarding the mice etc. There's plenty of owls, foxes and such like around here, and they'd likely very quickly take any dead or dying mouse or vole that they came across. There'd be no trace of the little sods after the larger predators and scavengers had dealt with them. Rats of course, are a different kettle of fish. If there are any more dead ones around, then I'm afraid I can't help you, but..."

"But what, Mr. Sweeney?" asked Trent.

"Well, the other day, Nobby did say that he'd found something strange. When I asked him what this 'strange' thing was he seemed to clam up on me. He became a bit vague, you know? It was as though he didn't trust me with whatever he'd found. I pressed him a bit and all he would say was that he'd found the 'enemy in our midst'. Nobby liked his brandy, Doctor and I'll tell you now, I thought he'd just been at the bottle a bit too much and could be a bit drunk, if you know what I mean. He wouldn't say much more, other than that he was worried that 'they'd left it behind," whatever 'they' and 'it' were. I got a telephone call right about then and had to break off the conversation. When I got back to where I'd left him, he'd gone. I never spoke to Nobby again."

Trent and Hilary left Sweeney soon after. There was nothing else they could learn from him. As they walked back to the hospital marquee, Trent turned to Hilary with a worried frown on his face.

"D'you know what, Hilary?"

"No. What, Paul?"

"I've got a feeling that the best chance we had of finding out the real source of the infection here in Olney died while under our care a short time ago."

"Do you really think that Nobby Clark found whatever caused this outbreak?"

"I don't just think he *found* it Hilary. I think he found it, perhaps without even knowing what it was, and it scared him so much he wouldn't talk about it. I wouldn't be at all surprised if we one day learn that whatever he found was responsible for him catching the disease."

"Do you realise what you're suggesting, Paul?"

"Oh yes, Hilary, I realise only too well what I'm saying. If I'm right in my assumption, then whatever Nobby Clark found is responsible for what is no longer just an outbreak but an epidemic of plague in Olney St Mary. He talked about 'it' and 'they' which means he found something that shouldn't have been here in the first place, and could have been left behind here, maybe by accident. In other words, Doctor Newton, I'm saying, as you well know, that if we believe Nobby's story, as related by him to Michael Sweeny, then the source of this goddamned infection was brought to Olney St. Mary *from the outside.* Someone or something brought it here. If that's true, then we must assume that this is no natural outbreak!"

Hilary looked at him in shock, her mouth hanging open until she managed to form just two words that seemed to sum up both of their feelings at that moment.

"Bloody Hell!"

CHAPTER 21

"You can't be serious! It's the most preposterous theory I've ever heard, Doctor Trent. D'you really think that someone has deliberately infected this village with pneumonic plague, man? That wouldn't just be foolhardy; it would be tantamount to rank stupidity. How could whoever did such a thing hope to contain an epidemic without possibly infecting the whole country, and what could be their possible motive?"

Angus McKay had stood and listened incredulously as Trent and Hilary Newton had confronted him with Trent's wild theory about an outside agent being responsible for the outbreak. His reaction had been predictable, his anger and dismissal of the theory being exactly what Trent had expected. Now, Paul Trent would take the matter one step closer to risking an all-out war with the Scotsman. His reply to McKay's dismissal was sure to evoke an aggressive response from the little man.

"Doctor McKay, you ask how someone could contain such an epidemic. Well, they'd do just what you are doing now! To be fair, I don't mean you personally, but you do work for the Ministry, don't you? As for that Ministry, tell me which one you work for. Are you employed by the Ministry of Health or by the

Ministry of Defence? After all, you turn up with all these military personnel, give orders as if you're used to being obeyed, and seem to have unrestricted access to unlimited medical supplies, not to mention the ability to summon RAF helicopters at a minutes notice. Come on Doctor McKay, who do you really work for?"

"My God, Trent, just who the hell d'you think you're speaking to young man? If it wasn't for me and the people I've brought with me this whole village would probably be dead by the end of the week."

"You know that for a fact do you, Doctor?"

"What the hell are you suggesting Trent? That I'm part of some great conspiracy to wipe out Olney St. Mary? That the Ministry of Defence or the Ministry of Health have somehow conspired to infect the village in some sort of biological experiment? You've gone completely mad if you think such a thing. We're here to help you and these people, Trent. Don't you understand that? What on Earth could be the motive for such a foolhardy and reckless action by a government agency? You've lost your mind if you believe that theory for even a minute."

"I don't know. Maybe the infection was a mistake, something got out that shouldn't have, and now you and your people have to perform a damage limitation exercise to wipe out any trace of your mistake. That could explain the motive couldn't it?"

"Bloody hell, Trent! I'm not the cause of this infection man, neither is the government of this country, either directly or indirectly."

"Then how do you explain the over the top response. Surely this isn't the normal way to go about controlling a plague outbreak."

"I'm responding to the orders I received from my superiors, Doctor Trent, and their orders came from the Ministry of

Health, passed down via the Ministry of Defence, for whom it's true I work."

"Ah, so you admit to working for the MOD."

"Yes, I do Doctor Trent, though it has no relevance to the outbreak here in Olney. Like I said, we're simply here to help and were sent because we could respond faster to the emergency than the Health services own people could do."

Feeling that he had the little Scotsman backed slightly into a corner, Paul Trent decided to go for the jugular. It was time for some straight talking.

"OK, Doctor McKay," said Trent determinedly. "If you really want me to believe you and trust you, then level with me. Tell me the truth. You admit you work for the MOD, so tell me exactly what you do for them, and where you work."

Angus McKay looked at Trent and saw a steely glint in the eyes of the man who had taken him on face to face, something that few people ever did. He had to admit to a grudging respect for the man, though he kept that respect buried as he replied to Trent's question with quiet solemnity and in a slow voice, aimed at maintaining his own dignity. It would never do in his book to be publicly shown to have been bested by a man like Paul Trent. McKay knew though that he would have to give Trent something in the way of information if he was going to expect to continue to receive the co-operation of not only the man himself, but the doctors and nurses who had worked with him from the beginning of the epidemic.

"Very well, Doctor Trent. I'm not really authorised to tell you this, but I shall do so in the hope that it will help to put an end to this stupid hypothesis of yours and will stop the time-wasting such arguments are causing when we should be treating the villagers. First of all, I work for the MOD as a consultant in the effects of certain biological and nerve affecting toxins and other man-made agents on the human body."

"Biological warfare!" Hilary exclaimed.

"Please, Doctor Newton, if I may continue."

Hilary fell silent.

"I am an expert in the handling and treatment of numerous 'exotic' diseases and am employed to help prevent the spread of such diseases should they ever, God forbid, be unleashed against our own people. So you see, doctors, I work *for* the people of this country, *not* against them. That's why I and my rapid response unit were despatched here. It was obviously thought that our rapid containment and eradication procedures could help bring a speedy end to this outbreak, and, if you people will help me by letting me get on with my job, that is precisely what I intend to do. Now, do I have your co-operation or not?"

"You haven't quite answered my questions in full yet Doctor. You were gong to tell me exactly where you are normally employed to do this work of yours?"

McKay hesitated. He knew that despite what he'd just said, his next words would probably throw the cat among the pigeons once again as far as Trent was concerned. He stood as tall as his short frame would allow however and looked Trent straight in the eye as he spoke.

"Doctor Trent, I don't want you to read anything sinister into what I'm about to tell you. I believe that you'll have heard of the place where I usually work. It's called Porton Down."

That was it! The cat was out of the bag. Trent couldn't help himself; he began to laugh. Hilary Newton, perhaps not quite as well-informed as Paul Trent looked surprised at his reaction.

"Paul?" she asked, concern on her face. "What's so funny? What is it about this Porton Down place that you find so hilarious? Do you know something I don't?"

"Hilary, this man works at a place where they conduct experiments and research into the effects of biological and chemical warfare. It's the government's main source of research into the nasty bloody weapons they can create to destroy people while leaving buildings standing. If you want to find a supply of any known toxin or lethal bacteria, then Porton Down's your place, and this man expects us to believe that they had nothing to do with what's happening here?"

Just then, Guy Dearborn poked his head round the flap of canvas that divided McKay's workspace from the rest of the marquee.

"I'm sorry," he said, "but I heard raised voices. Is everything alright, Doctors?"

"Come in, Guy," Trent invited. "Doctor McKay here was just explaining something to us. You might find it very interesting."

McKay groaned inwardly and began once more to justify his presence in Olney, and to deny any government involvement in any so-called conspiracy to infect the village. It would take him some time, but eventually he managed to placate the three doctors with a promise to let Trent speak to Group Captain Forbes the next time McKay was in contact with him on the field radio. Trent and the others weren't yet entirely convinced of McKay's innocence, but as he reminded them, they had patients to attend to, and for now they agreed to a kind of truce, until Trent could speak to McKay's boss, and to his own superior, Malcolm Davidson, for advice.

The first thing McKay did when the others left him to begin a round of the isolation ward was to send for the RAF Regiment men. They were soon despatched to various locations around the village with orders to search for rat 'graveyards'. At least McKay seemed to have taken some of Trent's words to heart, though whether he believed in parts of Trent's theory or was reacting to something he already suspected, no-one could have known, at least not at that point in time.

CHAPTER 22

BY THE FOLLOWING DAY, THE SUBJECT OF TIME HAD BEGUN TO weigh heavily on the minds of all those attempting to stem the spread of the plague. Though still localised within the parish of Olney St. Mary, the signs weren't good. Time had become the enemy, almost as much as the disease, as the hospital marquee continued to fill with new cases and suspected cases, and the recovery statistics remained at one. So far, Emily Bradley was the only survivor from those who'd contracted the plague, making the future look bleak for those who languished in the beds of the little field hospital.

A rapidly held post-mortem had revealed that Nobby Clark had suffered from an undiagnosed heart and lung condition that would have made his chances of withstanding the onslaught posed by the plague bacillus very slim indeed. This at least told the doctors that the disease itself might not after all be a super-virulent fast acting strain of the plague, and that Nobby might have just been unlucky.

Late the previous evening, as dusk fell the RAF searchers had discovered a second 'graveyard of the rats' in another dry ditch that ran almost parallel to the one previously discovered by Clark. The ditch was on the far side of the children's playground, though it lay outside the boundary of the area, which was enclosed by a green metal fence, and had to be entered through a gate of the same material. Had they not been told what to look for the RAF Regiment men might have missed the huddled remains of thirty rats that had crawled into a crevice on one side of the ditch. The senior NCO of the RAF party, Flight Sergeant Eric Taylor, thought that the crevice might lead to a tunnel which itself would lead them to a rats' nest that lay somewhere underground. Bad light had prevented them checking his theory until the next day. At least they'd been able to provide the medics with some physical evidence at last. Perhaps the rat's bodies could provide a clue to the cause of the epidemic. Doctor Harry Blaine, one of McKay's epidemiologists, had volunteered the information that he'd received a small amount of veterinary training and had thus found himself detailed to carry out post-mortem examinations on a representative quantity of five rats. If necessary, McKay ordered him to examine every one of the dead rodents.

Back in the field hospital, twenty five of the forty camp beds provided by the Porton Down people were now occupied, and not one of the patients who lay suffering in those beds showed any sign of responding to the treatment offered by the medics. With only fifteen beds available, and with the expectation growing that they'd need far more before the outbreak was contained, McKay had ordered a further supply of fifty which would be airlifted in sometime that day.

Those already hospitalised provided the doctors and nurses with a fairly even spread across the generation spectrum in Olney. The disease seemed to have no preference for young, old or those in-between. Worse still, the incubation period from initial contact to the exhibiting of symptoms couldn't be determined until the source of the infection was known, making the task of those trying to treat the disease that much harder.

Paul Trent was still waiting to speak to Group Captain Forbes. McKay had tried to contact his boss the previous evening only to be told that Forbes was in a meeting at the Health Ministry and wouldn't be available until the morning. That morning had now dawned, and Trent was anxious to speak to the senior RAF man. He still felt in need of reassurance. His own instincts continued to send warning signals to his brain, and he found it impossible to trust McKay entirely, despite the man's attempts at honesty the previous day.

It was a great surprise to all concerned therefore, when at just after nine a.m. that day a black Wolseley saloon car pulled up in the centre of the village. As a light drizzle began to fall, a WRAF corporal emerged from the driver's door and moved to open the rear passenger door. The girl saluted as the officer within the car alighted. The man placed his hat on his head before returning her salute. Group Captain Forbes had arrived in person!

At his meeting with Ryan and Macklin the previous evening, Forbes had insisted on taking personal charge of the operation in Olney St. Mary. It was the only way he felt able to continue to support the operation. Like Paul Trent all those miles away in Olney, the RAF man still had misgivings about the part he'd been asked to play in the current situation. At least by being 'on the spot' he could oversee developments as and when they occurred, and would be better placed to act on any unforeseen events that might transpire. Much to his surprise, Ryan had agreed to his proposal without argument, agreeing that it might be an advantage to have a senior man in place to control the relief operation. Forbes would keep in touch with his base at Porton Down through the radio in his staff car, and a link would be established from Porton to allow him direct communication with Ryan at his office, if required.

At six feet two inches in height, and looking imposingly resplendent in his uniform, Forbes looked every inch the model of a senior officer in Her Majesty's armed forces. As he strode across the village green towards the field hospital, the few villagers who were out on the street that ran in front of the green couldn't help but turn their heads to look at the tall man who had suddenly appeared in their midst. Somehow, the appearance of the man, the way he walked and the uniform itself had a reassuring effect on those who saw him that morning. The RAF had after all saved the country from invasion by its exploits in the Battle of Britain not too many years before. Perhaps this man could save the village from the ravages of the disease in its midst. At least, that was the way the small group of residents viewed him. Whether he could convince Paul Trent, Hilary Newton and the others of his ability to control the situation was another matter entirely.

As for Paul Trent, his mood had darkened when, at just after eight a.m. nurse Patricia Knowles had joined the ranks of the infected. She now lay in one of the beds in the hospital, coughing and suffering along with those already admitted. Patricia had done sterling work in helping to care first for Emily Bradley and since then, the other residents of the village. Now, despite her having taken the prophylactic doses of streptomycin, she too had fallen victim to the disease.

As Forbes entered the marquee, being directed by one of the Porton Down nurses to McKay's 'office', Trent and Hilary were in attendance at Patricia Knowles's bedside, aided by Christine Rigby. The four had become a close-knit team in a short space of time, and Trent and the others were determined to do all they could to try and save Patricia from what appeared to be the sadly terminal outcome of the infection.

McKay was bent over his desk, lost in thought as he perused the results of Harry Blaine's first two rat autopsies. So engrossed was he that he failed to detect the curtain that delineated his personal space within the marquee being drawn back as Forbes entered.

"Good morning, McKay," The Group Captain's voice boomed.

"What the heck? Oh sorry sir. Good morning. I didn't expect you here today."

"If at all eh, McKay? Well, I'm here and from the looks of things we've got a real job on our hands."

McKay had reacted with shock at his boss's unexpected arrival and had managed to gather himself a little before continuing.

"Aye sir, I'll admit I never expected you to show up in person, but I'm glad you have. I could use your expertise and your opinions on a few matters, that's for sure."

"Well then, I'm glad you approve of my decision to join you."

"Yes, of course I'm glad, sir. May I ask how you got here? I didnae hear any sounds of a chopper arriving."

When he was nervous, McKay's Scots accent had a habit of showing itself to a greater degree than was usual. The unannounced arrival of Forbes had disturbed his equilibrium enough to bring such a manifestation to the surface.

"Ah, there you are, you see, McKay. I can surprise you yet. I came down by car. I thought I'd test the effectiveness of our external perimeters. I was pleased to see that the men on patrol and manning the road barriers were on the alert and doing a dammed fine job."

"That's good, sir. Can I ask what reason they're giving to the people they're turning away from the area?"

"Military exercises with live ammunition! It's rather good really McKay. Just one mention of live shells and bullets flying around is usually enough to deter anyone from venturing beyond a military check point. The commander of the troops has patrols out in the countryside as well, just in case any hikers or birdwatchers and the like happen to stray into the exclusion zone. I think we can safely say that we've got Olney St. Mary pretty well sealed off. Now all we need to do is find the cause of this bloody outbreak and find a way to control and cure those affected by it."

"I'm glad you're happy with the security," said McKay. "What about your driver, sir? Will she need accommodation? I presume it was Sally Hughes, your usual driver who brought you here? Things are a bit tight in that department here at the moment."

"Don't worry about it McKay. I've sent Corporal Hughes back to base with the car. There's no need for her to be unnecessarily exposed to the plague. If I need to leave, I'll call for a Sycamore to airlift me out. As it stands, I intend to say here until this thing is sorted one way or the other."

"Aye sir. Well, let me just say that finding the source of the plague and discovering the way to control it might be a little more difficult than we first imagined."

"Oh, how so, McKay?"

Pointing to the papers on his desk McKay gave Forbes a quick rundown on the discovery of the dead rats, and the rodent post-mortem examinations carried out so far by Harry Blaine. He proceeded to give Forbes a brief outline of Blaine's initial findings.

"You see sir; Blaine has found some remarkably interesting though disturbing facts about out little rodent friends. It would appear that the rats themselves were killed by the plague, which is normal enough, as the rat fleas then move on to a new host, usually the human victims. In the case of the two rats autopsied so far however, Blaine has found no sign of flea infestation. The skin of the rat when the fur is removed should show evidence of the rat flea or fleas having been present through bite marks and swellings on the skin where the fleas would have fed. In our rats however, there is no sign whatsoever of them having been attacked by fleas. Blaine says that under a microscope he would easily be able to identify the bites of the wee beasties, and he'll swear that they're not there on either rat."

"Could the plague have simply been passed on to the rats by other infected animals, as the pneumonic version does with humans?"

"Well sir, according to Blaine that's nigh on impossible. The rat has to be directly infected for it to succumb to the disease. Blaine also says that most rats would carry a number of fleas and that as these rats have been dead for some time, there should have been the odd dead flea in their coats. They wouldn't all have been able to find new hosts when the rats died. It's not logical. There's something else sir, something more disturbing."

"Go on McKay, tell me the worst."

"Well, when Blaine examined some of the rat cells under the scope, he wasn't sure what he was seeing at first."

"In what way?"

"The plague normally attacks the respiratory system in a rather predictable way, as we all know. In the case of the two rats however, it looks as though the respiratory organs have been literally eaten away from the inside, as though the plague itself had been helped in some way by another disease having been incorporated into the bacillus. The only way that could have happened would have been if someone had altered the nature of the protein make up of the plague bacillus."

As McKay spoke, Forbes felt the blood in his veins chill. His mind went back to the private meeting he'd had with Douglas

Ryan, and the fears he'd harboured that day came back to haunt him once again.

"Do you realise exactly what you're implying, McKay?"

"Aye sir, I do. And what makes it even harder to swallow is that Doctor Trent came to me yesterday with some wild theory about the plague having been introduced to Olney by some outside agency. He implied it was a government trial or experiment that had gone wrong. I tried to tell him that no government would endanger its people in such a way, but I don't know if I managed to convince him. I managed to placate him in the end by promising that you'd speak to him on the radio and reassure him that the British government has no part to play in this outbreak."

"I see. Well, I'll have to do what I can McKay, won't I? As for the government I think we're safe to assume that there's no British involvement in this."

"Then you think it could be the work of a foreign power? The Russians perhaps?"

The Cold War was of course in full swing in nineteen fifty-eight. The mistrust and almost open hostility between the nations that comprised the Warsaw Pact and those of the NATO convention had left the world in a state of expectancy, as the threat of nuclear war, or worse threatened the day to day existence of the people of the opposing factions.

"I don't know McKay. I just don't know. I'm sure the Soviets are as advanced as we are in the art of biological warfare, but I don't believe that they'd go so far as to actually launch a biological attack against this country. If they did, I'm pretty sure they'd want us to know about it, and I doubt they'd choose somewhere like Olney St. Mary as their proving ground for any trial of a new weapon. They'd target a town or a city where the effects would be greater, and they could evaluate the weapon on a grand scale."

"Then where the bloody hell has it come from?"

The shouted question came from an irate Paul Trent, who stood in the entrance to the office area. He'd obviously heard the last part of the conversation between the two men, and now he wanted an explanation, and he wanted it fast, especially when he announced:

"Someone had better have some answers for me, McKay, because I want to know who the hell is responsible for the death of one of my nurses. Patricia Knowles showed the first symptoms two hours ago, and she's dead, she's bloody dead!"

A silence fell over the small space, a silence that could have been cut with a surgical knife. Paul Trent hung his head. Despite his outburst he had the look of a defeated man. McKay looked stunned, and Donald Forbes knew he had some explaining to do to Trent, though in truth, he hadn't a clue what he could explain, or where on earth to begin.

CHAPTER 23

THE EARLIER DRIZZLE HAD TURNED INTO A STEADY DOWNPOUR by the time Paul Trent emerged from the marquee/hospital after his conversation with Group Captain Forbes. Somehow, the RAF man had managed to convince Trent that they were all working on the same side. As he pointed out, Douglas Ryan was the government's chief virologist. His job entailed working to protect and indemnify the people of Great Britain against just such an eventuality as they now faced in Olney St. Mary. Any thoughts of some sinister plot being behind the current plague cases must be cast aside and all attention and resources diverted to treating those infected, and if possible, to prevent further cases occurring. As Forbes spoke, Trent realised that the man was sincere in his words, and in his commitment to solving the crisis. As to the theory that the Russians or some other foreign intervention had led to the plague outbreak, Forbes would neither confirm nor deny something of which he had no knowledge, nor any evidence on which to base such a theory. He did however make it clear to Trent that he thought such an event highly unlikely. The Soviets, he'd explained, knew that the western powers were just as well armed in terms of biological weapons, horrific though they may be, and would surely be aware that if they were proven to have launched such an attack on the

UK, the chances were high that the NATO allies would retaliate in kind. No, he'd eventually come down on the side of it being extremely unlikely that the Russians were involved. Yet, he agreed that the source of the outbreak and the nature of the symptoms presented by those infected, did suggest that a new strain of the plague bacillus was at work in Olney, and that the number one priority for all of those working to contain the epidemic had to be to discover that source. Having obtained Trent's promise of co-operation in achieving his aims, Forbes had asked McKay to give him a tour of the ward so that he might assess the situation and see the effects of the plague for himself.

So now Paul Trent stood under the awning at the front of the marquee, the rain falling steadily and giving him the impression that the world and perhaps God himself was crying for the loss of poor Patricia Knowles and the others who'd already succumbed to the plague. He felt a presence moving behind him and turned to see Hilary Newton no more than a yard behind him. She'd approached him quietly and seeing him apparently lost in thought had stopped in that position, not wishing to intrude upon his private thoughts.

"Hilary," he spoke her name softly.

"I'm sorry, Paul. Would you prefer to be alone?"

Seeing the red rings that betrayed the tears she'd cried herself for Patricia Knowles, Trent did his best to produce a semblance of a smile.

"I'm just watching the rain. Funny isn't it, how some things never alter? Not long ago, Nurse Knowles was alive and breathing and the rain was falling just as it is now. Now she's gone forever, but the rain keeps on falling just as it did before, as though nothing's changed."

"In some ways it hasn't, Paul. Patricia died doing what she wanted to do, the thing she loved more than anything in the world. She told me that last night, you know? That of all the things she could have been when she grew up, nursing was always her one immovable ambition. The chance to come down here and help to try and cure a plague epidemic was, for her, the most rewarding thing she'd ever done, that's what she told me Paul, honestly."

"I'm sure you're right Hilary, but when Davidson asked for volunteers to come to Olney, I'm sure none of those who put their hands up thought that there was a real chance that they wouldn't be going home."

"I know, but that's a chance we all take when we enter this profession isn't it? There's always a possibility that we'll be hit by the very diseases that we try to treat and cure, and that goes as much for the nursing staff as it does for us doctors. We have to go on as before Paul, as though nothing's changed, because that's the way Patricia would have wanted it."

For a minute or two it was as though their roles had been reversed. Paul Trent was after all the senior doctor. Hilary had been a mere junior on the staff at Ashford when they'd worked together. Now, here she was, comforting him and trying to give him the will to go on in the light of the loss of one of his nurses. She understood his sense of responsibility to Patricia Knowles, but she also understood the need for a perfectly focussed and fully functional Doctor Paul Trent at that moment.

Trent looked at Hilary for a long moment, then turned and looked upwards into the brooding sky, at the clouds that continued to disperse their liquid load upon the earth below. He disappeared into the world of his own thoughts for a few seconds, then smiled at Hilary once again.

"You know, Doctor Newton, you'd make a damned fine psychological therapist, did you know that?"

"I'll remember that if the General Practitioner business goes sour on me. The way things are going here in Olney, I may not have many patients left to serve if we don't find a way to stop this bloody plague from spreading."

"You're right of course, Hilary. Come on, let's go and see what this new RAF bigwig has come up with while I've been feeling sorry for myself."

Together they walked back into the marquee, and for a fleeting moment, perhaps for no more than two or three seconds, Trent took hold of Hilary's left hand in his right. She didn't resist the small intimacy, but it ended almost as soon as it began, as they saw Guy Dearborn walking towards them.

"Hello Guy"

"Hello, Doctor Trent, Doctor Newton. That new chap, the Group Captain, is arranging for a small fleet of ambulances to come and remove the bodies of the deceased. He wants full and exhaustive post-mortem examinations carried out on them, post haste. They're to be taken to Ashford, where Mr. Davidson will work with the medical examiner to oversee the autopsies."

"And just how have you become privy to the Group Captain's plans so quickly young Guy?"

"Ah, well, there you are you see sir. It's not a matter of what you know, but who you know as happens so often. The Group Captain asked me my name and surprised me by telling me that he knows my father rather well. After that the old Groupie was quite effusive and seemed quite happy to let me know what his immediate plans were. After all, we're not exactly going to go running off telling anybody, are we?"

"That's a good point, Guy. As you say, we're not going anywhere." Trent grinned.

"At least he seems to be doing something positive," Hilary chimed in. "And he's got the authority to make things happen a lot quicker than any of us possess, or so it would seem"

"You're right, Hilary. When I last spoke to Malcolm Davidson he told me that the Ministry had put some top people on the job of solving the Olney situation, but I never thought we'd get the deputy director of special projects at Porton Down making a personal appearance here."

"And just how do you happen to know the man's job title, may I ask?"

"Ah, I must confess to not being much of a Sherlock Holmes in that regard. On my way out of the hospital I simply asked one of McKay's people what the Group Captain did at Porton down. He told me, that's all. There's no mystery involved I'm afraid. I wish to God I did have some sort of psychic ability, then I might be able to work out how to put an end to all this."

Guy Dearborn stood listening to this small exchange, and then, almost as though he felt as though he were intruding on their private grief, he cleared his throat to gain attention and spoke very quietly.

"It's a damnable shame about Patricia, er, I mean Nurse Knowles. I hardly knew her of course, certainly not as well as the two of you did, but she was a really nice girl from what I could tell, and she certainly worked hard and didn't deserve for this to happen to her."

"Thanks Guy," said Trent, and Hilary nodded in acknowledgement of his sympathy. Trent's composure had returned, and he now assumed the senior role once more. "She was part of the team, and we all knew the risks before we came down here. That's why Davidson asked for volunteers. We all knew something like this could happen."

"Of course, Doctor Trent. It's still a tragic shame though."

"Yes, it is Guy. Now, we have to do whatever we can to prevent such a fate befalling anyone else."

As they spoke the easily recognisable figure of Michael Sweeney appeared at the entrance to the marquee. There might be infection present, but it seemed that the indomitable local undertaker wasn't the kind of man to be put off by such 'trivialities'.

"Good day, Doctors," he called.

"Good morning, Mr Sweeney," Trent replied on their joint behalf. "I'm afraid this isn't the best of times. One of my nurses died just a short time ago."

"Oh God, I'm sorry to hear that. Is there anything I can do to help?"

"Not on this occasion, Mr Sweeney. The body is going directly to Ashford along with the others for immediate post-mortem examination, as soon as the ambulances arrive that is."

"Who was it, Doctor Trent?"

"Patricia Knowles."

"What a waste of a young life," said Sweeney. "They're both nice girls, those that you brought with you, Doctor. You must be shocked to have something like this happen."

"Shocked? Yes, that's a good way to put it. We're all very shocked that she's gone, but even more so as it happened so quickly. Now, was there something specific that you wanted to talk to us about, or was this just intended to be a social call?"

"Well, now that you mention it, there was something I wanted to tell you. I heard through the village grapevine that you've found another cluster of dead rats, am I right?"

"Can't we keep anything secret for more than ten minutes?" Trent groaned.

"Not around here I'm afraid, Doc," said Sweeney. "The local jungle drums were beating out the news about five minutes after your RAF chaps found the bodies of the little critters. Anyway, the point is this. I don't know if it's important or relevant, and I know he wouldn't tell you himself, but in the pub the other night I was talking to Billy Wragg and..."

"Billy who?" asked Hilary.

"Billy Wragg, Doctor, and the reason he wouldn't talk to you directly is that he earns his living as a poacher. Everyone knows about it, but he thinks its best not to come out in the open too often, if you know what I mean."

"Right, and what was this discussion you were having with him?" asked Trent bringing the conversation back on track.

"Well, if anyone knows what's afoot with the local wildlife it has to be the local poacher. According to Billy, there hasn't been a rabbit seen alive in the area for over two weeks. He's found a fair few dead ones, but they were too far gone to be fit for eating, as he put it."

"Rabbits?" Came the one-word comment from Dearborn.

"Aye, rabbits. They're rodents as well as rats aren't they Doctor? Now my question for you learned gentlemen and lady is this. I'm no expert on the plague of course, that's your field of expertise, but, from what I've read in books, and I've read quite a few, I've never heard of plague striking at the general animal community, apart from the rats of course. Now can you tell me if I'm right?"

"I'm sorry to disappoint you Mr. Sweeney, but it is quite possible for rabbits to carry plague fleas as well as rats," came the response from Trent. "I'll admit though that it's strange that all the wildlife in the area seems to be dying out before the plague strikes at the human population. Normally I'd have expected it to run concurrently within the two communities. Do you think that this Billy Wragg character might be persuaded to come and talk to us?"

"I'll try talking to him, Doctor. If I tell him how important it is and that he won't get into any trouble he might be persuaded to come and have a word with you. But apart from that, my information isn't of much use then?" asked the undertaker.

"Far from it, Mr Sweeney. You have at least provided us with another link in the chain towards finding the source of the infection. It now seems clear that whatever set off the train of events that ended in the outbreak here in the village, it hit the animals first and moved on to the humans some time afterwards. That could be highly significant. Thank you. I'll pass the information on to the new man in charge."

"You mean the Group Captain?"

"How on Earth did you know about...don't tell me, I know, jungle drums."

"You're learning, Doctor Trent, I'll give you that," said Sweeney as he turned and waved a cheery goodbye as he left the three doctors and departed from the hospital, intent on going about his normal day to day business.

"Now that's a man I'd like to have on my side in an emergency," said Hilary. "I think there's a lot more to Mr Michael Sweeney than meets the eye. He seems far too intelligent to be living out his life as a village undertaker or whatever else he does around here."

"He's certainly keen enough to help us whenever he can, and he's not afraid to put himself in harm's way. Look at the way he just walked up to us in this place. None of the villagers will dare to set foot on the village green, never mind walk into the hospital, for fear they'll catch the disease," said Dearborn.

Before they could discuss the matter further, the sound of approaching vehicle engines heralded the approach of the ambulances summoned by Forbes. Within minutes, and before they could speak to Forbes about the information from Sweeney, the Group Captain emerged from the marquee with McKay to supervise the loading of the bodies. Less than half an hour later, the first of Olney St. Mary's dead left the village for their date with the medical examiners knife. The rainfall had become a downpour. It seemed to suit the mood of the morning.

CHAPTER 24

THE INCESSANT RAIN HAD CAST A PALL OF GLOOM OVER THE already beleaguered village of Olney St. Mary. Most of the inhabitants took the decision to stay in their homes. The daily business of the village became suspended in time as fear gripped the hearts and minds of the people. Legions of dark, brooding clouds marched across the sky and the smoke from the chimneys of the houses and cottages rose through the falling droplets to meet them. Gradually a thick smog formed that enveloped the entire community. To the outside world, it was as if Olney St. Mary had been spirited away into a nether world, a place where sounds were muffled by the smog, and where the rain-sodden streets lay empty and deserted, a ghost village, inhabited by the dead and the dying.

Even those who had found it in themselves to express anger at the loss of their telephone service fell silent, and the only signs of activity in the village were to be found at the hospital marquee and the doctor's surgery. Even the newly pasted posters listing McKay's do's and don'ts and emergency regulations for the villagers had begun to sag and droop, the rain dissolving the paste that held them to walls and telegraph poles until they hung like limp rags, forlorn and unreadable.

The trees, most of which had retained their leaves long after the end of the season now surrendered to the onslaught from the clouds, and wet and sodden leaves fell in a dying cascade upon the roads and fields in and around the village. Soon, a sodden carpet of russet and brown lay all around, and many of the trees eventually stood naked of their summer garb, their bare branches pointing like accusing fingers up towards the unrelenting rain clouds.

The sound of the rain drumming on the roof of the hospital marquee became a symphony of sorrow for those incarcerated under the canvas. They might be dry under the tarpaulin covering, but they were all captives who couldn't escape the nightmare thudding of the watery aerial cascade above their heads.

Within hours the picture postcard appearance of Olney St. Mary had become transformed. The locals, who were well used to such events at this time of year, would have taken such a day in their stride if not for the plague that threatened them all, but for the newcomers, it only added to the misery of their situation. Not only were they so far incapable of finding a way to halt the spread of the plague, but the storm that sent the rain lashing down upon the village also prevented the searchers from continuing their task. Apart from providing the best care they could for those already infected and those who continued to trickle into the hospital every hour or so, there was little the medical staff could do until the rain relented. Even the promised helicopter delivery of camp beds found itself on hold until the weather cleared. In the simple cottage garden of the late Mabel Thorndyke, as in many others around the village, the last remnants of summer blooms that had held firm in the light of the late spell of good weather now released their grip on life. Pansies, Dianthus and Petunias bowed their heads and surrendered to the power of the torrential downpour.

As the doctors and nurses worked feverishly to try to hold back the symptoms of the plague in those already affected, one brave soul ventured out from his home and made his way to the hospital marquee. Timothy Grafton had decided that it was time he paid a call on his suffering parishioners. The vicar had pulled on his galoshes and a long belted fawn raincoat, topped off with a rather worn, brown trilby hat, and had sloshed his way across the main street, navigated the best route possible across the sodden village green and now stood dripping in the awning that formed the entrance to the hospital.

Having at first been refused admission to the isolation ward by one of McKay's nurses the reverend gentleman had made such a fuss and hullabaloo that his voice carried into the office where McKay, Forbes and Trent were in conference. The three doctors appeared seconds later, and it was finally agreed, with some pushing by Trent, that the vicar be allowed to minister to his flock on condition that he wore the necessary protection against airborne infection. Though he initially resisted the wearing of a mask and gown, saying that his parishioners should see that their minister wasn't afraid of the illness that ailed them, he finally agreed when it was made forcefully plain by Forbes that masking up was the only way he'd ever get to see those in the ward.

As he led Grafton into the ward Paul Trent took the time to take hold of the vicar's arm for a second, halting him in his tracks.

"Before we go in Vicar, can I ask you a question?"

"Of course Doctor Trent, what is it?"

"Well, yours is the only church in Olney, right?

"That's correct. What of it?"

"It's just that yours is an Anglican church, serving the Church of England, so what about those of the population who are

Catholics, or other denominations? Where do they worship? I'm just interested to know that's all."

"Now Doctor, let me enlighten you. In a place as small as Olney St. Mary, there is little time for such things as religious intolerance and division. Though I'm sure the Pope wouldn't quite agree with the practice, many of the Catholics in the village, and there are very few by the way, occasionally attend my services, if they feel the need to visit a church. As for confession and so on, I believe that those who take their religion very seriously visit the nearest Catholic Church from time to time. Unfortunately, it's over twenty miles away, in the village of Hopwood, and most of the inhabitants of Olney don't own cars as you know. So visits to St. Saviours are quite rare. If anything Hopwood is smaller than Olney, so I've always wondered how a Catholic church ever sprang up there. Does that answer you question?"

"Yes, thank you, apart from the other denominations."

"Yes, well, as far as I know we have no members of the Jewish faith here, and the few Methodists and Presbyterians are happy to use my little church. We even have one family, the McIvers, who are members of the Episcopal Church of Scotland. I don't think there are followers of any other religions in the village, Doctor, and as I always say, we all follow the same God anyway. It's only in the format prescribed by men of contradictory faiths that the way we worship Him differs. Now, may I go and minister to my flock?"

"Of course, Vicar. Just a moment please."

Trent called quietly to Edith Kinnaird who was stationed at the desk that served as the nurses' station for the isolation ward. She was instructed to accompany the vicar on his rounds. Though he was about to protest that he needed no chaperone, Grafton quickly decided to hold his tongue. Young Edith Kinnaird promised to be as unobtrusive as possible, and Trent had just informed Grafton that some patients were far sicker than others, and Edith would ensure he stayed at a necessary distance from the bedsides of those who appeared to be in the most infective stage of the disease. Grafton wasn't stupid enough to believe that his calling would afford him protection from the plague, and as he began his round of the ward, he felt grateful for the comforting presence of the young Scottish nurse at his side. Soon, the sound of quiet prayer could be heard from the bedside of the first patient to be visited by Grafton.

Leaving the Reverend and Edith to their task, Trent moved slowly along the central aisle of the ward, nodding and smiling reassuringly at the patients who remained sufficiently cognisant to reply with a brief, often pained attempt at returning the gesture. As he moved through the hanging canvas partition that separated the ward from the rest of the marquee, he stopped and looked upwards. Though he couldn't see through the canvas roof of the marquee, his ears told him that the rainfall had lessened considerably in its intensity since Grafton's arrival. Pulling back the tarpaulin that allowed him into the inner sanctum of McKay's office, Paul Trent pondered on just how close a relationship with the Almighty, the Reverend Timothy Grafton enjoyed. However strong or tenuous it might be, Trent thought that any prayer would be a good one at this time and allowed himself a silent plea to the God he'd thought little of over the last few years. The reason for his earlier question to the vicar was apparent as he repeated the opening of a Roman Catholic prayer, "Hail Mary, Mother of God..."

CHAPTER 25

DOUGLAS RYAN FELT DISTINCTLY UNCOMFORTABLE, NOT AN everyday occurrence within the four walls of his own inner sanctum. Today however, he was in the position of being outranked and outgunned by the man sitting in the leather armchair on the visitors' side of his desk. Sir Robert Blake was the Chief Undersecretary of State for Health, and the stern countenance on his face reinforced the mood of the meeting.

"There are worries being voiced in various quarters of the government, Douglas, rumours that seem to have emanated in some part from your department. There's talk of something going on down in Kent, and that you're using an inordinate amount of resources to keep a lid on whatever situation has developed."

"I'm sorry, Sir Robert, but I can't be held responsible for every rumour that emanates from within the corridors of Whitehall."

"I never said you could, but what I want to know is if there's any truth in those rumours."

"Perhaps if you tell what they're saying, Sir, I might be able to confirm or deny whatever it is I'm supposedly responsible for."

"Very well, Douglas. In a nutshell it's said that you have an epidemic on your hands in Kent, and that said epidemic is of a highly virulent and potentially disastrous plague that could spread out into the general population. Not only that, but you've called in help from the Ministry of Defence and are employing military personnel to virtually keep a large area of the county sealed off from the public. Telephone services have been cut off, and the dead are reportedly piling up in the streets because you haven't made provision for on the spot burial or cremation, and there are no ambulances to carry the bodies to the nearest mortuary in Ashford. Armed soldiers are patrolling the Kent countryside and you've even called in the Deputy Director of Special Projects from Porton Down to co-ordinate your on-the-ground operations. Have I missed anything out, Douglas?"

Ryan was stunned. Though he firmly believed he'd been acting in the way expected of him, in the space of a few minutes Sir Robert Blake had managed to make him feel as though he'd taken part in some great conspiracy and should be hanging his head in shame, or at the very least, making a grovelling apology for his actions. He searched for an adequate response to Blake's accusations, for that in fact was what the man's words amounted to.

"I'm waiting, Douglas," said Blake, impatiently.

"I'm sorry, Sir Robert," he replied. "I was just wondering who filled your head with such slanderous allegations."

"No 'allegations' as you call them have been made, Douglas. If you must know, Air Commodore George Bright, the head of research at Porton Down, contacted me because he was concerned about both the safety and the legal position of his people. They, after all are the ones who you've apparently placed at the greatest risk by sending them to Olney St. Mary."

So, Blake not only knew something of what was going on he also knew *where* it was going on. Ryan felt aggrieved that Forbes had obviously made such an issue of his plans that Bright had felt the need to speak to a higher authority, as if Ryan himself couldn't be trusted to handle the situation. Douglas Ryan had forgotten that the military code of ethics meant that people such as Bright and Forbes would act to protect and cover each other before they would a civilian bureaucrat such as himself.

"Look," said Ryan, "in the first place, Sir Robert, it's true that the General Practitioner in Olney St. Mary sent two patients to the hospital in Ashford when they exhibited symptoms she thought might be a highly contagious form of influenza. One of the patients, a teenage boy, died on the way to hospital, the other soon after being admitted. Doctor Malcolm Davidson, whom I've known for many years and his assistant, a Doctor Paul Trent, discovered the boys were suffering not from influenza, but from pneumonic plague."

Ryan paused, expecting a response, but Blake said nothing, waiting instead for the virologist to continue. He cleared his throat and went on.

"In an attempt to prevent a mass outbreak of the plague, which I'm sure you know is far more deadly than the bubonic strain, I took what I thought to be the appropriate steps to contain it to the local area in which it had occurred. In order to do so, I called in the man who, after myself and Charles Macklin is reputed to be the leading expert in the field of epidemical control in the country. That man is Group Captain Donald Forbes. He is an exceptionally brilliant virologist and I knew that he would have the power to mobilise the resources I would need to achieve the results we require. His military background enabled me to gain rapid use of helicopters and personnel who have been put to use in treating the sick and in attempting to discover the source of the epidemic in order that we may prevent any outbreak into the general population. I can categorically state that there are no 'bodies piling up in the streets' of Olney St. Mary. The sick are being cared for in an admittedly primitive though adequate field hospital provided thanks to the efforts of Forbes, and he, Paul Trent and the local GP are working with a team of experts from Porton Down to eradicate the plague from the community. It's true I requested that the governor of the GPO cut off the phones in the village apart from those of the local doctor and the police house, but that was done with the objective of preventing unauthorised news of a plague outbreak reaching the general public and causing a widespread panic. The troops are positioned around the Kent countryside to try and prevent outsiders stumbling into a plague epidemic, while at the same time preventing anyone who may be infected from leaving and spreading that infection. My priority is to safeguard the lives and security of everyone in the village. I never had any intention of misleading the minister, you, or anyone else, Sir Robert. I took whatever actions I felt necessary in order to protect the citizens of this country, including those in Olney St. Mary, and will continue to do so to the best of my ability, unless you or anyone else in authority decides to relieve me of my position in this office."

Ryan's last words had done the trick, and he knew it. There was no-one in the United Kingdom better qualified to handle such an outbreak, and he'd now placed Blake in such a position that he would have to endorse his methods or fire him. The Under-Secretary of State dissolved into deep thought for a few seconds before he responded to Ryan's explanations.

"Listen very closely, Douglas. There are other 'reservations' shall we say, that have been voiced regarding your handling of this situation. I am not going to talk about them at this time. Suffice it to say that there are people better placed than I in the government hierarchy who do not want to hear rumours that there is or there has been some sort of conspiracy to mislead or deflect the British people from the truth. If I find at some later date that that has been the case, then it won't matter a fig that you're the leading man in your field, and that you hold a great deal of power in the department. You will be summarily dismissed and will probably find it difficult to get a job working as a junior researcher in a pharmaceutical lab. Do I make that absolutely clear?"

"Really, Sir Robert, there's no need for such threats. I'm not deceiving anyone and have never intended to do so. Having said that, your threat is abundantly clear, though unnecessary."

"Good! Then, Douglas, I think I shall leave you to get on with whatever you have to do, but bear in mind that this matter has now been brought to the attention of Mr. MacMillan himself, who has expressed grave concerns about the possible repercussions if your strategy proves, how shall we say, inappropriate?"

Mention of the Prime Minister's name certainly wasn't lost on Douglas Ryan. Harold MacMillan was the leader of the new Conservative government and would certainly not be pleased to have to explain to the House of Commons, or to the public for that matter, any kind of scandal or incompetence by the Ministry of Health in the handling of a potentially disastrous pneumonic plague epidemic. Sir Robert Blake may have been forced on to the back foot by Ryan's 'back me or fire me' tactics, but such was the political guile and intelligence of the man that he'd managed to turn the situation around once again. Ryan was now left in no doubt that if his plan were to go wrong in any way whatsoever then the Prime Minister would require a scapegoat who could be offered up in sacrifice to the media and the people. Blake had just made it abundantly clear who that scapegoat would be and Douglas Ryan, for all his wealth, power and knowledge, suddenly felt that he knew how a tethered goat might feel when offered up as bait in order to catch a rampaging lion.

Blake soon took his leave of Ryan, who reached for his decanter as soon as the heavy door closed behind the knight of the realm. As the hot fiery Scotch whisky drained down his throat, Ryan hoped that he would be proved right in the matter of the plague in Olney. For many reasons, including one he'd failed to divulge to Sir Robert, he now knew just how much he stood to lose.

CHAPTER 26

A WEEK HAD PASSED SINCE YOUNG EVAN PARKES AND DAVID Bradley had become the first victims of the Olney plague. To the beleaguered doctors and nurses who were fighting the battle to save the village from the ravages of the disease it felt more like a month. No matter how hard they'd tried, the search parties of RAF Regiment personnel, aided by the local knowledge of Police Constable Greaves and the ever willing volunteered assistance of Michael Sweeney had drawn a blank in discovering anything that might shed a clue as to the original source of the plague's introduction to Olney. In the light of the ever-rising death toll, even the local poacher Billy Wragg had been persuaded by Sweeney to join in the hunt for anything unusual that might explain how the disease had infiltrated the community. After all, as Wragg had said when introduced to a grateful Paul Trent:

"Aye, well, there's little else for me to do around the village is there? A man can't catch what's not there, and right now the place is bare of anything worth putting in a cooking pot."

Trent thought that Wragg might be the best man to locate anything out of the ordinary. As a poacher, he would know of nooks and crannies that might escape the eyes of searchers from the outside or even locals who didn't have his keen sense of what might be seen as out of place in the fields and hedgerows that surrounded Olney St. Mary. Yet so far, even Wragg had come up empty handed. Of course, not knowing what exactly they were looking for didn't help.

So far, Forbes had ordered the closure of the village school, and the Post Office, banned the Reverend Grafton from holding services in the church and to the horror of most of the men in the village, The Beekeepers Arms had been instructed to close its doors until the epidemic was declared over. The terrified people of Olney stayed for the most part within their homes, afraid to venture out except when absolutely necessary. As the General store and the butcher's shop began to run low on fresh food supplies, and the supply of canned and dried foods ran low, Group Captain Forbes ordered an air drop of supplies, and four Sycamore helicopters made their by now familiar approach to the village, landed and took off within ten minutes and for a time, the situation was stabilised. For the duration of the epidemic the residents of Olney would have to get used to the old wartime tastes of powdered milk and canned meat once again.

Forbes knew that if the situation went on much longer the aerial supplies would have to be repeated on a frequent basis. To the pilots who flew those much-needed supplies into the apparently deserted village, from the air Olney St. Mary resembled little more than an abandoned ghost town.

Guy Dearborn and Edith Kinnaird had joined a small team who were working with Doctor Naylor to carry out as many rat autopsies as possible. So far, they'd managed to conclude that the rats all died of the same strain of the disease, but they couldn't explain the apparent change in the biological make up of the bacillus as presented within the rats remains. Dearborn, brilliant as he was, could only go back to the already discounted theory of

163

outside contamination. He'd been told by Group Captain Forbes to look deeper, explore further, and aided by Edith Kinnaird, he decided to do just that. His research had now taken a new direction, which for the time being he would keep to himself and Edith.

Trent and the others, Forbes and McKay included, were becoming increasingly concerned by the rising death toll within the village. Though no more of the medical personnel had joined the unfortunate Patricia Knowles on the obituary list, the figures were looking disastrous. Of eighty-five reported cases so far, sixty had died, twenty-two were still under treatment in the hospital marquee, and in addition to Emily Bradley, only two others appeared to have begun a full recovery from the plague. Poor Emily Jones had been reunited in death with her great friend Mabel Thorndyke, though for the doctors the hardest to bear of all the deaths had been the fourteen children who'd so far perished. The statistics were not heart-warming. John Dempsey and Alice Tate, the two additional survivors had presented exactly the same symptoms as the others, and had received the same treatment, yet they'd survived whereas the others had died. The big question the doctors were now asking themselves as they met not in the marquee's small 'office' but in the more comfortable surroundings of Hilary Newton's surgery was, why?

"The rate of fatality is far higher than I would have expected," said Forbes as he sat sipping Earl Grey tea from a bone china cup that was a part of Hilary's best and only tea service. "This is more akin to the death rate experienced during the dark ages from bubonic plague rather than an outbreak in twentieth century Britain with all of our modern antibiotics and clinical know how and expertise."

"There's definitely something not quite right about the way the disease is affecting those who contract it."

This comment came from Paul Trent, who had been listening to the theories of Guy Dearborn just before the meeting had begun.

"Aye, I have to say that Doctor Trent is right," said McKay, who no longer seemed quite as officious as he had when he first appeared in the village. The magnitude of their situation hadn't been lost on McKay, who now knew that he and the others were involved in an all-out war with the plague bacillus, a war that they couldn't afford to lose if it were to be contained and eradicated.

"I agree," was Forbes's reply. "For whatever reason, and the sooner we discover that reason the better, the bacillus has changed it's tactics from the established method of disease progression we were previously aware of. It's imperative that we find out how and why and then set about finding a way to stop it. So far, it seems that the antibiotics are having no effect, or that at most, they delay the inevitable for a short time."

"Are you saying that those who survived did so *in spite* of the streptomycin as opposed to *because* of it?" asked Hilary, herself drinking hot coffee from a Horlicks mug.

"I really don't know, Doctor Newton. It's possible that they would have died if we hadn't given them the antibiotic, in which case it did save their lives, or maybe they just have some in-built resistance to this strain of the disease. Don't forget that you and the others here administered prophylactic doses to the whole village just before the disease went on the rampage. So we can't say for sure whether the drugs are helping or not."

"Uh, sir," Dearborn tried to speak.

Paul Trent backed him up.

"Group Captain Forbes, I think you should listen to what young Doctor Dearborn here has to say. He has a theory that might seem a little wild, but it's better than no theory at all, and certainly beats anything we've come up with so far, which of course is absolutely nothing."

"OK, young Dearborn. Let's hear what you've got to say."

"It's just this, sir. Some days ago, God it seems like years, someone had the idea that the outbreak might be the result of a biological attack."

"I know all about that, Dearborn. It was a preposterous idea and quickly discounted."

"Yes, I know sir, but wait. I'm not saying this is a biological attack as such, but what if it's biologically based in the past?"

"Good God, can't you make some sense Dearborn? What the hell are you trying to say man?"

"What I'm trying to say is this sir. We all know that England was ravaged by the plague hundreds of years ago. In fact there's evidence that the plague was still quite common in small clusters right up until the end of the last century. Now, I don't know anything of the history of Olney St. Mary, but here's what I think might have happened."

As Dearborn paused for breath the Group Captain looked at young doctor, nodded and said: "Go on, Dearborn."

"Well sir, let's suppose just for the sake of argument that Olney St. Mary was affected by the plague hundreds of years ago, perhaps at the time of the Black Death. Right, so, the people of the village as it then was would have presumably done what everyone else did at first. They'd have buried the dead in the graveyard with all due reverence. Then, when the deaths began to escalate out of control the normal burial rites would have been suspended. I've heard of plague carts being wheeled around towns and villages into which the dead were dumped as the cart passed the houses. That's where we get the phrase 'bring out your dead' from."

"Yes, yes we all know that. What then, man?"

"As you know, when the epidemic reached such proportions the dead would be buried in mass graves or 'plague pits' often not as deep or as well dug as we would today deem healthy. Now, this is my theory, and of course it is only a theory sir."

"We understand that, Dearborn. Please continue."

"OK. Let's assume that the scenario I've outlined really did take place. We all know that bacteria can, under certain circumstances survive almost indefinitely until they one day find a new host and can begin their cycle of infection all over again. What if something like that happened here, but with a difference? The bubonic plague bacillus lies dormant in the soil, perhaps in the remains of a plague burial, or even in a crypt in the graveyard, someone who wasn't earlier identified as being a plague victim perhaps, and wasn't buried but just laid to rest in a stone coffin. Then, over the years, the modern world encroaches on Olney, and modern farming methods begin to be applied to the soil. I know that modern manures and pesticides often contain small amounts of chemicals. What if one of those chemicals triggered a rebirth of the bacillus, and also caused a chemical change at a fundamental level, causing the bacillus to mutate and become highly virulent in the pneumonic variant?

Then, one day, along comes one of our local rats or rabbits and disturbs those remains, feeding off the bones of a corpse perhaps, and thus releasing the plague once more into the world. The rat then goes on to infect his own kind and the other rodents in the area and it's not until those two boys come into contact with one of the rats that the plague finds its way into the human population of the village once again. Because it's changed its face, so to speak, the plague now acts differently both in the way it kills the rats and in the way it presents itself in its human victims. I know it sounds crazy sir, but I believe there's a chance that such a thing just might have happened. The reason therefore that the disease appears different to us is because it *is* different! It's changed, grown, evolved into something even more deadly than we might previously have imagined. That's about it, sir. That's my theory."

Silence greeted the end of Dearborn's hypothesis. Everyone in the room seemed to be holding their breath waiting for a response from Group Captain Forbes. The RAF man seemed to be holding his breath too, but then he sighed, exhaled, and looked deep into Dearborn's eyes. When he spoke Donald Forbes did so with a hint of admiration in his voice.

"I don't know if your theory is anywhere near the truth, young Dearborn. But, by God sir, it's the nearest we've come so far to a workable theory as to what's going on in this God-forsaken village. Brilliant, young man. Quite brilliant. Now, before we can explore your idea, we need to know if there was indeed any connection between Olney and any previous plague epidemics. Any ideas, anyone?"

It was Hilary Newton who provided the answer that might lead them a step closer to a solution to the puzzle.

"The parish records, sir. If they go back far enough, they should tell us if there was any plague epidemic here in the past, large or small. The deaths of everyone going back for years should have been recorded there."

"Then, Doctor Newton, gentlemen, I think it's time we all went to church."

CHAPTER 27

THE REVEREND TIMOTHY GRAFTON WAS NOTHING IF NOT surprised to see a delegation of doctors standing at the door to the vicarage. The quaint cottage that served as the home of the incumbent of the post of minister of St. Mary's stood in a small walled garden less than twenty yards from the church. He'd opened the front door to his home before anyone had knocked on it, having seen the four men and Hilary Newton walking up his garden path.

Without waiting to inquire as to the purpose of their visit he politely invited them in. He directed them along the hall and into the parlour that served as his office and place for meeting parishioners who might require spiritual help and guidance.

"Now, what can I do to help all of you distinguished and learned medical people?" he asked smilingly.

"We need to see the parish records dating back to...maybe to the seventeenth century if they go back that far." Group Captain Forbes had elected himself as spokesperson for the group, though he'd asked Dearborn to relate parts of his hypothesis if necessary, to the vicar.

"You're searching for records that indicate incidences of plague in the past I presume?" said Grafton.

"You're very quick on the uptake, Vicar, I must say. Why would you think that?"

"It's only logical, Group Captain. After all, we're in the middle of a plague epidemic here in Olney. I would have thought that you might be looking for a historical record of plague in the village, though I don't know what bearing the plague of the seventeenth century might have on what's taking place today."

"I'll allow Doctor Dearborn here to clarify that point if I may," said Forbes, handing the gauntlet of explanation to the young doctor.

Guy Dearborn kept the explanation of his theory as simple as he could and five minutes later Grafton sat back in his chair with a dispirited look on his face. He stared at the assembled group of medics and then spoke slowly and gravely, each word clear and striking home like arrows, gradually puncturing Dearborn's theory.

"I'm sorry to disappoint you," he began, "but the parish records do indeed go back to the time period you mentioned, even further in fact. Unfortunately, they make no mention of the Black Death, or the plague ever being recorded in the village. I'm sure if anyone in Olney St. Mary had ever been the victim of such a pernicious disease it would have been recorded by the incumbent priest of the time."

"Unless the priest himself was a victim too," said Dearborn, trying to salvage the remnants of his theory.

"There would always have been someone available to record such a death," said Grafton. "You're all welcome to read through the records, but I assure you there's nothing there that could help you."

"How can you be so certain, Vicar?" asked Forbes.

"I'm quite a historian, Group Captain. When I arrived in Olney, I did all I could to research the history of the village and its inhabitants over the centuries. The first thing I did was read the parish records. They are always a valuable source of local information to a new priest. They tell you which families have lived here for centuries or just for a generation or two. They can inform the reader of things such as you are looking for. The great 'flu epidemic of nineteen eighteen for example claimed a number of lives here in the village. The plague would have been recorded in a similar fashion I assure you."

"May we see them anyway?" asked the disappointed Group Captain.

"Certainly," replied the vicar who proceeded to lead the party through the back door of his home and into the church via a side door. There, he produced the records they sought to peruse and left them to their research with a request that they lock the side door and return the key to him when they'd finished. The heavy brown leather-bound volume that held the records of the parish of Olney St. Mary stood ready to reveal its secrets, if any existed.

"The vicar's right," said a disconsolate Guy Dearborn after an hour and a half of searching through the records. There's absolutely no mention of anything in here that would indicate an outbreak of plague, and we've gone back over five hundred years. There's consumption, flu, deaths from open wounds becoming infected, almost everything under the sun, but nothing that might indicate a plague outbreak, however small."

"You say there's mention of influenza," said Hilary. "Could they have mistaken the symptoms of plague for the flu as I initially did?"

"We're talking about bubonic rather than pneumonic plague in the time frame we're covering. I doubt they'd have missed the obvious differences in physical symptoms, even way back then," Dearborn replied.

"I suppose you're right Guy," Hilary went on. "I wouldn't think we can do any better here, can we, Group Captain?"

"I'm afraid not, Doctor Newton. We've drawn a blank I'm afraid. It was a good try though young Dearborn. I suggest we go back to the surgery and try to find another avenue to explore. McKay, why don't you and Doctor Dearborn return to the hospital and see what you can do over there? The rest of us will reconvene our 'think tank' and try to come up with some other way of finding the source of this damned pestilence."

"Aye, we'll do that, sir," said McKay, and he nodded to Dearborn who followed him out of the church and across the road towards the marquee. As soon as the two men were gone, Group Captain Forbes turned to the two remaining doctors and said, very quietly, as though in deference to their cloistered surroundings.

"I didn't really think that young Dearborn's idea would bear fruit, though it was worth exploring. I just thought that he, perhaps as well as the rest of us could do with something to focus on outside the confines of the hospital ward for an hour or two. His theory of the bacillus surviving in the ground for centuries and then mutating from contact with modern day chemicals didn't really have much of a chance I'm afraid, but it kept his hopes up, and that had to be a positive don't you think?"

"A spot of therapy eh?" asked Trent.

"He's been working very hard, too hard in fact," said Forbes. "I've watched him in that ward. The man's energy has been boundless. I don't know when he last slept. I've nothing but admiration for him. Trouble is, if he doesn't take a break, he's going to burn himself out and that wouldn't help either Dearborn or the rest of us who certainly need men of his calibre at the present time."

"Perhaps the time's right for everyone to take a break," said Hilary. The two men stared at her as though she'd gone mad and she quickly qualified her remark.

"I don't mean all at once of course, but I do think we should look at the possibility of giving some of our people a rest. They can't possibly work at their best if they continue at their current rate. We should make them take a few hours at a time off work, instead of a quick break here and there as they're doing at present. If they had the chance to refresh their bodies and recharge their minds they might be better focussed when they step back into the ward. Guy isn't the only one who's working himself to a standstill in there. That young nurse, Edith Kinnaird has been by his side almost constantly, caring for the sick, and most of your people have worked tirelessly as well, Group Captain."

"I think you may have a good point, Doctor Newton, though I think that young Nurse Kinnaird's closeness to Doctor Dearborn might have its roots in a more personal attachment."

Hilary and Paul Trent looked at one another and smiled. They'd also thought that the young doctor and the pretty nurse might be becoming romantically attracted to each other and were glad that the Group Captain had seen the signs as well. In the midst of the terror being wrought by the plague, they were all quietly pleased that the everyday business of human attraction could still work its magic between two people.

Agreeing with Hilary's suggestion, Forbes instructed Trent to liaise with McKay to produce a rest and relief rota for the medics and nurses employed in the hospital marquee. Though there was nowhere to go and little chance of recreational pursuits in the plague-stricken village, at least a few hours rest might help his people to recharge their batteries ready for a fresh assault on the disease that had afflicted so many.

As Paul Trent turned the ornate iron key that locked the heavy wooden door to St. Mary's church and the three doctors prepared to return to their task of treating the sick, Donald Forbes placed a hand on Trent's arm. Trent turned to see the Group Captain smiling at him.

"Whatever you do, Doctor Trent, when you and McKay draw up that rest rota you will make sure that Doctor Dearborn and Nurse Kinnaird are given their time off together won't you?"

Trent said nothing but nodded and winked at the Group Captain in agreement. Perhaps during the pestilence, despite the village being the centre of untold misery and death, Cupid's arrows might be helped to score a point or two of their own.

CHAPTER 28

"D'YOU THINK WE'LL WIN, GUY, OR WILL THE PLAGUE DEFEAT all of our attempts to rid the village of it?" Edith Kinnaird felt a little uncomfortable using the parlour of Hilary Newton's house and being there alone with Guy Dearborn. She was trying to keep the conversation trivial, impersonal, though she knew that she felt something far more personal for the young doctor than propriety allowed.

"I thought we agreed not to mention the plague while we're here, Edith."

"I know, but, well, what would people think? You're a doctor and I'm..."

"An unbelievably beautiful woman Edith, that's what you are. Do you really think anyone in Olney cares a brass farthing for the fact that we're here together? You're not in the nurse's home in Ashford now, and there's no matron breathing down your neck checking to see if you've broken curfew or are spending time with a doctor or anyone else for that matter. They've all seen the way we are together, and don't forget that it was Doctor Newton herself who suggested we use her home to spend a little time together. We don't have long Edith. Why don't we just spend the

175

time in relaxing and perhaps get to know each other a bit better?"

Guy Dearborn had been surprised when Hilary Newton had virtually ordered him to take Edith out of the hospital and make sure she relaxed for a while. His surprise was compounded when she then told them that her home would be available for them to spend some rest and relaxation time together, undisturbed for the next four hours. Paul Trent had been standing behind Hilary when she'd given Guy his instructions and had nodded his approval to the young medic. He'd had to work quite hard to get Edith to agree to join him at the house, but eventually his charm and personality, and the fact that the girl had strong feelings for him managed to outweigh her reticence, born of the proprieties of the day. Now, they sat together on Hilary's sofa, he in his white coat and crumpled grey suit, Edith in her less than perfectly starched uniform of blue dress and white apron. Even her stockings had a slight run in the left leg, though Guy wouldn't have noticed if she'd been wearing sackcloth. He was alone with the girl of his dreams at last. He switched Hilary's radio on and waited for it to warm up, at the same time as he waited for Edith to speak.

As the strains of Perry Como's 'Magic Moments' began to fill the room Edith smiled and Guy felt a breaking down of some of the barriers that existed between them.

"You're right Guy," she said, using his Christian name for the first time. She'd been so scrupulous in addressing him as 'Doctor' or 'Doctor Dearborn' when on duty, attempting to disguise her feelings for the handsome young man, who she knew had ensnared her heart. She'd obviously not done too good a job at camouflaging her feelings, if Hilary and Paul Trent's knowing looks had been anything to go by.

"I just don't want to cause any trouble for you or myself when we get back to Ashford, that's all."

"Listen Edith, I don't care what anyone says, especially Matron. The old dragon has probably never had a romantic thought about anyone in her life, but I'm damned if she's going to come between us now we both know how we feel."

"Do we Guy, know how we feel I mean?"

"I certainly know how I feel Edith, and I'm not going to let a little thing like a plague epidemic prevent me from spending some time with you whenever we get the chance. I rather think that Doctors Newton and Trent are attempting to play Cupid on our behalf, and to tell the truth, I rather like the idea, don't you?"

"Well, yes, I suppose I do," she replied coyly.

"I think that's just the right song for us, don't you?" he asked suddenly. "*Magic Moments*. Isn't that what this is Edith, a 'magic moment' for both of us?" Guy reached across the short space that divided them on the comfortable sofa and took Edith's hand in his own. She made no attempt to stop him, or to withdraw her hand from his. Perry Como's voice began to fade into the background as the record came to its close, but the two young people hardly noticed. They sat, holding hands for what seemed an eternity, looking into each other eyes, until Guy Dearborn at last moved closer to Edith, placed his spare hand around the back of her neck and gently and lovingly pulled the girl towards him. When they kissed, it was as though all the tension and fear that had found its way into their systems during the last few awful days simply melted away. Edith returned his first tentative kiss, and then pulled away, uncertain of herself. Guy pulled her to him once again, and this time, she didn't pull back. The second kiss seemed to last for an eternity, and when they finally separated, they simply sat looking deeply into each other's eyes.

The voice of Connie Francis was now emanating from the radio on the sideboard, the song, 'Who's Sorry Now?'

"I'm not sorry, are you?" asked Guy as he recognised the tune.

"No Guy, I'm not sorry at all."

"What do we do now, I wonder?" he enquired of the girl who replied somewhat sheepishly,

"I'm not sure I know what you mean."

"Oh, I think you know very well what I mean, my dear girl," said Dearborn with a wink. "Didn't Doctor Newton say we had the place to ourselves for a whole four hours?"

"Guy, really!" said Edith, trying to sound as shocked as she could, though not really succeeding in fooling Guy Dearborn for a second.

As Guy led the beautiful young nurse from the parlour and they began to ascend the stairs, the sound of Doris Day's 'Secret Love' began to filter through the room.

"Shouldn't we go and turn it off?" asked Edith shyly.

"Leave it," said Guy. "After all, as the song says, *Our secret love's no secret anymore*', and it isn't, is it Edith?"

Looking up at him with love and admiration in her eyes Edith replied,

"No, Guy. It isn't a secret any more, is it?"

As he closed the bedroom door behind them Guy looked at his watch. They still had two and half hours to themselves!

CHAPTER 29

BY THE END OF THE WEEK, THE POPULATION OF OLNEY HAD got used to the sight of the military personnel, the medics and the giant marquee and it's smaller cousins that had grown up to form the hospital complex and accommodation for those working within it. Those who ventured out onto the almost deserted streets of the village had established an almost other-worldly relationship with those from the outside, nodding politely to the doctors and nurses without really acknowledging them. The newcomers were certainly not treated as friends, even though their purpose in being in the village was to help and if possible, protect the residents from the disease that had ravaged their community. They were treated almost like aliens, there to carry out a task whilst remaining suitably detached from the everyday life of the village, though 'everyday life' was certainly not as it used to be.

As for the villagers themselves, those in homes that hadn't been affected so far by the plague tried to keep themselves apart from those families who had members in the hospital. In this way, it became gradually apparent that a 'them and us' mentality was springing up in the village. Group Captain Forbes and Paul Trent were both quite concerned by this development, as they both agreed that such attitudes could lead to friction and perhaps to eventual violence. Forcible segregation wasn't something that either man would have liked to see happening, certainly not when self-imposed for the wrong reasons. Though Sweeney had assured them that the people of Olney were too close for such a thing to happen, neither of them quite believed him, and Forbes was heard to have given Sweeney quite a lecture on his 'countrified sense of naivety'. Forbes took the matter so seriously that he asked McKay to prepare a leaflet that would be distributed to every home, informing the people of Olney that the disease was transmitted in the air, and that isolation in the home wouldn't necessarily afford complete protection. The leaflet urged the residents to continue to take the prophylactic doses of antibiotics, and to seek help at the first sign of illness. Whether it would do any good was yet to be seen, but Forbes felt, and Trent agreed, that they had to do anything they could to foster a sense of togetherness amongst the people, rather than allow them to alienate themselves from one another. This was a time to pull together, not drift apart.

In an effort to restore a sense of normality to the village, Forbes agreed to Trent's suggestion that The Beekeepers Arms be allowed to open for a short time each day, and so the local pub reopened for business, albeit restricted to just two hours at lunchtime and the same in the evening. Forbes hoped that by restricting the length of time available for the consumption of alcohol, the additional problem of drunkenness fuelled by tedium at the lack of worthwhile activity in the daytime would be avoided.

The hospital was now filled to capacity, with more beds ordered by Forbes expected to arrive by helicopter at any time. The death toll had continued to rise, the only bright spot having been the recovery of two of the patients, both children. With a total of three recoveries from ninety-six cases, the prognosis for the village as a whole didn't look good.

"We can't possibly sustain fatalities at this rate for much longer," said Trent disconsolately. He, Forbes and McKay were holding yet another crisis meeting in Hilary's surgery. Hilary and Guy were working hard in the hospital with Forbes's people, trying to stem the tide of the rampaging plague.

"Aye man, I agree with you, but what the hell can we do? We've failed miserably so far. All we can do is make the poor bastards comfortable and then stand back and watch them die before our eyes."

"You gentlemen sound as if you're giving up," said Forbes, with a look of anger on his face. "And giving up is the one thing I absolutely refuse to do. We have a responsibility to these people, and by God, we're going to discharge that responsibility to the best of our ability. Got it?"

"We're well aware of our responsibilities, Group Captain," Trent responded with equal angst. "Doctor Newton, myself and Guy Dearborn, plus our three nurses were here before you and McKay and his team arrived, I'll ask you to remember, and one of those brave nurses has been lost to the plague as well. I certainly don't need reminding of my bloody responsibilities, thank you."

"I didn't mean to imply any lack of resolve, either," McKay spoke apologetically to his superior, "but it's true that we don't seem to be getting anywhere in our search for either the source of the plague or the means to combat what appears to be a highly virulent and almost unstoppable version of the disease. We need some answers, and maybe more help than we have at our disposal. Perhaps the Minister of Health might be prepared to divert more resources our way?"

"You're right of course, McKay, and you too, Doctor Trent. I apologize if I gave you the impression I was questioning your commitment. I know you both want to find a way to stop this bloody disease before it claims any more lives."

Trent and McKay nodded their acceptance of Forbes's apology. The Group Captain hesitated, thinking for a moment before adding to his response. When he spoke again it was with a new resolve and a hint of steel in his voice. Forbes had had enough. It was time to take a more positive approach to the dilemma that he and the others faced. Weighing up his words carefully before speaking he took a deep breath and then went on.

"I think it's time I paid a visit to London, gentlemen. When the chopper arrives with the new consignment of beds, I'll hitch a ride and drop in on our friend Douglas Ryan. The Ministry's chief virologist has been less than honest about some things, I'm sure of that, and it's time I got some answers. This time I'll not be leaving his office until he provides me with some!"

This was the first time that Trent had detected anything akin to a crack in the normally unflappable and composed veneer in the character of the Group Captain. Sensing that Forbes might know something he himself was unaware of, Trent tried to learn more.

"You think this Ryan character has been keeping us in the dark about something?" he asked.

"I shouldn't really be telling you this, Trent, but I've already voiced my concerns about this operation to my own superior officer, and on one occasion I tackled Ryan himself in his office. On the surface of it he gave me a perfectly plausible set of reasons for his actions, but something has always niggled away at the back of my mind about the whole situation here in Olney. My boss even took my worries to a higher level in the government and I believe that Ryan has been visited by someone with much more authority than I possess. I'm not privy to what took place at that meeting, so I've no idea what is going on back in London, but I'm damn sure going to try and find out."

"But he's a doctor, like us, isn't he? He surely wouldn't be involved in anything suspicious or underhanded, would he?"

"Listen, Trent. The one thing you must remember about Douglas Ryan is that first and foremost he's a bloody civil servant, a pen pushing administrator who's probably forgotten what it's like to actually deal with real flesh and blood patients. Yes, he's the Ministry of Health's top virologist and there isn't a better man in the country when it comes to overall knowledge of the type of thing we're dealing with, but, Douglas Ryan is keeping something back, I know it, though I've no idea what it could be. I mean, come on man, why all the secrecy about this outbreak? It's not as if we've never had medical emergencies in the country before, and I'm bloody sure the people of England wouldn't have flown into a blind panic if news had leaked about a small plague outbreak in the Kent countryside. Ryan reckoned that we're still getting over the war and that such news would be too demoralising for the nation to accept. I find that a ludicrous and wholly inadequate reason for his reaction. Sealing off the village and severing communications with the outside world, and then placing troops at strategic points to ensure the village's isolation is tantamount to declaring martial law in Olney St. Mary, and I can see no justification for his actions."

"D'you really think you can achieve anything by going to see him again then, sir?" asked McKay, feeling braver now that Forbes's anger had dissipated.

"Whether I can, or I can't, McKay, I'm sure as hell going to try."

"You really do think there's something not right about the situation don't you Group Captain?" said Trent, becoming more than a little concerned that the man in charge was beginning to question his own orders and the reasons behind them.

"I didn't at first and was quite prepared to believe that this was a simple mission of medical mercy, but things have changed. We're no nearer to reaching a solution to the mystery of how the plague began, we have dead rats in clusters, people dying at an alarming rate, and despite what we have here in terms of equipment and personnel, it's nowhere near enough to cope with what this is turning into. If we're not careful Olney St. Mary will cease to exist as a viable habitat for its residents. I keep asking myself why Ryan didn't simply initiate the normal quarantine procedures when this outbreak was first reported, or why he seems determined to keep it a secret."

"We could always phone the press ourselves from Hilary's phone," Trent suggested.

"Which would achieve precisely what?" the Group Captain retorted. "It's too late for that I'm afraid Trent. We would just have a very angry Ryan on our backs because he'd know exactly where the call came from, and we have to rely on getting at least some support from the man as we try to deal with the situation here. No, the press is no longer a viable option for us. It's expert medical and logistical support we're in dire need of. I don't know how much longer my people can carry on in these conditions. They're working round the clock, getting next to no sleep, and tiredness is the first enemy of efficiency in my book. If we don't find something to lift people's spirits soon, we're going to have a very demoralised set of doctors and nurses on our hands, and mistakes are going to be made. I want to avoid a situation like that if I can."

"So, what do you suggest we do next, while you're in London?"

"Carry on doing what you've been doing, Doctor Trent. Do your best for the poor souls in the ward and my searchers will carry on trying to find a clue as to the nature of the original infection source."

Before any further conversation could take place the ubiquitous sound of approaching helicopters announced the arrival of the latest consignment of camp beds. The three men rose and walked to the door of the surgery, looking up to see the four dragonfly shaped aircraft as they approached the village green once again. As the first Sycamore touched down Trent looked at Forbes, nodded and said simply.

"Your taxi has arrived I think, Group Captain"

Forbes shook his hand, touched the peak of his cap in a quick salute of encouragement to Trent, and strode across the wet turf to the helicopter. Two minutes later, its load discharged, it lifted off with its passenger on board, bound for his meeting with the increasingly mysterious Douglas Ryan. Trent watched as it disappeared into the distance, and he knew that Forbes was right. Something was very wrong in Olney, and he shared Forbes's feeling that Douglas Ryan knew just what it was.

CHAPTER 30

AS THE SOUND OF THE SYCAMORE CARRYING DONALD FORBES
receded into the distance and the sun broke through the clouds
to cast an aura of warmth and brightness over the village, in the
home of Police Constable Keith Greaves, the policeman and
Michael Sweeney looked up for a second, though their eyes
found only the ceiling of the policeman's kitchen. They'd been
talking for some time, being served fresh tea from time to time
by Greaves's wife, Tilly, accompanied by freshly baked scones
laced with butter and jam. Tilly had made them herself as usual,
though the butter supply was growing critical. She thought that
the men deserved it though. Soon they'd be reduced to using
the margarine that she kept on a shelf in the cool of the pantry.
Tilly wished that she and Keith could buy one of those new-
fangled refrigerators, but their kitchen was quite small and she'd
no idea where it would fit if they obtained one. Still, most
people nowadays seemed to be buying them, even some of the
residents of Olney, and sooner or later she and Keith would
catch up with the modern age. It would help her keep fresh
foods longer as well. She'd heard that food could be stored for a
whole month or more in the latest models! After refilling their
cups from the steaming pot of fresh tea she'd just made, Tilly
left the men in peace to continue their deliberations. She didn't

want to eavesdrop on their conversation, so she shut the kitchen door as she left the room and made her way upstairs to the front bedroom, the one she shared with Keith. There, Tilly wiped her brow with her handkerchief, and placed a hand on her chest. She felt tightness and a shortness of breath that hadn't been there when she'd put the kettle on to boil a few minutes earlier. Feeling as though she needed to rest for a while, the policeman's wife kicked her pink slippers off, raised her legs onto the bed and placed her head on the pillow. She thought it wouldn't hurt to rest, just for a while. Tilly Greaves was asleep in less than a minute. Downstairs in the kitchen the conversation continued.

"So what do you think we should do, Keith?"

"I can't say as I really know what the best course of action would be, Michael. I've got the phone of course, like the doctor has, but usin' it for anythin' other than official police business has been banned by the Group Captain, and they'd soon find out if I'd said anythin' to anyone outside the village."

"But just what the hell have you been telling your superiors? Don't they have *any* idea what's going on here?"

"Oh, they know somethin' alright. As far as I can tell from what my sergeant in town says, the Ministry of Health have informed them that a 'situation' as they call it, has developed in Olney St. Mary that has meant they needed to isolate the village to prevent contamination of the surrounding area. Those officers at the station who've been allowed to know about it have all been made to sign the Official Secrets Act, so that they can't speak of it to anyone without placing themselves in serious hot water. If they talk to any unauthorised persons about what's happenin', they stand a chance of being arrested and charged under the Act, which could put them in jail for a very long time if convicted."

"Bloody hell," said Sweeney. "They seem to have thought of everything. Everyone's hands are tied, and we just have to sit here while our friends and families suffer."

"The doctors and nurses are doin' their best you know, Michael."

"Oh, I know. I'm not knocking those who've arrived to help us. Even that bloody-minded McKay character seems to be sincere after all. It's the government Keith, they're what's worrying me."

"The government?"

"Yes, well, the Health Ministry at least, or whoever sent the military in to seal us off from the world. Look Keith, this just isn't the British way of doing things. It smacks of panic somewhere in high places. That's why I think someone, somewhere, knows just what's happening to us and doesn't seem to be able to come clean with the truth."

"I'm still not sure I know what you're gettin' at, Michael. Why would our own government want to cover up the fact that the people in Olney are sick? What's to be gained from such a thing?"

"I've told you I don't have the answers, Keith, just lots of unanswered questions. Look, we've lost about half the population of the village to the plague already. Don't you think they should have evacuated everyone from Olney by now, moved us all to a nice secure and safe isolation hospital somewhere? Ask yourself why they haven't done that, Keith. Either they won't, because they know they can't contain the plague, or they can't, because they know that we're all bloody doomed anyway, and someone has given orders that they want to keep the bloody thing bottled up here in the village."

"You're talkin' about a conspiracy at a high level by the sounds of things, Michael. It's all a bit far fetched if you ask me."

"That's exactly what I'm doing, Keith for God's sake. I want you to ask yourself if this is right, what's happening here."

"Bloody hell, Michael, you're serious about this, aren't you?"

"Too bloody right I am. Something stinks here right now, Keith, and it isn't the sewers, let me tell you."

As he spoke those last words, a thought was born at the back of Michael Sweeney's brain, a thought that would take a little time to reach his full conscious mind. He couldn't quite formulate it at first, but something began to niggle at the undertaker, and wouldn't go away.

"Hey, are you listening to me, Sweeney?"

Michael Sweeney snapped back to the present moment. He hadn't realised that he'd drifted away from Greaves and their conversation as the thought had begun to grow in his mind. He realised that Greaves had been saying something to him and that he'd not been paying the slightest of attention.

"Eh, yes, sorry Keith, I was just thinking. What did you say?"

"I was just sayin' that we ought to try to help the experts out a bit more than we've been doing so far. After all, no-one knows the village and the surroundin' area like we do."

"I agree with you, but will they accept our help?"

"They don't have much choice really, do they, Michael? They must surely be prepared to listen to us. It's all of our lives that are at stake after all. They've even lost one of their own nurses for God's sake. They're runnin' around like chickens with their heads cut off and can't find the source of the infection. From what I've heard from talkin' to some of the doctors, until they do find the source, there's not much they can do to stop the number of cases from risin'. We could all be bein' exposed to it every day without us realising it."

"But what can we do that hasn't already been done by them?"

"We know the area better than they do. We might be able to find somethin' they've missed."

"But what? And where? They're not fools after all, and they must have some idea of the types of places to search to find what they're looking or."

"I don't know exactly Michael, but I do know that if we just sit back and wait, there's every chance that we'll all be dead by the end of next week."

It was at that moment that the thought that had been gestating in the mind of Michael Sweeney at last achieved its birth in his consciousness.

"Bloody hell, Keith. I think I might know where to look. Something's been bugging me for a while and I've just realised what it is."

"Come on then man, tell me. What are you thinkin' about?"

"Sewers Keith, that's what I'm thinking."

"They've already searched the sewer pipes under the village man, you know they have, and they found nothing."

"Yes, I do know that, Keith. I'm not stupid but listen. When we were talking earlier and I said that something stinks, but it's not the sewers, something started to play on my mind. The sewer pipes in Olney were all re-laid after the war if you remember. You know that and I know that, but do the doctors and the RAF people know that? There are God knows how many yards of disused tunnels and pipes that would have been sealed off or just discontinued when the work was done. Don't forget, the field on the edge of the village that used to belong to Simon Parkes was ripped up and turned into the kids' playground, and I remember seeing all sorts of pipes when the tractors and machines were working there. My point is, there are places that they don't know about where some clue might be to what they're looking for."

"By God, Michael, you just might be on to something. Of course, the pre war sewers were the original ones, laid down at the beginning of the century. They led to an old open sewer pit about ten miles from the village if I remember rightly. The sewage was then regularly carted away in trucks and taken to the reprocessing plant in Ashford for treatment. After the war they laid the new pipes that carried the raw sewage directly to the sewage treatment works under ground all the way."

"Exactly! The old pipes, or even the old pit, might be harbouring the infection for all we know. They should be told about it right away."

"You're right. Let's go together and see Doctor Trent."

"What about McKay?"

"I'd rather talk to Trent. He can tell McKay, can't he?"

"Well yes of course he can, I suppose."

The two men rose from the kitchen chairs, grabbing their jackets which hung loosely draped over the chair backs.

"I'd better tell Tilly where we're going," said Greaves.

"Tilly, Tilly, we're going across to talk to Doctor Trent."

When his wife failed to answer his shout, Greaves said,

"Poor love. She's been feelin' tired lately. I'll bet she's fallen asleep. I'll go up and wake her and tell her."

Two minutes later an ashen-faced Keith Greaves rushed down the stairs where Michael Sweeney waited for him. As soon as he saw his friend's expression, Sweeney knew instinctively what Greaves was about to say, but he waited for him to say it anyway.

"Michael, I think you'd better go and bring Doctor Trent over here if you don't mind. I think my poor Tilly has caught the bloody plague. She's asleep and I can't wake her, and she's fair burnin' up. Please go, please hurry."

Sweeney said nothing; he just nodded and was out of the front door in seconds. As soon as he hit the fresh air, he broke into a run. He knew that time was of the essence if anything were to be done for Tilly Greaves. His talk with Trent would have to wait just a little longer. Keith Greaves went back up the stairs, sat on the side of the bed he shared with his wife, and held her hand, talking softly to the only woman in the world who mattered to him. The policeman was well aware of the appalling rate of survival among those so far infected by the plague, and hot tears stung his face as he waited for what seemed an eternity for Sweeney to return with the doctor.

CHAPTER 31

"YOU'RE SURE, ABSOLUTELY SURE DOC?" ASKED KEITH Greaves after Trent had conducted a half hour examination of Tilly.

"There's no doubt about it Constable. Your wife most definitely does *not* have the plague."

"But her symptoms..."

"I'll grant you that at first glance you might think she has the same disease as the others, but I assure you she hasn't. Like I said a minute ago, Tilly has a severe cold, and is running a high temperature, and I suspect that your wife may also be suffering from the early symptoms of angina, which would explain her chest pain, but, I'll repeat again, she *doesn't* have pneumonic plague!"

Keith Greaves had been so relieved at the news of his wife's reprieve from a diagnosis of plague that he hardly took in the fact that she could be suffering from angina, which would have an effect on her heart for the rest of her life.

"As soon as the village is released from its current quarantined status, we'll get her heart checked out in Ashford and with the correct medication she should be able to lead a fairly normal life," Trent went on.

"Yes, yes, of course. Did you hear that Tilly? You're goin' to be alright, my darlin' girl!" There were tears in the policeman's eyes as he spoke, though his smile was as broad as his face.

"Of course I heard it, Keith. I'm in the same room as well you know. I'm not dead or deaf you big softie."

"I know, I'm just so happy that you're okay. Doctor, why couldn't I wake her up?"

Trent grinned at Greaves, who was unable to keep still and seemed on the verge of nervous exhaustion, such was his sense of relief.

"She was simply exhausted, that's all. You told me she'd been working herself extremely hard lately and stayed up late last night baking those scones you mentioned. With all the worry about what's happening in the village it's not surprising that she just needed to rest for a while. The cold virus itself can be quite debilitating when it strikes hard as well you know."

"Right, I'm sure you're right, Doctor. I can't thank you enough for what you've done."

"I haven't really done *anything*, Constable."

"Of course you have, Doctor. You've put my, our minds at rest, that's what you've done, hasn't he, Tilly?"

"Yes Keith," she replied. "Now, don't you think we should let Doctor Trent get back to treating the people who really need his help?"

"Oh, God, yes. I'm so sorry Doctor Trent. Here's me rabbiting on and keepin' you tied up here when you should be over in the hospital lookin' after those poor people."

"It's not a problem, really," said Trent. "There are plenty of people over there taking care of the ward. It's just as important that we check out everyone like your wife, to make sure the plague isn't spreading. We have to remember that people will still get sick, like Tilly has, with other illnesses apart from the plague, and we mustn't panic and think that everyone who falls ill is infected with the pestilence."

"I suppose I panicked, didn't I? That's not so good for a policeman is it?"

"Don't be daft man. It was your wife who was ill, and you were naturally worried. You did the right thing, Greaves, believe me."

"Well, if you're sure, Doctor."

"Believe me, you did what anyone else in the same circumstances would have done."

"I'm just so glad she's goin' to be okay, that's all."

"Of course you are. Now, just keep her warm, give her a couple of aspirins, and plenty of hot drinks, and she should be fine in a couple of days. As for the angina, I'm giving you some nitro-glycerine tablets. If Tilly complains of pains in her chest or has pain in her left arm that lasts for more than a couple of minutes, make her place one tablet under her tongue. It'll dissolve fast and will take away the pain. I'd rather treat her as having angina as opposed to waiting for confirmation from the hospital which could take some time to arrange with all this going on."

Trent reached into his black bag and took out a small bottle of pills. He removed a few and placed them in a small brown envelope which he also took from the bag. These he gave to Greaves, who instantly placed them on the small table that stood on his side of the bed. He'd look after his wife if anything happened, of that Trent was certain.

As Greaves led Trent down the stairs some minutes later, Michael Sweeney stood waiting for them by the front door.

"How is she?" he asked.

"It's a cold Michael, just a bloody cold. I panicked, that's what I did," Greaves replied.

"Yes, but it could have been something much worse couldn't it? You weren't to know that were you, Keith?"

"That's exactly what I said, Mr Sweeney, said Trent. "Try telling your friend here that he has nothing to reproach himself for in calling for me. He did the right thing."

"Of course he did. Don't worry, Doc, I'll not let him fret for long."

"Good man," said Trent and moved to place his hand on the door handle prior to leaving the house.

Before his hand encountered the polished brass surface of the handle however, Michael Sweeney reached out and placed his own hand on Trent's arm.

"Before you go, Doctor Trent, might Keith and I have a word with you in the privacy of the living room? I think we may be able to help you in your search for the source of this bloody plague."

Trent needed no further invitation and within a minute the three men were ensconced in the warmth of the constable's living room, where Sweeney began to relate his tale of the rebuilt and re-laid post war sewers to the doctor. Ten minutes later, Trent was convinced that the two men just might be on to something.

"So you're saying that there may be tunnels and disused sewer pipes lying buried in the vicinity and that we haven't a clue as to where they are?"

"Oh, there'll be plenty of clues," said Sweeney. "All you need to do is speak to the clerk of works on Ashford Council and he'll surely have all the plans and drawings that were used when the original work was done. They must have diagrams or something that show the location of the original sewers as well as the layout of the new pipes."

"And that's not all, "Greaves added. When I came to the village, they were in the middle of converting one of the fields that bordered the village into a children's playground, the one you see now on the outskirts of the village. It used to belong to Simon Parkes."

"Evan's grandfather?" asked Trent.

"Right. Well anyway, they dug up lots of old pipes from around that field, and that's where the RAF chaps you've got searching out there found the rats."

"I thought that was a drainage or irrigation ditch."

"It was. Well, drainage anyway, from when the land was a field. My point is that the ditch would probably have run into the sewage system at some point, so there would have to be an opening, or a joining point somewhere wouldn't there?"

"And you're saying that the rats of today could have found that opening and come into contact with...what exactly?"

"With whatever it is you're looking for, that's what. Don't ask me to tell you what it is Doctor, that's your job after all. We just thought you might be able to do something with the information that's all."

"I'm sure we can, Constable. Thank you, and you too Mr Sweeney. Your help could just prove to be invaluable."

"We just want to help to stop anyone else dyin' that's all Doctor," said Greaves.

"Well, this information may just do that," said Trent. "I'm sure Group Captain Forbes will be most grateful as well when he gets back from his meeting with Doctor Ryan."

Trent had used the name of the chief virologist without thinking. Little expecting the reaction he now received from Michael Sweeney.

"Ryan? Did you say Doctor Ryan? That wouldn't be the same Doctor Ryan I ran into in this very village just after the war would it, Doc?"

Trent was stunned.

"What? I don't know what you mean Mr Sweeney. I'd think there are lots of Doctors called Ryan in the country."

"Maybe there are, but it seems a bit of a coincidence."

Trent thought that too, but for the moment he held his tongue, waiting to hear what Sweeney had to say.

"Tell me more about the Doctor Ryan you met," he said to Sweeney.

"Well, I'd just been demobbed at the end of the war, and I'd made my way back here to the old homestead. There was a bit of a fuss going on because a German aircraft had crashed here during the Battle of Britain and they, the RAF that is, were removing the remains of the aircraft from the field where the playground was eventually built. I heard tell that the wreckage is now on display in a museum somewhere. Anyway, when they were excavating the aircraft from the field, some of it had sunk deep into the ground. They had to stop the work for a few days. Seems they found some unexploded ordnance, bombs that is, and needed the Bomb disposal boys to come down and sort out the problem. Anyway, me being fresh from the army like, the RAF boys weren't averse to a spot of conversation over a pint or two in The Beekeepers after work. All told they were here three days, and even they'd had to stop work for a while during that time because they'd found something a bit dodgy."

"In what way, dodgy?" asked Trent.

"I never found out properly. I don't think the Bomb Disposal lads did either. They told me that they'd found some bombs that didn't look like the usual Luftwaffe stuff and their boss had called for a 'second opinion'. Whoever gave that opinion must have called in extra help because the next thing I knew was that the whole site, not just the bit where the bombs were found, was cordoned off until it could be totally cleared. Then, this bigwig from the Air Ministry showed up accompanied by none other than this Doctor Ryan character. None of the lads knew who he was or what he was doing there, or even what sort of a doctor he might be, but they concluded he must be some sort of boffin employed to investigate new bomb types or something. I met him just once, when I was standing watching the men at work on the site from outside the roped-off area. He must have stopped to take a break, because he walked over to where I stood and said good morning, and asked how long I'd lived in the village, and was I here when the airplane crashed? When I told him I'd been away serving in the army he turned away and walked back to the crash site, without so much as a 'by your leave', rude bugger. The next day, they were all gone. The field was empty, and Simon Parkes was kind enough to sell the land to the village for a cheap price, to be used as a playground for the children. The parish council provided the funds to build the equipment that's in the playground to this day."

Trent was now more than a little concerned that his possible 'coincidence' of names was no such thing.

"Did you ever manage to hear what this Doctor Ryan's first name was, Mr Sweeney?"

"As a matter of fact I did, Doc. A couple of the RAF Bomb Disposal chaps were talking in the pub that last night and I heard one of them say to the other something about 'Doctor high and mighty bloody Douglas Ryan.'"

Paul Trent's heart sank. Now, more than ever, he knew that Group Captain Forbes was on the right track. Not only that, but Trent now realised that Ryan could be a dangerous man to cross. It was obvious that something profoundly serious had taken place in Olney, and that Ryan was apparently prepared to go to enormous lengths to cover it up, whatever it was. Forbes could be walking into danger without even being aware of it. As his mind focussed on what he'd just heard, he was suddenly brought back to the present by the voice of Michael Sweeney.

"Well Doc, was it him? Is it the same Ryan that your Group Captain has gone to see? Is he something to do with what's going on here in Olney?"

Trent was unsure for a moment or two just how much he should reveal to Sweeney and Greaves. Then, deciding that the two men stood out as the most stout-hearted and reliable men in the village he made his decision.

"Yes, Mr Sweeney, I think it was the same man, and no, he wasn't some 'boffin' who worked on new types of German bombs. He was then, and still is, the leading virologist in this country, and is now the government's chief virologist for the Ministry of Health."

"But what's virology whatever that is, got to do with the pneumonic plague and what's happening here in Olney right now?" asked Keith Greaves.

"Oh, Constable," said Trent with a very heavy sigh, "I think that we're about to find out that it's got *everything* to do with what's happening here in Olney St. Mary. Allow me to explain my theory to you both..."

CHAPTER 32

Guy Dearborn stood beside the bed of the latest admission to the plague-besieged hospital marquee. The Reverend Timothy Grafton was trying to maintain a cheerful disposition as Edith Kinnaird tried to lower his temperature by the application of cold flannels to his forehead. In the next bed lay poacher Billy Wragg, whose attendant nurse Christine Rigby was trying to get the man to take some nourishment of warm soup, without much success.

"I'm sorry to be such a bother to you all," said the vicar.

"You're no bother at all, Vicar," Dearborn replied. "You've done your fair share of ministering to these poor folk in the past few days. It's only fair that you get the best of attention now that you need it."

"I suppose you think it's my own fault, for having placed myself in such a precarious position by visiting so many of the sick, and now I'm getting my just desserts."

"Rubbish!" snapped Dearborn. "You're a brave man Reverend Grafton, that's what you are. A lot of people, men of God or not, would have baulked at the idea of walking into a plague ward when they had no real need to. You showed how much you cared for your flock by being here for them when they needed you, without thought for yourself. So, we'll hear no more of that talk, right Nurse?"

"Of course, Doctor. He's right you know, Vicar. Most of the villagers have virtually barricaded themselves in their homes to try and avoid contamination, but you've just gone about your business as usual. Doctor Dearborn said it for us all. You're a very brave man."

"Here, here," echoed Christine Rigby from the side of Wragg's bed.

Grafton smiled up at the medics. He felt worse than he'd ever done in his life, but his faith and his forbearing resolve gave him the strength to think of others even at a time like this.

"How's Billy doing?"

"Oh, I'm sure Mr. Wragg is doing just fine, right, Nurse Rigby?"

"Of course, Doctor," Christine replied, though in truth there was little that they could do for the unfortunate village poacher. Dearborn thought to himself that perhaps the vicar's prayers and the intervention of The Almighty might be the only things that could save Billy Wragg now.

"Listen to me, Vicar," he said. "I'm the doctor and you're the patient, so that puts me in charge, and I want you to get some rest, is that clear?"

"If you insist Doctor," the vicar agreed, still managing to maintain that smile in the face of adversity. He went on:

"You know, you make a lovely couple."

"What? I beg your pardon, Vicar."

"You and Nurse Kinnaird, here. Oh come on, did you really think that you could keep it hidden. It's written all over your faces. I'm pleased and happy for you, and who knows, when I'm well you might even want me to perform a little service of some kind for you one day."

Dearborn and Edith both blushed uncontrollably. Christine Rigby turned to face them and beamed up at them with a knowing grin. It seemed that the whole village, sick or not, had become privy to the knowledge of the feelings that had sprung up between the young doctor and nurse.

"Yes, well, we'll talk about that when you're better shall we, Vicar?" said Dearborn.

Edith Kinnaird smiled at Guy. She quite liked the idea that people were aware of their feelings. Now that she'd grown accustomed to her own feelings for the young doctor, she felt less self-conscious about their relationship, and after their impromptu love-making session in Hilary Newton's house, she felt closer to Guy Dearborn than she had to anyone in her life.

"Now, rest, Vicar," Dearborn ordered once more, and he and Edith walked slowly from the bedside and moved along the ward, checking the other patients as they went.

"Do you think he'll pull through, Guy?" she whispered as they reached the end of the row of beds.

"Who can say?" he replied. "We've not had much of a success rate so far, have we? Maybe his God can help him; we sure as hell can't do much until we find out why the plague has changed from what we've always known it to be. There has to be something we've missed, there just has to be!"

Angus McKay was just walking out of his canvas-doored office as they passed.

"Hello Doctor Dearborn, Nurse Kinnaird."

"Doctor McKay, hello," Dearborn replied.

"Doctor Trent has just been to see me. He's got some rather important information that he wants to share with us all. He thinks we should have a meeting in the surgery as soon as we can possibly convene one. Are your patients fit to leave in the care of my people for the time being?"

"As fit as we might expect. Whether it's me or your own doctors, I doubt it'll make much difference to these poor souls. We just don't know enough about what we're dealing with Doctor McKay."

"Aye, well, that's what Trent wants to talk to us about apparently. Seems he's been given some new information that might help us in our search for the source of this damnable plague."

Guy Dearborn became instantly alert. His frustrations were beginning to get him down. Perhaps Trent had at last discovered the key that would unlock the mystery of the changing face of the plague that had hit Olney St. Mary.

"Right then, I'll be right with you. Doctor. I'll be back as soon as I can. Nurse, keep a close eye on the vicar, won't you?"

"Yes, of course, Doctor," Edith replied in as official a voice as she could muster. Neither of the pair were fooling anyone though, as McKay turned to the young nurse, winked at her and said, lilting into his pure Scottish brogue for a few seconds.

"Aye, you do that lassie, and I'll be sure to bring yon laddie back to ye as soon as circumstances permit."

———

Paul Trent had busied himself by making a fresh pot of tea as he waited for the others to arrive. Hilary had been making a series of house calls around the village, checking on the general health of the residents. She wanted to be sure that no-one was avoiding treatment out of a false sense of 'I'll be alright', which could prove disastrous to the whole population. Luckily, not one of the remaining survivors of the original population of the village was exhibiting any signs of infection, of the plague or any other minor ailments. As soon as she returned, she helped Trent in providing biscuits to go with the tea, and then all they could do was wait.

McKay and Dearborn were surprised to see Michael Sweeney and Keith Greaves in the sitting room of the surgery when they arrived. Trent explained that the two men had been the source of his new information and that they should be there to corroborate what he was about to tell the small gathering. Once everyone had been served with tea by Hilary and Trent, he began:

"It seems you were right in your earlier supposition, Guy. The root of the problem does indeed appear to lie in the past, though not quite as far back as you envisaged."

That certainly got everyone's attention. McKay, Hilary and Guy were transfixed, not one of them taking their eyes from Trent's face as he continued.

"We only need to go back just over ten years to the war years. Mr Sweeney and P.C. Greaves have I think stumbled upon the key to the mystery. A German aircraft crashed here during the war, and it wasn't until hostilities were over that the remains of that aircraft were removed by the RAF. At the time of the removal it appears that some unexploded ordnance was discovered in the wreckage. Mr Sweeney, who was in the army during the war, recognised the plane as a Messerschmitt Bf110 which was in fact a fighter as opposed to a bomber. That was unusual enough to begin with when looked at in retrospect. Why would a fighter be carrying bombs when at the time of the Battle of Britain the Germans were sending over droves of bombers almost every day?

Anyway, there was obviously sufficient about the aircraft to arouse interest at a high level in the Ministry of Defence, because it wasn't long before a team of specialists arrived to disarm the bombs. Unfortunately, something was wrong, and they called in yet more experts. One of those men who attended the crash site is the government's chief virologist Douglas Ryan, the man co-ordinating the operation to treat this outbreak in Olney."

Trent hoped that he'd said enough. Without further facts to give them, he felt unable and unprepared to answer any questions that might arise from his statement, hence the presence of Sweeney and Greaves. They after all knew more than he did about the strange aircraft that had crashed in the field not far from where they now sat. He needn't have worried. McKay was the first to speak.

"The miserable bastards," he almost screamed in his anger. "The Germans must have had some sort of biological weapon on board that aircraft, but something went wrong, and it got shot down before it could release its payload."

"I said it could be a biological weapon," said Dearborn, "but everyone scoffed at me."

"Aye, well they're no scoffing at ye now, laddie," said McKay, inwardly and outwardly seething.

A sudden realization struck Dearborn.

"Hang on Doctor Trent. What you're saying is that this Douglas Ryan fellow knew about the bombs or whatever they were all along, going back to the war years. If that's true, then the bugger knew from the beginning what was happening here, and yet he seems to have chosen to keep us all in the dark."

"That's the way it looks to me," said Trent, "and if he knew what was in those bombs, he could have said or done something that would have enabled us to evacuate this village before things got out of hand."

"Bastard!" said Dearborn, in an uncharacteristic show of emotion and profanity.

"But why?" the question came from McKay. "Why would he keep it covered up and put the village and us at risk like this?"

"I suspect, Doctor McKay, that your boss has been harbouring his own suspicions about what's going on here, and that that is precisely the question that Group Captain Forbes is putting to Doctor Douglas bloody Ryan even as we speak."

No-one spoke. There seemed little that anyone could say until they heard from Forbes upon his return. For now, a sense of betrayal and a feeling of impotence set into the minds of the medical personnel. What could they do against an unknown, possibly man-made chemically or biologically engineered enemy? As things stood at that moment in time, they knew the answer, and it worried the hell out of every one of them.

CHAPTER 33

IF A MAN OF HIS AUTHORITY COULD BE DESCRIBED AS squirming, then that was exactly what Douglas Ryan was doing at this precise moment, as he faced the three men who sat stony-faced across from his position behind his expansive desk. Despite the warmth of the sunshine that flooded into the office through the large windows, the atmosphere in the room was decidedly frosty.

Forbes had decided he needed back-up before facing Ryan and had called ahead from the helicopter, and his own boss Air Commodore George Bright had arranged to meet him prior to Forbes entering the Health Ministry building. What the Group Captain hadn't known until he arrived at the entrance to the building was that Bright had himself enlisted reinforcements in the shape of Sir Robert Blake, who now acted as spokesperson for the trio.

"You're a bloody liar, Ryan, that's what you are. You knew what was causing the plague in Olney St. Mary, and for some reason neither I nor anyone else could possibly comprehend, you decided to keep quiet about it. I'll have your bloody head on a platter for this, man. What the hell did you think you were doing?"

"I didn't know, Sir Robert, well, that is not for sure."

"Good God, man. Either you did or you didn't. Stop prevaricating and tell us the truth, will you?" What are you trying to cover up?"

"It's not a cover up, Sir, I assure you..."

"Then what the hell is it Ryan? Go on, tell me, and convince me that I shouldn't have you damn well arrested for placing God knows how many people's lives in jeopardy!"

"It's a long story, and I really didn't think that anyone would ever be harmed by what happened in Olney all those years ago. Even now I can't be sure if there's a connection, not for certain anyway, but I had to take precautions, you must see that."

"What d'you mean, man? All those years ago? You're not making any sense at all Ryan. Have the Russians launched a biological attack against this country? Are you a bloody traitor, in league with the Soviets?"

"It wasn't the Soviets, Sir Robert. It was the Germans," the words almost fell from Ryan's lips in a babble. Blake and the others looked stunned. As yet they were unaware of the developments back in the village, and this was hardly what they'd expected to hear.

"Explain yourself Ryan. How are the Germans involved? Is that what you meant by 'all those years ago'?"

Ryan sighed heavily and his shoulders drooped. Suddenly, he didn't look quite so powerful and self-assured as he normally appeared. His voice seemed to be coming from a far away place as he began to speak again, this time in a monotone that implied his thoughts were far from the confines of his oak-panelled, comfortable office. Douglas Ryan's mind was travelling back in time and his audience could only sit and listen to his incredible story.

"It seems a long time ago," Ryan began, "but it was only just over ten years ago. During the Battle of Britain a Messerschmitt Bf110 was brought down by one of our Spitfires and it crashed into a field in Kent, in Olney St. Mary to be precise. Of course, the main targets for our fighters were the German bombers, and when they were shot down the ordnance people soon moved in to dispose of any unexploded bombs that might be on board any sizeable wreckage. Shot-down fighters weren't considered to be dangerous, and the wreckage of any number of Messerschmitt 109s and 110s lay in fields around the country for years in some cases. Most of the aircraft that crashed in Olney slammed into the ground so hard that it almost buried itself in the field where it was left until the end of the war, and the RAF moved in to dispose of the remains. You must understand that no-one had any idea of what was to come when the RAF teams moved in to excavate the wreckage and remove it for display in some museum somewhere. Well, the first thing they found was that the aircraft had several bombs attached to racks under the wings. That was unusual in the first place, as the Bf110 was, as you know, a fighter and not usually armed with bombs. They were primarily used as a bomber escort, though the 110 was slow and cumbersome compared with the 109, and just couldn't compete in an aerial dogfight with our Spitfires and Hurricanes. 'Canon fodder' our fighter pilots called them, and they were right. I doubt a 110 ever brought down a Spitfire or Hurricane in the whole of the war."

"For God's sake man, get to the point." This was Air Commodore Bright.

"Yes, I'm sorry. Where was I? Oh yes, well, when they found the bombs, they sent for the bomb disposal people, who soon arrived on the scene. When they got there, they could tell straight away that the bombs were unlike anything they'd encountered throughout the war. That was also the time when we perhaps encountered our only slice of luck in the whole affair.

The Squadron Leader who headed the bomb disposal team that day had spent some time during the war working in Intelligence and he recognised certain markings on the bombs that immediately warned him that he might be dealing with something very, very dangerous."

"Markings?" asked Sir Robert. "What sort of markings?"

"There was some wording on the bombs, in German of course, that identified them as having been manufactured at the Straub factory."

"I never heard of it," said the Air Commodore.

"I'd be surprised if you had," Ryan replied. "The Straub factory was a highly secret establishment set up by the Nazis in the depths of the Bavarian forests to conduct research into the use of biological and chemical weapons. Only a few of our own people in the Intelligence community were aware of its existence."

"Why wasn't it bombed and destroyed then? asked Bright.

"Because the Air Ministry were afraid of what might be unleashed if the contents of the factory were released into the atmosphere. They couldn't be sure just what the Germans had produced within the factory, and any bombing might have caused a catastrophe of Biblical proportions, or at least, that's the way the thinking went at the time. It was considered better to let it stand and hope that the Nazis could be defeated before they perfected any weapons that could be used against us. Attempts to infiltrate the place were made of course, but all resulted in the loss of some highly trained and very valuable agents.

To continue, the bomb disposal man knew what the bombs might contain, and so he called in a specialist team that existed to investigate any such incidents. I was one of that team!"

"Now we seem to be getting somewhere," said Bright. Ryan continued.

"In addition to the Straub factory markings, I should add that each of the bombs carried a skull and crossbones emblem. We knew enough about the German psyche to guess that such a mark identified the bombs as being of a different nature to the usual high explosive or incendiary types we were used to seeing, and that they weren't anything like the 'butterfly' bombs that the Germans had dropped on our cities during the war. They released lots of tiny bomblets that exploded long after the bomb had dropped and maimed or killed hundreds of innocent civilians as you know."

The others nodded, all being aware of the effects of the hideous 'butterfly bombs' that the Germans had deployed to devastating effect. They waited for Ryan to go on. After a short pause, he carried on with his tale.

"The reason I was included in that team was because I had been on stand-by through the last two years of the war for just such a possibility. It had been suspected that the Germans might try an experimental drop of some nerve agent or chemical or biologically engineered gas or similar substance, and so I was just one of a number of specialists who were ready and waiting to handle any situation like the one that now presented itself. I wasn't the only one, you see. There were chemists, physicists, engineers, munitions experts, scientists from every field who were seconded to the team. Anyway, when we got there and saw what we were potentially dealing with the decision was made to remove the bombs from the crash site and have them rendered safe at a secure government facility. They were taken to a secret underground establishment..."

"Where?" asked Sir Robert.

"I'm sorry Sir Robert, but that location was and still is covered by the Official Secrets Act."

"I said *where,* Ryan? Everyone in this room is cleared to Top Secret level and you bloody well know it."

"It's on a remote Scottish island called Magavin. It's only two miles long by a mile wide and has never been inhabited by anything but seabirds. It's a research and development establishment."

"For biological weapons?" asked Blake.

"No sir, far from it. Magavin exists for the purpose of finding antidotes to what we believe may be the next generation of chemical, biological and nerve toxins. Its existence is kept a closely guarded secret because of the nature of some of the elements stored and experimented upon within its walls. If an enemy were to discover just what we have stockpiled there, well, you can imagine what might happen."

"Indeed," said the peer. "Go on, Ryan."

"Magavin was new when we moved the bombs there. It had only been in existence since the end of the war and was staffed by a small group of dedicated scientists and doctors who knew how vitally important it was to protect the country from attack by such terrible weapons. The trouble was, we were relatively inexperienced in the safe handling procedures necessary for dealing with some of the samples that passed through our hands. There were a number of, how shall I put it, accidents? The worst of those took place when we tried to disassemble the bombs from Olney St. Mary. I wasn't in the lab at the time, luckily for me, though I was viewing the procedure through a plate glass viewing screen.

A bomb disposal expert and two of our scientists began the task of opening the first bomb. I intended to join them when the bomb was made safe. The detonator and the trigger were safely removed, but then when they tried to remove a vial of liquid from within the bomb casing, a booby trap kicked in, They'd missed a thin wire attached to the base of the vial, and when the bomb disposal expert eased the vial from the casing it snapped, causing the bottom of the thin glass container to split open. There was no explosion, but a fine vapour was released into the room."

"A vapour?" This was Forbes, at last breaking his silence.

"Yes, like an exceptionally fine mist, but definitely visible to the eye. We all knew straight away that something dreadful had probably been released into that room, and we had no idea whether the masks and gowns our people were wearing would afford them sufficient protection."

"What happened to them?" asked Bright.

"Well, the room was sealed from outside of course. There were two airlocks that had to be negotiated in order to enter or leave the room. They couldn't be opened simultaneously, thus preventing accidental exposure to any toxins within the lab. Not only that, but the air was filtered in the best way we knew how with the technology of the day. The whole place was a bit like a submarine below the ocean. The air was scrubbed, filtered and then subjected to the whole process again in order to filter out any contaminants. The filters themselves were untouched by hand and were ejected from the scrubbing machine into a duct that carried them directly to an incinerator below the lab. New filters automatically replaced the old ones before the ejection took place, so the risk was always minimal. Any residue of actual contaminants was thus sent straight to the fires of hell."

Bright spoke up once again, a hint of impatience evident in his voice.

"I asked you what happened to those poor people in the lab Ryan."

"After the scrubbing procedure was completed and room fully vented the three men were extracted from the lab and taken straight to the isolation ward we kept on site for just such an eventuality. They were kept under constant observation for the next few days. On the second day, the first one fell ill. Within two more days all three were infected. We soon identified the symptoms as being those of pneumonic plague, but we could do nothing to stem its progress. It was so fast; we could only stand and watch helplessly as those men died. It was obvious even then that the bacillus had been changed or added to in some way to make it even more lethal than usual, but we didn't know how, nor could we access the actual toxic liquid to investigate it, not without risking another release of the vapour. What was worse was that two of the doctors who'd initially treated the three men all contracted the disease as well. There were no survivors. You must understand, Sir Robert, that there was nothing we could do. Don't accuse me of being heartless or uncaring, because those men were all my friends and colleagues, but they knew the risks they were taking, as we all did."

"But how did you cover up the five deaths?" asked the Air Commodore.

"We staged an air crash at sea, in deep water, just off the coast. Officially the men were on board when the aircraft went down without survivors."

"And the pilot?"

"One of our men, he parachuted to safety before allowing the aircraft to ditch in the sea. The bodies were cremated on site at Magavin. We went through the correct procedures for an air/sea rescue and a search was mounted but of course no bodies could be or indeed were found. The families surely wouldn't have wanted to know what a horrible death their men suffered. This way was kinder."

"And a pack of downright lies," Bright said accusingly.

"All for a good reason, Air Commodore. The government of the day, or at least, someone with the power to decide what to do, ordered that the whole incident be discreetly 'buried' so to speak. Nothing could bring those men back and it would have caused a massive political stink if the affair had been made public. It was the last news the country needed right then."

"So there were no more cases?" asked Sir Robert.

"None. We believed that the Germans had formulated the toxin in such a way that it had a limited life span when it reached the air. That way, if they'd used it in a large-scale attack they would only have had to wait a certain length of time for the infection to spread amongst the population, and then their invasion troops could safely move in."

"That's monstrous," Forbes interjected.

"But probably true," said Bright. "They wouldn't want to put their own troops at risk, would they? Making the disease self-destruct after a certain period of time would make sense."

"What happened to the rest of the bombs, Ryan?" asked Sir Robert. "Why didn't you carry out further tests?"

"We were ordered to dispose of them, they were too dangerous to carry out further tests on. They were only twelve inches long, each one, and they were easily sealed in concrete containers which were then loaded into a specially adapted torpedo, loaded onto a submarine, and taken into mid-Atlantic where they were fired into deep water, and where they probably still lie today. There's little chance of them ever being found, or ever finding their way out of the concrete."

"But why didn't someone contact the Germans. Surely there must have been people who worked on the project at Straub who could have told us if there was an antidote to the toxin?"

"The war was over, Sir Robert, and the country was in a state of rebuilding. So was Germany. It was deemed inadvisable to raise the subject of biological warfare with the new democratic administration in Germany. Don't forget that the posturing between the Russians and the West had already begun, and Germany was no longer seen as the enemy. With the bombs gone, that was the end of the matter, or so we thought."

"Until now," said Blake. "You knew all along about the bombs, and yet you said nothing."

"I've just told you, Sir Robert, that there was nothing we could do for those people in Magavin, any more than we can do for the people of Olney St. Mary. That's why I sent such a small team to the village and cordoned the area off. Don't you see, the whole place is probably infected?"

"You callous bastard," said Forbes vehemently. "I hope you realise that I've spent the last few days there, so I'm possibly infected myself, and might just pass the disease on to you as well Ryan."

"I hadn't..."

"Thought of that? No, I'll bet you bloody hadn't." Forbes went on.

"If you knew all this why did you bother to send anyone to Olney? Why didn't you just let them die, you unfeeling worm? Then you could have gone back to your cosy little life behind your desk as if nothing had happened."

"I had to be seen to be doing something," Ryan said apologetically.

"And you've quite possibly condemned a lot of innocent people to their deaths," Sir Robert said accusingly.

Ryan fell silent as the others stared at him with real menace in their eyes.

Air Commodore Bright had been silent for a while, lost in thought. Now, he spoke once more, with an urgency in his voice.

"Maybe it's not too late to do something. How many were there, Ryan?"

"Eh?"

"Bombs man! How many did you extract from Olney?"

"Six. That's all we found, and there were bomb racks under the wings of the aircraft for three bombs on each, so that was it. We got them all."

"No you didn't you bloody idiot. If you had, we wouldn't be facing this damn crisis now, would we?"

Ryan looked quizzically at the Air Commodore.

"Listen, if you'd got them all there'd be nothing left to infect the people of Olney. What you didn't allow for was German efficiency and ingenuity. They would have utilised every available space for bomb placement on the 110. That would have meant another single bomb rack slung beneath the belly of the fuselage, something like the arrangement on the Stuka dive bomber. Did you examine the underside of the fuselage, maybe near the underside of the cockpit?"

"That was the most damaged area of the wreck. There wasn't a lot left to identify."

"Then that's where you missed it," said Bright. "I'll bet you that somewhere under the field in Olney there was another of those bombs. It's lain there, dormant and waiting for over ten years until something has disturbed it and cracked the casing open, releasing the toxin into the air. We need to find it, and fast, and then we must find someone who worked on the original German project. They must have had an antidote available in case of accidental infection of their own troops. They wouldn't have dared risk using it otherwise. You've been a bloody idiot, Ryan. You should have thought of that yourself."

Sir Robert stood.

"You know, I think you just might be right, Air Commodore. You leave the German end to me. The diplomatic side of things is my area of responsibility. Don't worry about me pussy footing around. That won't happen. I'll get some back-up from the ministry of Defence. We'll put as much pressure on the German government as it takes to locate someone with the knowledge we need. You and Forbes had better lead the search for the bomb and take every precaution you can. It may be that the toxin has burned itself out as Ryan suspects it was designed to do. If that's the case you should have no more incidences of the plague, but you still have a lot of sick people on your hands."

"Very well, Sir Robert," Bright replied, himself rising from his chair, followed closely by Forbes.

As the three men moved towards the door Douglas Ryan stood up behind his desk.

"What do you want me to do, Sir Robert?" he asked.

"You Ryan? What do I want you to do? I want you to sit behind that desk of yours and contemplate what little future you have left in this office. What do I want you to do? I think you've done more than enough already, don't you?"

CHAPTER 34

Bright and Forbes watched as the chauffeur-driven Bentley carrying Sir Robert Blake disappeared from sight along Whitehall. Traffic was light and the traffic noise at a minimum. A bright red double-decker bus thundered past, crowded with shoppers and commuters, then all fell silent once more. The morning was warm, the sunshine casting a ruddy autumnal radiance on the streets of London. Even the greyest of buildings assumes a cheerful glow on such days, and so it was with the majority of the government and other office buildings that surrounded the place where they stood. For the two men in uniform however, it might as well have been blowing a force ten gale and snowing, such was the mood that prevailed upon them.

"How could he have done that, sir? Ryan, I mean. He could have told us right at the beginning about the biological bombs, and we'd at least have known what we were dealing with."

"I agree with you Donald, but what's done is done I'm afraid. As much as I can condemn Ryan, I must admit that he was only acting according to whatever orders he received years ago. He must have thought he was doing the right thing. I simply can't believe that a man of his experience and position would just sit back and let all those people die without doing anything."

"Couldn't he have checked with whoever issued those orders in the first place? Surely that person would have given him the go ahead to inform us what was going on?"

"That would depend on certain factors Donald. First, is that person still involved in the government? There've been changes since 1945 remember. It's possible that it might have been an MP, someone who's no longer in office. A civil servant might still be in his job or could have moved on to another department. Our own people must have been involved to some extent and I intend to make inquiries at the MOD as soon as we part company. I think it may have been hard for Ryan to find someone to give him the authority he needed to reveal the truth, and his own sense of responsibility to his paymasters would have ensured his silence, at whatever tragic a cost."

"It's bloody stupid, sir, that's what it is. He put us all at risk, just because some bloated jackanapes somewhere wanted the whole thing kept quiet."

"Like I said, Donald, I agree with you, but Ryan is now the least of our problems. If, as he says, the altered bacillus only has a limited life span then we must hope that it is reaching the end of that period by now. If there has been a leak from an undiscovered bomb in Olney then it must have been a slow leak, and the toxin released over a lengthy period, weeks perhaps, otherwise everyone would have been infected at once. The bombs only held a small vial of the stuff, so we must hope it's all dissipated into the air by now. We'll know if the cases stop being reported in the next day or so."

"I think I'd better be getting back to Olney then sir, if that's okay with you."

"Yes, of course Donald. In the meantime we can only hope that Sir Robert comes up trumps in his search for someone in Germany who has knowledge of what the Nazis were up to. If there is an antidote it could help to save at least some of those who are currently languishing in your hospital."

"We can only pray that he's successful. You know sir; I should have known that Ryan was playing a crooked game when I first got to Olney."

"Oh, how so?"

"Well, he'd said that serious cases of the plague would be airlifted to a special isolation ward in Ashford, but when I arrived in the village I received a sealed envelope he'd sent in advance for my attention, and it was made abundantly clear that all cases were to be treated on site. He never intended to allow any of those people to leave the village. I should have known straight away that something was amiss."

"Perhaps you simply trusted him too much in the beginning Donald, as we all did. After all, no-one knew that he had a different agenda to the rest of us. Now, forget about Ryan. It's up to the rest of us to sort out this damned mess now."

"Right sir, I'll be off then."

"Very well. And Donald?"

"Yes sir?"

"Be careful, won't you?"

"You bet I will sir, don't worry about that."

With that the two men parted, Bright walking the short distance to the building that housed the Ministry of Defence, Forbes to the underground car park nearby where his driver was waiting for him in the black Humber saloon car. A smooth and relatively quick journey took him to RAF Northolt where his helicopter waited to return him to Olney St. Mary.

Within minutes of his arrival he was once more in the air, the rotor blades of the Sycamore churning their way through the warm air, guiding the Group Captain back to the village where the next few hours could prove critical to the chances of anyone in Olney making a recovery from the plague. As he stared down from the helicopter at the huge expanse of buildings that made up the vast metropolis that was London, Forbes did at least feel grateful that the long hidden bomb hadn't been left to decay in the rubble of a burned out bomb site somewhere in the city. The number of deaths that such an eventuality would have caused were simply too horrendous to contemplate. Soon however, the sights of the city gave way to the swathes of green and brown as the helicopter clattered across the fields of southern England, into the heart of the Kent countryside. Soon, he knew he'd be on terra firma once more, in the midst of the greatest horror to have hit the country since the declaration of war by Neville Chamberlain not so many years ago. Trouble was, this time no-one in the country knew about it, apart from a small number of people in authority, those who were suffering from the effects of the plague, and those few trying to treat them and hold back the spread of the infection.

Farms and villages sped past below, many of them much like Olney St. Mary, he thought. They, however, weren't sealed off from the outside, left to the ravages of a disease that few could envisage because of what he saw as the misguided loyalty of a senior civil servant to orders he'd received over a decade ago. Forbes grudgingly admitted to himself that Ryan had been very clever in his handling of the crisis. As far as the outside world was concerned, Olney St. Mary was simply in the centre of a top-secret military exercise, and the phones had been cut off as part of that exercise. Anyone phoning the GPO to report that they couldn't get through to a number in Olney would be told the same story. Friends and relatives of the residents might be concerned at the lack of contact with the residents of the village, but again Ryan knew that the plague had a limited life, and eventually the phones would be turned back on, the troops removed from the surrounding area, and Olney would be left to get back to something close to normal life once again.

That was the moment when a stark and terrifying realisation hit Group Captain Donald Forbes. Ryan had wanted the whole affair kept secret. He couldn't afford to let anyone know what had taken place in Olney. If the troops left and the village was opened up once again there would be survivors left to tell the tale. In any epidemic, even a man-made one like this, there would always be a small percentage of human beings who would have an in-built resistance to the disease-inducing agent. Ryan had expected all along that there would be no survivors, he expected the whole village to die, and if that were the case, that meant he also expected Forbes and the unfortunate medical team to join the villagers on the death list. How had he planned to ensure such a result? Forbes remembered the first meeting in Ryan's office when the man had told himself and Macklin that he would not let the plague spread from Olney under any circumstances. The man had been deadly serious. Forbes now knew that if the plague hadn't claimed the lives of everyone in the village, Douglas Ryan had made plans to destroy not just the place itself, but anyone left standing after the disease had run its course. What Forbes couldn't decide, as the Sycamore breasted the low hill that announced it's approach to the stricken village, was whether that plan still existed, whether Ryan had given instructions to a person or persons unknown to implement his deranged scorched earth policy. The Group Captain realised that he only knew a part of the grotesque plan that had been the brainchild of Douglas Ryan. Was there more to come, and if so, could Forbes actually trust anyone, either back in London, at the Air Ministry, or amongst his own people on the ground in Olney St. Mary?

The Sycamore's skids touched down gently on the grass of the village green, and the pilot nodded a salute to his passenger who exited via the side door, keeping low to avoid the wash from the still rotating rotor blades. As the helicopter lifted off, Forbes looked up and waved to the pilot. Seeing Trent and McKay waiting for him at the entrance to the hospital marquee, he walked purposefully toward them, straight back into what he believed to be his own version of a modern-day hell on earth.

CHAPTER 35

"THE BLOODY JUDAS!" ANGUS MCKAY EXCLAIMED WHEN Forbes finished his report on his meeting with Ryan.

"He expected us all to die, didn't he?" said Trent with anger in his voice.

"How could he?" asked Hilary Newton, incredulously.

"Because the man works according to a set of rules and adheres to orders received on the subject over ten years ago, from someone who we haven't yet identified." Forbes replied.

He'd asked that the others refrain from informing him of their news, as anxious as he could see they were, until he'd passed on his own version of events in London. Now, the small office section of the hospital marquee reverberated to the sounds of angry words as everyone present vented their feelings regarding Douglas Ryan. Perhaps the most vehement critic of the virologist was Angus McKay, who of course had led the relief team into Olney, and thus would have been one of the first to become infected and die according to Ryan's plan. It was Paul Trent who suddenly stated the so far overlooked fact:

"But, you're still alive and well, Doctor McKay, as are me and all of your team. The only member of the medical staff we've lost is poor Patricia Knowles, and that was days ago. If what the Group Captain here has told us is correct, then Ryan thought we'd all have succumbed by now."

"By God, Trent! I think you've hit on something!" This was Forbes himself. "If the bacillus is as virulent as Ryan led us to believe, then we should all have been infected by now. It can only mean one of three things. Either it's not as infectious as the German manufacturers thought it was, or the bacillus had outlived it's time before we arrived"

"And the third option?" asked Trent.

"It could be that certain sections of the population are immune to it. Maybe people with certain blood types, or with a particular mix of antibodies already in their blood, I don't know," Forbes replied.

"I'm sorry but there's a flaw in your theory sir," said Guy Dearborn, who'd remained silent so far, preferring to listen and absorb what he'd been told.

"Go on young man. What is it?"

"Well, you said that it could be that the bacillus had reached the end of it's infective period before we arrived, but if that was the case, then why did so many of the villagers continue to fall ill after we arrived?"

"That's a good question, Dearborn. It may be that they had already been infected by the disease before we arrived but that it took longer to gestate and show itself by way of physical symptoms in some of the residents. Again, some of them may have been able to fight it off for longer than others before it took a firm hold on their systems."

"In other words, the German arms manufacturer didn't do a particularly good job," said Trent. "The bacillus is only partly effective against a sizeable population."

"Maybe that's why it was never used against a large town or city. I know Olney appears to have been an accident, as the German aircraft was shot down by one of our fighters, but what if this was the intended target? They could have selected it as an ideal test site for their new weapon. Olney is small, quite isolated, and the Spitfire could have caught the Messerschmitt just before it commenced its bomb run. It does seem odd that there were no other German aircraft found that day or afterwards with these bombs on board. I think that we've hit on the truth. Olney was a trial that the Germans thought had failed because the aircraft carrying the bombs was shot down and they received no reports that the payload had been delivered. Maybe they only had enough of the altered plague bacillus to try once. If it had worked, they might have gone ahead with a rush of production and then used it on a larger scale. Who knows?"

They all took a few moments to let Forbes's words sink in. The whole thing was so horrendous to contemplate. Everyone in the office now knew that the Germans had intended to try to infect the British people with a deadly plague of Biblical proportions and that only a stroke of luck in the form of an unknown Spitfire pilot had prevented a successful trial of the fearful and despicable weapon.

That realisation did little to solve their current dilemma however, as Dearborn quickly reminded his more senior colleagues.

"We still have to decide which of the Group Captain's options is the one that applies though, don't we? Why have some of the residents continued to become infected while some of them, and us, have remained immune?"

"Quite correct, Guy," Trent replied. "We'll need to apply ourselves to that question, and fast."

"On that very subject, have we had any further admissions since I left this morning?" asked Forbes.

"No sir, we haven't," McKay answered. "And only the two yesterday."

"So, it could be that the plague bacillus is dying out, as the German chemists intended." Forbes said hopefully.

"Let's hope so," Trent ventured. "If it is, we still have a ward full of patients who need our help, and we still don't have any idea if there's an antidote."

"But, that's another odd thing about the plague." Dearborn interjected once more.

"Go on Guy, what's odd?" asked Hilary.

"Well, when the plague first raised its ugly little head, most of the victims contracted the disease and died within two to three days. The later victims have all survived for longer periods before succumbing, and some of the most recent admissions don't seem to be quite as badly affected by the symptoms. I think there's a chance that the recovery rate will improve, statistically speaking, as the latest round of admissions progresses through the phases of the infection."

"I think he's right sir," McKay spoke in agreement with Dearborn. "Maybe the toxin loses some of it's virulence as it begins to lose its potency. That would fit with what you've said previously."

"I agree McKay. Well spotted Dearborn. Perhaps we'll beat this thing yet. Now, all we have to do is find the bloody source of the leak. There must be a bomb casing somewhere quite close to the village, somewhere that allowed the rodent population to become infected first and then the people secondly. Maybe the two boys played regularly in one place, close to the source, and picked up the infection that way. It may even have been moved from its original location between the time the rodents became infected and the human population contracting the disease."

"Aye sir, you could be right," said Angus McKay. "Now, on that very subject, as you've now had your say, I think you ought to hear what we've been finding out while you were enjoying putting Doctor Ryan on the spot."

Forbes realised that the others had been anxious to tell him their news. He now relaxed a little and sat back in his chair as Paul Trent related to him the events of that morning, his conversation with Greaves and Sweeney, and the correlation between their story and what he'd learned himself from Ryan. By the time they'd finished, he knew that it couldn't be long before they found what they were looking for. It was Guy Dearborn, once again, who provided them with the inspirational thought they were looking for.

"From what I've heard here, and from what PC Greaves and Mr Sweeney have been saying, I think the solution is now pretty obvious. The German plane crashed in the field over there," he pointed in the direction of the crash site, "so it's safe to assume that the bomb would have originally fallen quite close to the aircraft. But, after the war, the remains of the plane were taken away, leaving the bomb somewhere under the ground perhaps. Then the field itself ceased to be a field and..."

"The playground! The bloody children's playground!" Forbes exclaimed. "It has to be in the vicinity of the playground."

"But the whole area was searched before by the Regiment chaps, sir," said McKay.

"Now well enough it would seem, Mr McKay. "Not nearly well enough at all."

CHAPTER 36

By the following day, the situation in Olney appeared to have stabilised somewhat. There'd been no new cases of the plague admitted to the field hospital, and those already committed to the beds in the marquee showed no signs of further deterioration. Even the Reverend Grafton was sitting up in bed, joking with the nurses, as was his neighbour, Billy Wragg, who'd seemed so close to death the previous day. Wragg was less inclined than the vicar to believe in divine intervention but couldn't help joking that his close proximity to Grafton as he'd prayed might just have helped.

"If God reached out to touch the vicar, then maybe a little bit of his goodwill spilled over to reach my bed," he'd said to Edith Kinnaird that morning.

Whatever the reason for Grafton and Wragg's improvement, the same could be said for almost everyone else. The death toll appeared to have stopped rising, and the doctors and nurses allowed themselves a brief and cautious hope that the worst might just be over.

Every patient was being given extra doses of streptomycin in the hope that any residual infection could be fought off by use of the antibiotic. In addition, on orders from Forbes, they were all receiving additional doses of a variety of sulphonamides, which had been used successfully to treat plague in minor outbreaks since the nineteen thirties. Anyone living beyond the fourth day of infection was to be considered as being in the recovery phase of the illness. Though the normal course of the disease saw patients dying after three to four days, the new strain had been killing the infected patients within two to three, so any survival beyond that point was seen as a victory for both the patient and the medics.

As a peace of sorts descended upon the hospital marquee, the main focus of attention fell on establishing the location of the one remaining unexploded bacterial bomb. Forbes had asked Trent to arrange a meeting early that morning with Greaves and Sweeney, who he felt were best qualified to help him and his people in finding the lethal weapon in their midst.

Now, the four men, plus Dearborn and Hilary Newton were once more sat around Hilary's kitchen table, with plans of the village laid out before them. Forbes had wasted no time in having detailed maps and plans of Olney St. Mary flown from the County Council's Headquarters in Maidstone the previous evening. He also had the RAF's own reports of the removal of the crashed German fighter plane at his disposal, provided from the archives at the Ministry of Defence, and flown in on the same helicopter as the village blueprints. Now all he and the others had to do was make sense of them and identify the likely resting place of their target.

"Look, this is where the aircraft crashed," said Forbes, pointing to a small cross marked on the RAF's own grid plan of the crash site.

"Right in the middle of where the playground now stands," said Trent.

"Yes, but we have to remember it was a field back then," Sweeney added. "The ground would have been soft and would have allowed the aircraft and its wreckage to sink into it, as we know it did. The bomb could have been thrown from the wreckage and ended up quite a way from where the fuselage came to rest."

"So, where would you think is a good place to begin Mr Sweeney?" Forbes asked.

"It would have to be somewhere we've overlooked so far, or at least somewhere that wouldn't have been searched too closely. I remember after the war, when they'd cleared the wreckage it was a number of weeks before Simon Parkes announced he'd sell the field to the village. Then, a few months later, the diggers moved in to dig up the field and the foundations were laid for the playground. It's my guess that the bomb was probably dug up by one of the excavators, and possibly reburied in the sub-soil beneath where the playground now stands."

"But the playground was concreted over," said Hilary. "How could the bomb have found it's way to the surface after all these years?"

"I think I have the answer to that question," the constable replied. Greaves went on:

"About six months ago, the council paid for a new kiddie's roundabout to be installed in the playground, d'you remember Michael?" he directed the question at Sweeney.

"Course I do," said Sweeney, "and I believe I know what you're going to suggest, but go on Keith, you tell 'em."

"In order to put in the new roundabout, they had to take away the old one," said Greaves. "To do that they had to bring in an excavator to break up the concrete around the existin' equipment which was sunk into the ground. Then, the new one was installed, and fresh concrete laid around the thing. That could have been when the bomb was dislodged."

"And," Sweeney added, "When they dug out the old one, they dumped a certain amount of rubble and clay-like soil in the old drainage ditch on the far side of the playground, just over the fence, where it couldn't harm anyone, the kids in particular."

"And I'll bet if we look carefully, we'll find fragments of the bomb casing, or even the whole thing, leaking slowly, somewhere under that rubble, which is where a lot of kids play regularly," said Forbes.

"Of course," Trent came into the conversation. "The men you've had searching would have looked all around that rubble in the ditch, but without being certain of what they were looking for they wouldn't have thought to look *under* it."

"It's not just that, there's a lot of the stuff, and they'd have needed an excavator or at least a hell of lot of muscle to shift it. Three men wouldn't have been able to do it," said Sweeney.

"Well, Group Captain?" asked Trent. "What's our next move?"

Forbes was silent only long enough for his thoughts to formulate a plan of action. In seconds he responded to Trent's question.

"Does anyone in the village or on one of the local farms have anything that can do the work of an excavator PC Greaves?"

"I'm sure there'll be any number of farms that have something we can use."

"A tractor with twin forks for lifting bales, that's what we need," said Sweeney. "We can use the forks, with boards attached, to lift rubble from the ditch."

"It'll do for now," said Forbes, "until I can get a full-sized excavator here, which I'm going to organise right away. In the meantime, Doctor Trent, perhaps you'll be kind enough to go and ask McKay to get onto our people at Porton Down and arrange for a supply of NBC suits to be airlifted to us?"

"NBC suits?" asked Greaves.

"Nuclear, Biological and Chemical Warfare protective suits Constable," Forbes replied. "They'll afford a high level of protection to anyone working in close proximity to the bomb. It may be that the bacillus has lived out its altered life cycle, but we can't afford to take any chances. Until those suits get here, no-one goes near that playground. Can you see to that, Constable?"

"Leave it to me, Group Captain. I'll make sure it's sealed off. Can I borrow a couple of your RAF Regiment chaps?"

"They're at your disposal," said Forbes, with a look of grim determination on his face. "Now, until we hear if Sir Robert has had any success with the Germans, it's up to us to do what we can to solve this problem at its source. I suggest we all get to work!"

The meeting broke up. Greaves left first, heading for the RAF men's accommodation tent where he quickly enlisted the assistance of two of the men within it to begin the task of sealing off the playground from public access. Hilary accompanied Sweeney to Simon Parkes' farm, where they soon managed to convince the farmer to loan his forked tractor to them. Sweeney drove it into the village with Hilary 'riding shotgun' on one of the tractor's large rear mudguards. They were keen to begin, but knew they had to wait for the NBC suits to arrive. Forbes had assured them the helicopter containing them would arrive in les than two hours, once McKay made the call, which he did within a minute of Trent arriving in the hospital office and passing on Forbes's order.

A new sense of purpose seemed to emanate from every one of those involved in the relief operation. Even those of Forbes's people who were working hard in the hospital soon picked up the growing mood of optimism and expectancy. Guy Dearborn began to whistle a happy tune to himself as he attended to the needs of the Reverend Grafton.

"All things bright and beautiful, Doctor Dearborn? My, my, things must be looking up in Olney St. Mary. I haven't seen anyone so cheerful in days, and I suspect it's not all to do with the delectable Nurse Kinnaird on this occasion."

Dearborn blushed at the mention of Edith but smiled cheerfully at Grafton.

"Perhaps I shouldn't be saying this yet, Vicar. It's a bit premature, but, well, we think we may know what's caused the plague in the village, and we also think we can put a stop to it without losing any more patients."

"Well, well. So you think there's hope for me after all, eh Doctor?"

"I think there is, Reverend. I think there just might be, yes."

"See, I told you them there prayers would help," came a voice from the next bed.

"Yes, Billy Wragg, of course you did," said Timothy Grafton sceptically and he and Dearborn looked at one another and began to laugh uncontrollably.

As the sun broke through the scattering of clouds that had lain over the village for most of the morning and shafts of bright rays shone down upon the village, Olney St. Mary began to look less like a plague encampment and slowly began the task of resurrecting itself from the darkness of despair, and moving back into the light of the world of the living.

Hope had been reborn!

CHAPTER 37

SIR ROBERT BLAKE REPLACED THE TELEPHONE RECEIVER ON ITS cradle. The black Bakelite instrument was hot from having been in contact with his hand for so long. Following his meeting with Ryan the previous day, Sir Robert had set the wheels in motion that he hoped would finally lead to a solution to the problem of the plague in Olney. First, he'd spoken to the Minister of Health, who'd professed himself appalled at Ryan's scrupulous and slavish adherence to orders he'd received so many years earlier. The Minister, Andrew Dodson had immediately ordered Ryan's removal from his position at the Health Ministry, though in order to maintain a level of normality and not arouse suspicion Ryan would be allowed to resign on 'health grounds' and leave his office at the end of the month. For all practical purposes however, Charles Macklin was now in operational control of Ryan's department. Next, Dodson had spoken to the Prime Minister, who authorised him to contact the German Government in an attempt to trace anyone with knowledge of the bombs manufactured at the Straub factory. A call to his counterpart in the Federal Government of West Germany brought immediate co-operation and led Blake to a little-known official in the German Interior Ministry, Klaus Haller.

Haller was an expert in the Nazi's secret weapons programmes of World War Two, his father having been a Bavarian scientist conscripted to work on various projects by the Nazis, eventually to die when a chemical explosion destroyed the factory complex he was working in. On reaching manhood, the young Haller had made it his business to find out all he could about Hitler's munitions industry. He was sure that many children must have lost their fathers or mothers in similar circumstances, some of them foreign nationals press-ganged and deported from their own nations by the Nazis and forced to work on the weapons programmes. Haller wanted to be able to provide information for any such victims of the Nazi years, and his cause had become something of a Holy Grail to the young German.

Haller spoke excellent English and during a one-hour telephone conversation with Blake, he'd revealed much that Sir Robert found terrifying and surprising. The Germans had apparently been well ahead of the Allies in the technology of delivering biological or chemical weapons during the Second World War, a fact that unnerved Blake. Haller informed him that he was aware of the type of weaponry undergoing research at the Straub factory, though he'd been unaware that any actual field trials such as the Olney St. Mary bombs had been authorised or carried out. At one point in the conversation he'd left Blake hanging on the telephone, and Sir Robert had heard the sounds of filing cabinet drawers opening and closing in the background.

Eventually, after what seemed an age to Blake, Haller returned to the telephone. Apologising for the delay, he'd explained that he'd been searching for specific files that not only listed the projects carried out at the factory, but also those involved in working on them. This had not been an easy task, as each project proceeded under a code name, so there was no file that listed 'Plague Carrying Bombs' for example. In fact, he explained the word 'plague' appeared nowhere in the Straub files. Blake was at first crestfallen, but Haller had told him that he had found something interesting, and that it might be what the Englishman was looking for. In a file headed 'Biological splicing of bacilli' Haller had discovered the results of a series of trials carried out by a group of doctors under the direction of Doctor Hans Dreschler. Here at last he'd found reference to the plague, and an attempt to introduce a secondary bacterium into the genetic make-up of the plague bacillus. This experiment had failed, but the German research team had found a way to add a synthetic catalyst into a controlled environment that caused the plague bacillus to alter its characteristics sufficiently enough to make it almost twice as fast acting in its assault on the bodies of those infected by it. It had been trialled in a sealed laboratory at the Straub factory, and at first had produced satisfactory results when used on rats, mice, and other rodents. Horrifyingly, Haller reported to Blake, the new bacillus had then been unleashed on a number of Russian prisoners of war, transported to the factory from the concentration camp in which they'd been imprisoned.

A separate document within the file showed that most of the prisoners had died within forty-eight to seventy-two hours of exposure, thus proving that the scientists had successfully accelerated the effects of the plague by at least twenty five percent. All the prisoners had died, without receiving medical care of course, and here was the first reference of something going wrong with the experiment. In addition to the prisoners, two doctors and an orderly involved in the experiment also contracted plague and died from the disease, at which point work had been suspended pending discovery of a fail-safe means of delivering the toxin and at the same time protecting those using it as an offensive weapon.

The answer had been found a month later, when one of the team working on the project added a microscopic amount of mercury to the liquid suspension that contained the bacillus. The amount of mercury was so small that it had no initial effect on the bacteria but over a period of time the plague cells began to die and were eventually rendered harmless. The document reported that the scientists and doctors involved in the experiment had been delighted with the results of their work and a second trial using prisoners was carried out almost immediately. Once again, the prisoners all died, but this time they'd been left unattended by any of the research staff. After death, the bodies were left where they lay for six days, the time estimated for the bacillus to be degraded and killed by the mercury infusion. A new group of prisoners was sent in to remove the bodies, and that group was then placed in a sealed room and monitored for seven days. None of them contracted the plague, though they must have been in a pitiful state by the time the Germans extricated them from that room, having been left with only water and a small supply of bread and cheese to maintain them throughout their nerve-wracking wait to see if they too would die the horrible death imposed upon their countrymen.

Haller made a point of telling Blake that no further mention was made of those prisoners who'd cleared the bodies. Both men could guess their fate! Having survived the experiment they would have been of no further use to the research scientists and they would have been placed on the first available transport to an extermination camp.

Sir Robert Blake listened to all of this with a mixture of shock and revulsion. Though the world had learned much of the brutality and inhumanity of the Nazis at the end of the war, certain facts relating to their callous treatment of Russian prisoners were still coming to light, and the power of such testimony could still invoke horror in those hearing of it.

Now, however, he had a priority other than that of pursuing ex-Nazi war criminals. As Haller had completed his statement of the facts surrounding the plague experiments at the Straub factory, Blake had voiced the questions he'd been waiting to ask.

"Herr Haller, is there anything in the documents you possess that mentions an antidote to the altered plague bacillus, and secondly, is there anyone who worked at that facility who might be able to help us?"

"I'm afraid there is no mention of an antidote or a cure of any description, Sir Robert. That is not to say of course that such a thing does not exist. It may well be that the information regarding such an antidote is contained in another file, perhaps somewhere else in my registry or perhaps locked away in the memory vault of one of those who participated in the experiments."

"Which leads us back to my second question?"

"Ah yes, of course. I'm afraid that Hans Dreschler will be of no help to us. He was an ardent Nazi, who, rather than face up to the fact that Germany had lost the war, preferred to blow his own brains out in his office at the factory on the day that Berlin fell to the advancing Soviet army. We have better luck with two of those who worked with him, however. Like my father, they were both forced to work for Straub, their families having been taken hostage and held in concentration camps to ensure their co-operation. Franz Adler was last heard of living in...no wait, I'm sorry, Sir Robert. Adler died last year in a road accident. He was hit by a tram while crossing the street. That leaves us with Wilhelm Koenig. He was only young, just twenty-six when he was forced to work for the Nazis. He had a brilliant mind by all accounts, and his records say that he left Germany after the war. The Nazis didn't keep their word about his family of course. His Mother, Father and two sisters were gassed at Auschwitz."

"Do your records show where he went, Herr Haller?"

"But of course Sir Robert. We Germans are known for our efficiency in keeping records are we not?"

"Quite so."

"Ja, well, let's see." There was a short pause, and Blake could hear the rustle of papers as Haller searched through the file before him. Then, "Here it is. Mein Gott! You won't believe this, Sir Robert."

"What is it Haller? Tell me man, please."

"Well, this is too good to be true. When the war ended, Koenig left Germany and worked for the Rausch Corporation in Zurich. He had been absolved of any blame for the events at Straub, due to his family circumstances and his coercion by the Nazis. Then two years ago, he accepted a research post with the MacKinnon Foundation in England. He is currently, at least according to my records, working in their research and development laboratories near the city of Bristol. He cannot be far away from you, Sir Robert. Even now, the solution to your problem could be on your doorstep, as you English say."

Blake was impressed and delighted with the news and the co-operation he'd received from Haller.

"I can't thank you enough, Herr Haller. On behalf of Her Majesty's Government, I wish to place on record my appreciation of your help in this matter. Please pass on my thanks to your own superiors. Your information has been of immense help."

"Not yet, Sir Robert, but perhaps once you have spoken to Koenig, then you might have cause to thank me. By the way, he is probably the best man to help you with this problem. The records show that he worked directly under Dreschler. If anyone knows the answers to your questions, it has to be him."

The conversation ended with the two men's mutual goodbyes, and Blake's promise to keep Haller informed of progress. After all, The West German government would be highly embarrassed if word of the biological attack on England ever leaked out, and Blake had promised that full co-operation by the German authorities would ensure silence from the British government. Blake had been surprised to find someone as willing and able to assist him as Haller. He considered it great good fortune to have been connected to a man with such a belief in rooting out the old evils that still lurked within his country. Klaus Haller, he decided, was a good man.

Now, as the telephone cooled on its cradle, Sir Robert flicked a switch on the intercom that connected him with his secretary. Within minutes Blake was on the telephone once more, having been connected to the Chief Constable of the Somerset Police Force, the county police authority that covered the area where Koenig worked. Blake had decided that there was no time to waste on the niceties of life. The order had been given to pick up the German scientist and ferry him to the nearest RAF base, from where he would be flown directly to Olney St. Mary, where Group Captain Forbes and the others would be waiting for him. If indeed Koenig knew anything, he would be in the right place when it came to providing the answers they sought.

CHAPTER 38

THOUGH DONALD FORBES HAD BEEN NOTIFIED VIA HILARY Newton's telephone to expect the arrival of the German scientist, he was quite unprepared for the physical appearance of the man who stepped down from the latest Sycamore helicopter to land on Olney's village green. Of the two men who alighted from the helicopter and ducked and ran to avoid the downdraft of the rotors, one was dressed in the uniform of the RAF police, which meant that the other could only be Wilhelm Koenig. Forbes wasn't sure what he'd expected, but the fact that he'd been told that Koenig was a dissenter from the ideals of the Nazis who'd been forced to work on their weapons research programme had conditioned the Group Captain to expect a small, mousey and possibly cowed individual. The reality was far different.

The man who now strode purposefully towards him with the RAF police corporal by his side was young looking, tall, at least six feet, two inches in height, with the blue eyes and blond hair that so typified the perfect Aryan look extolled by Hitler and his cronies. His walk was that of a man of confidence, and as he drew closer to the Group Captain, Forbes could detect a look of anger on the man's face.

"Are you the man in charge?" the German asked as he stood face to face with Forbes. "Perhaps, if you are, you will be kind enough to inform me why I have been forcibly removed from my legitimate place of work, bundled into a police car, and then shoved into a helicopter that has brought me under guard to this place, wherever it is, without so much as a single word of explanation!"

"Herr Doctor Koenig, good day to you. First of all, yes, I am the man in charge, and please, I must ask you to calm down. My name isFGroup Captain Donald Forbes, and I, like you am a doctor, but in my case, of the medical variety. I'm sorry that you were treated so brusquely by those who came to collect you, but time is of the essence in the matter that has brought us all to this place, which, by the way, is the village of Olney St. Mary."

"And as to why I am here?"

Forbes had hoped that mention of the village's name might have struck a chord with Koenig, if indeed it had been a deliberate part of the German's wartime plan to target Olney, but his reaction suggested otherwise.

"You have been brought here Herr Koenig, because we believe you can help us with something of a medical dilemma, connected with the time you spent during the war working on certain research at the Straub Munitions Establishment."

Koenig's demeanour instantly changed. Gone was the belligerence and anger, replaced instead with a look of sadness and a hint of interest.

"Ah, those were bad times Group Captain. I must admit to a great sorrow whenever I think back to the things we were forced to do in the name of the Fatherland."

"I understand you were forced to work there against your will?"

"That is correct. My family were held hostage to ensure my co-operation, and even then, they were not permitted to live. I learned after the war that as soon as I was put to work in the factory, they were all killed. Letters I received from them were nothing but clever forgeries, to try to keep my sprits up and make me work harder in the belief that I would see them again one day."

"I'm sorry for your loss, Herr Koenig, but now we're faced with the awful consequences of something that was developed at Straub, and that we believe you were involved in creating."

Koenig looked around the area where they stood, and as if he hadn't taken it in before, his eyes now scanned the marquee, the tented accommodation around it, and the large red cross on its white background that adorned the canvas roof of the hospital itself. His mind appeared to be wandering, his eyes glassed over for a few seconds, then they closed all together as he allowed his mind to wander back in time, to remember things which perhaps he'd wanted to forget. Koenig's face suddenly flashed with the dawning of recognition as Forbes's words struck home.

"The Enhanced Plague Experiment!" he gasped as the awful realisation dawned upon him.

"One and the same, I'm afraid," Forbes confirmed.

"My God! But I never thought they would use it. It was too unstable," said the horrified scientist.

"You didn't know then?"

"No, on my life, Group Captain, I had no idea. We tried so many ways to make it work, but the life expectancy of the bacillus couldn't be sufficiently controlled. Some strains were infectious for only a few days, others for weeks. We couldn't have sent troops in after an attack with such an erratic time range of potential lethal exposures."

"Were you privy to all of Dreschler's work?"

"There were a few experiments that he kept to himself. Perhaps, even though I was forced to work there under threat I was still not totally trusted. It looks, from what you're telling me as though he found a way to stabilise the life of the altered bacillus sufficiently to allow a trial attack?"

"That's what it looks like Herr Doctor. Now, the thing we really need to know is this. I have to assume that, in addition to producing the plague bombs, some work had to have been carried out on an antidote to the toxin, in case of accidental exposure?"

"Ah, you mean Katya!"

"Excuse me?"

"Katya. Dreschler often gave his secret files female names, and he chose Katya for this one. I presume you have had someone in Germany looking into this and could find no reference to an antidote? If so, that is why. Who would think of looking at a file called Katya when searching for a cure for the plague?"

"So, there is a cure?"

"Of sorts, Group Captain. As you so cleverly surmised, it was imperative that we find a way to counteract any accidental exposure to our troops if they were to arrive in a still infected area. We found that the disease could be arrested in it's progression by administering large doses of a synthetic drug that Dreschler himself perfected. It combined the new antibiotics which had just been discovered with a small amount of liquid mercury, such as was used in the manufacture of the altered bacillus itself."

Good God man, you mean to say that you gave mercury, a deadly poison, to living human beings?"

"Yes, we did. The dose was so small as to have no lasting toxic effect on the patients, and it also served to kill off the plague bacillus as it did in the actual offensive compound of course. Are you telling me that you have severely infected patients here in this village?"

"That's the whole point, Herr Doctor. We don't know how badly they're infected because we didn't know how the disease worked on the human system. Also, we don't know if the worst is over. Most of the patients in the beginning died within three days, but some of the newer patients seem to be holding their own, having survived for a fourth or fifth day, and we hope that the disease has reached its point of dying out naturally. We still need to know the way to cure it though, as we haven't found the remains of the bomb used to deliver it yet, and there could be more of the toxin waiting to leak out."

"Then, Group Captain, we have little time to waste. Do you have access to a telephone from which I can speak to whoever is helping you in Germany?"

Forbes led the tall handsome man to the home of Hilary Newton. There, for the next half hour, the scientist engaged in conversation with Klaus Haller. For the sake of speed, they spoke in their native tongue and apart from occasional words and references to 'Katya', Forbes had little idea what the two were discussing. Eventually, Wilhelm Koenig replaced the telephone on its cradle, and turned to face the expectant RAF officer and a quizzical Doctor Newton, who'd been told little when the two men walked into her home other than that it was imperative that Koenig use her phone.

"Katya exists," said Koenig, smiling as he spoke, "or, at least, the file containing the formula for her production does. It is imperative of course that the correct dose is administered, to avoid poisoning the patients, but I'm sure that we can solve that small problem. Herr Haller is sending the file to your Sir Robert

Blake by fax as we speak, and you must find a way to get it to my research laboratory in Bristol as soon as possible. I presume you have no objection to me working on producing the antidote you require, Group Captain?"

"No objections at all, Herr Doctor. I'll have you flown back as soon as I can call up a helicopter, without the police escort this time, I might add. I'll make sure I ask Sir Robert to forward Haller's fax directly to your facility in Bristol so you can begin work right away. I have only one question."

"And that is?"

"How will you know how to gauge the strength of the antidote without knowing the exact strain of the bacillus that Dreschler used in the bombs? You said the examples you worked on were unstable, so how can you be sure that he didn't change it in some way before this trial specimen was cleared for use?"

"That, my good Group Captain, is the one imponderable. We must hope that the essence of the toxin was not altered in any significant way before they authorised the dropping of the bombs."

"The bombs weren't actually dropped remember. The plane was shot down, and they failed to go off as planned."

"Then for that we must be eternally grateful. It was typical of Dreschler I must say, to use a fighter plane as you have described to deliver his cargo of death. Your fighters would have been going for the bombers most of the time. He'd have hoped that one fighter carrying the small biological bombs would have got through to its target and released them without being shot down. Your Royal Air Force saved your country in more ways than one during the Battle of Britain I think, Group Captain Forbes."

"Do you think Hitler would have known about the bombs?"

"Of course he did. Dreschler knew him personally and was in fact on good terms with the Fuhrer. He would often go to Berlin and report in person to Hitler on his progress. You may count on it that the Fuhrer gave his full authority for any such attack on England."

"So, we live and learn," said Forbes. "If not for that Spitfire pilot we might have been looking at a holocaust situation of another kind right here in England."

"I'm afraid so," said Koenig, "but, now we have the chance to put an end to what should never have begun, do we not?"

"Yes we do, Doctor Koenig, yes we do, and thank you."

"Thank me later, Group Captain. Now, you mentioned a helicopter?"

"Yes, of course," said Forbes, picking up the telephone.

As soon as the arrangements had been made Forbes and Koenig did their best to bring a bemused Hilary Newton up to date with developments. Within thirty minutes the sound of approaching engines announced the arrival of the helicopter ordered by Forbes. As Forbes helped the German scientist into the Sycamore and wished him well, Hilary ran as fast as she could to the marquee where the others were still hard at work caring for the sick.

Seeing her face and the animated expression she wore upon it, Trent, McKay, and Dearborn all stopped what they were doing as she approached them, and Hilary began to deliver the latest news with the words,

"You'll never guess what's been happening..."

CHAPTER 39

THE EVENING SUN DIPPED SLOWLY BEHIND THE LAST WISPY cloud formations of the day as night cast its cloak over the village. Silence descended upon Olney St. Mary as the few villagers who still dared to venture onto the streets locked their doors and hid away from the terror that had gripped their lives over the last week.

In the kitchen of Hilary Newton's home, she and the two nurses. Edith Kinnaird and Christine Rigby were finishing the remnants of a meal prepared by the doctor as a small thank you to the girls. She'd witnessed the degree of effort they'd put into their work since arriving in the village, and, unlike the personnel who'd arrived with Angus McKay, these girls had after all volunteered for the work they were now involved in, and all of them still mourned the third girl, Patricia Knowles, who would not be returning to her room at the nurses home in Ashford when all of this was over.

"I'm sorry it wasn't much of a meal, girls," said Hilary, apologising for the Spartan fare she'd been able to provide. "There's not much fresh stuff left in the village, and even with the food supplies that the Group Captain organised, it's still a bit difficult to prepare anything really appetising."

"Please don't apologise, Doctor," Christine replied. "We appreciate the thought, and anyway, I love stew."

"Me too," said Edith.

"Yes, well, it's just a pity that there were more vegetables than meat in it, that's all," Hilary ventured.

"No, honestly, it was great," "Edith insisted.

"Anyway, let's hope that we won't have to put up with the situation much longer," Hilary went on, trying to change the subject.

"Do you really think the end to the plague could be in sight, Doctor?" asked Edith.

"From what I heard this afternoon, the German scientist they've brought in is working on an antidote to the toxin even as we talk, and the RAF men now have a good idea where to look for the remains of the bomb that led to all the trouble in the first place."

Christine voiced the feelings of both nurses when she spoke.

"I know there was a war going on, but I find it hard to believe that the Germans could have been so callous as to have used such a weapon against innocent people without knowing exactly how it would work."

Hilary had explained the full situation to the girls over dinner, and they were both completely up to date on all that had developed in connection to the plague bomb.

"It just goes to show how evil the whole Nazi regime was," Hilary answered.

"My uncle was killed in the war," said Edith. "He was a merchant seaman and his ship was sunk by a submarine while he was on convoy duty."

"I think we all know someone who lost relatives or friends in the war," Hilary responded. "The point is, we must all try to remember that the Germans are no longer our enemies. After all, Doctor Koenig is trying to help us, and a member of the German government is providing our people with all the information that he can in an effort to assist us."

"I think it's the least they can do," said Christine Rigby.

"I agree," said Edith.

"Yes, well, be that as it may, we must all do what we can to try to put an end to the plague, and without the Germans help, we'd still be struggling to find a reason for the outbreak in the first place, and we'd have no idea how to fight the altered plague bacillus."

"We know that, Doctor," said Edith. "It's just that we wouldn't be in this situation at all if it hadn't been for some mad German scientist in the first place."

Hilary felt that she needed to turn the conversation away from the plague. They'd lived too close to it for the last few days, and she knew the girls had seen a lot of people die in that time. She could hardly expect them to be grateful to the Germans at this point. She suggested they retire to her sitting room, where the television she'd recently purchased had sat in the corner, unused, for over a week. The wooden box with its rotary controls and small screen was hardly the most expensive model on the market, but Hilary had felt it necessary to move with the times. Most people seemed to be acquiring them lately, so she'd spent a reasonable sum of money on a mid-priced set, and the three of them now sat waiting as the machine warmed up and the picture came into view.

The three of them were soon entranced by the images that poured from the little screen in the corner of the room. They watched the game show 'Take your Pick' hosted by Michael

Miles, and then laughed at the antics of Bootsie and Snudge in 'The Army Game', and Hilary only rose to turn off the set when an episode of 'Emergency Ward Ten' came into view. They all agreed that they'd had enough of that sort of thing for one day. The reality of their situation was grim enough without having to sit through some TV producer's version of what their jobs were about. The picture receded from view, becoming a small white dot in the centre of the screen before disappearing completely.

As silence fell upon the room, Christine Rigby looked towards Edith with an impish grin on her face and voiced the question she'd been aching to ask all evening.

"Edith, what's he like? Do tell us about the handsome Doctor Dearborn, Is he a good kisser?"

Edith Kinnaird blushed.

"Christine, really, you shouldn't be asking such things."

"Oh, come on, we're all girls together. We all know you've been growing close to the good doctor in recent days. Don't keep us in suspense."

"Doctor Newton, tell her," pleaded Edith.

"I'm sorry Edith, but it does seem to be rather common knowledge around the village that you and Doctor Dearborn are getting rather close to one another. But really Christine, we shouldn't be prying."

"Matron would have a fit if she knew," said Christine, referring to the fearsome matriarchal figure who hovered over them from on high back at the hospital in Ashford.

"Not that anyone here will say anything, will they Christine?" asked Hilary, smilingly.

"Of course not," said the girl, "but you must tell us something, Edith, oh pleeease!" she implored.

"Oh well, alright then, but nothing much has happened, honest!" Edith proffered. She decided that she could tell them something without giving away the game completely. She knew that Christine would probably be shocked if she knew that she and Guy had actually slept together. For the next few minutes she gave Christine and Hilary a highly sanitised version of her relationship so far with Guy Dearborn, and amid much giggling and knowing winks Christine in particular teased scraps of information from Edith, though Kinnaird managed to hold on to her closest secret. Hilary of course, had worked it out for herself, though she said nothing in front of Rigby. She'd been the one who'd found the bed after the two young lovers had left her house. They'd remade it of course, but nobody made a bed quite like Hilary, and the hospital corners expertly created by Edith had showed themselves to be a little different to the ones earlier applied that day by Hilary. She maintained a diplomatic silence however, not wanting to embarrass the young nurse in front of her colleague, and the rest of the evening passed equitably in a plethora of girl talk and generalisms.

———

Just as the girl's evening was breaking up, with Edith going back to her room at the Beekeepers Arms, and Hilary and Christine retiring to their beds, in his laboratory not far from the great city of Bristol, Doctor Wilhelm Koenig, assisted by two research assistants was nearing the end of his first attempt to recreate the antidote to the plague bacillus, aided by the sheaf of papers that had been faxed to London by Haller.

"We have no way of knowing if this will work do we, Doctor?" asked Dave Seddon, his senior assistant. We have no way of trialling it before it's put to the test in the village you've told us about."

255

Koenig had been open and honest with Seddon and John Fellowes, his other assistant that evening. He considered that they would be rather more than diligent if they appreciated the urgency of the situation. He'd been right. Neither man had complained or made excuses about having to get home or having something that needed doing outside of the lab. They'd worked with him, non-stop since the papers had arrived.

"No David, we don't know. We can only hope that it will do the job. To test it as best as we can, I will give myself a small dose to ensure its safety to use on humans."

"But you can't!" Fellowes protested. "If anything happens to you, who will carry on with the work? Those people in Olney need a live Willie Koenig, not a dead research scientist. You must let me be the guinea pig, Doctor."

"No, I'll try it," Seddon volunteered.

"Gentlemen, I thank you, but I cannot let you take such risks."

"You have to, Doctor," Seddon replied. "John's right. You're too important to everyone concerned. You must allow one of us to test it."

Despite his protestations, Koenig knew that his assistants were correct in their assessment of the situation. If anything happened to him, the work of producing the antidote from the ageing papers written in the hand of Dreschler, and which he could read quite easily where others might not, could be disastrous for the people of Olney.

"Very well, you have won the argument," he at last responded. "As always, your logic is impeccable, both of you are fine scientists and I applaud you."

"So, which of us is it to be?" asked Fellowes. "I volunteered first."

"Hardly a logical way of deciding the order of precedence in a clinical trial old boy," Seddon replied.

"I agree David," Koenig intervened. "But in this instance, I will go along with John's statement that he was the first to volunteer. I will allow him to be my guinea pig on this occasion. You will help me to monitor his reactions to the antidote once it has been administered."

The argument was thus ended by Koenig's intervention and the three men retuned to putting the finishing touches to their work. An hour later, they stood back and stared at the clear, colourless liquid that was contained in a small test tube held in Koenig's hand. The liquid had a slight viscosity to it, caused by the small amount of liquid mercury that was contained in its chemical make-up.

"Gentlemen, we have it! John, it is time we tested the vaccine. We have little time for niceties. Any self-congratulation must wait until we know whether we have succeeded and that will not happen until we can deliver it to Olney. Before that of course..."

"I'm ready, Doctor," said Fellowes, removing his white lab coat and rolling up his right shirt sleeve.

Koenig quickly filled a small hypodermic syringe with a small dose of the liquid preparation and within seconds the needle penetrated the skin of John Fellowes, the liquid within quickly beginning its journey into the man's bloodstream. For now, the three men moved across the lab to Koenig's office where they could sit comfortably in the soft vinyl chairs he kept there for visitors. Neither Koenig nor Seddon took their eyes off Fellowes for a second. They sat observing his every movement, every flicker of his eyelids, every blink of the eye, waiting to see if the antidote would remain passive, or whether they had poisoned their colleague in their attempt to help the situation in the little village many miles away.

The hands on the electric clock on the office wall moved silently around the dial as they sat, waiting. There was nothing else they could do for the time being. Fellowes sat motionless, inwardly afraid perhaps that he might not witness the coming of the dawn, alert to every small feeling and sensation in his body, wondering if he was about to be hit by a fatal seizure caused by an error in their work that evening.

Back in Olney St. Mary, the light in Hilary Newton's bedroom went out as she put the book she'd been reading on the bedside table and lay her head on her pillow. As darkness enfolded her and she fell quickly into a deep sleep induced by the unrelenting tiredness she'd experienced for the last few days, in the office of Wilhelm Koenig in the laboratory in Bristol, three men sat...waiting!

CHAPTER 40

Paul Trent couldn't sleep. His mind was filled with questions for which he had no answers. At least, not yet. Would the German scientist Koenig find the right mix of chemicals and reproduce the cure to the altered plague bacillus? After all it had been over ten years since the man had worked with Dreschler at the Straub factory. Would they in fact need the vaccine? If the plague had burned itself out, then maybe those in the hospital would recover without it. Then again there was still a chance that more of the lethal toxin lay below the ground in the remnants of the wartime biological bomb. That led Trent to his next question. Would they be able to locate those remnants and make them safe without anyone being infected by any toxic residues left in the bomb? They had the NBC suits of course, but would they provide sufficient protection from the airborne plague?

As his mind pondered on these questions, thoughts of Douglas Ryan forced their way to the front of his consciousness. Though he'd never met the man, Trent knew of him by reputation, and he could find no reason why the man had jeopardised his entire career in order to keep the plague a secret. After all, it wasn't as if Ryan had been responsible for the bombing of Olney, was it?

That one single point was the over-riding factor that kept Trent tossing and turning that night. There had to be a reason for Ryan's behaviour, a reason that had so far evaded Forbes, Sir Robert Blake, and everyone else for that matter.

———

Edith Kinnaird also found sleep hard to come by that night. After returning to her room at the Beekeepers Arms, she'd gone straight to bed, and had plumped up her pillows and tried to engross herself in a novel that Hilary Newton had loaned to her. The story of a young English woman rebelling against her overbearing parents while on holiday in Athens, eventually running away to live with a fisherman on an idyllic Greek Island held little interest for her. Her bed felt cold, she was lonely after experiencing the feelings of feminine camaraderie that had existed earlier in the evening with the other girls, and she longed to talk to Guy Dearborn. Leaving the bedside lamp on, she placed the book to rest on the small table beside the bed and rested her head back against the pillows. Closing her eyes, she'd tried to drift into sleep by default, through sheer tiredness, but the relief of peaceful oblivion continued to evade her.

At just after two a.m. she heard footsteps on the landing outside her room. The sound of slippered feet made their way to the bathroom at the end of the landing, and she heard the door close as whoever it was entered the communal facility. A few minutes later she heard the WC flush, followed by the sound of the door to the bathroom opening as the occupant departed. As the soft treads of the nightwalker came to her door they stopped, and Edith sensed a figure on the other side of the solid door, ear to the door, listening for sounds within. She pulled the blankets up around her neck, and as fear began to mount in her mind, she heard the soft intonations of a familiar voice from the other side of the door.

"Edith? Are you awake in there? It's me, Guy. Your light's on, I can see it under the door."

Edith was out of bed in a second, and she quickly ran to the door and opened it, almost falling into Guy Dearborn's arms as she cascaded from her room onto the landing outside.

"Hey, what's wrong?" he asked as he held her closely against his chest.

"Nothing, Guy. Nothing at all, at least, there isn't now that you're here. I couldn't sleep and I was cold, and it sometimes gets rather lonely in there on my own at night and..."

"Want some company then?" Dearborn whispered in her ear.

Without saying a word Edith stepped back a little from Dearborn, though her hand still held his as tightly as ever. With the index finger of her other hand pressed close to her lips in a demand for silence, she pulled him gently into her room and in seconds, the pair slipped under the covers of her bed, still warm from where she'd lain earlier. Guy placed his arms around the now shivering Edith.

"You're cold," he said, softly.

"Not for much longer, thanks to you," Edith whispered softly as she snuggled closer into his chest.

Without speaking, Guy reached one arm across where she lay and turned off the bedside lamp. Edith felt his breath close to her face, and then his lips were on hers, and, very soon Edith Kinnaird once again found herself unable to sleep, but, this time, she didn't mind one little bit at all.

———

Wilhelm Koenig had slept a little, which surprised him. He must have been very tired. He hardly remembered feeling sleepy, so assumed that sleep had taken him by surprise such had been his state of mental exhaustion. He looked at the electric clock on the wall. Four fifteen a.m. He felt stiff and cold and as full wakefulness returned to his slightly befuddled mind, he realised that he'd fallen asleep in his chair. Suddenly he was wide awake! Of course, there were Fellowes and Seddon. Like him, they'd fallen asleep where they'd sat, and now both men were slumped in their chairs, fast asleep. At least Koenig hoped that sleep was the only thing keeping Fellowes from conscious thought. He swiftly prised himself from his chair and moved to Seddon's chair where he soon had his chef assistant restored to full wakefulness.

"Is he okay?" Seddon gestured towards the sleeping figure in the third chair.

"I hope so." Koenig said, softly. Together the two men converged on the figure of John Fellowes and Koenig reached one hand out, placed it on the man's shoulders, and shook him gently.

"John, John, can you hear me?" he beseeched the sleeping figure, shaking him again, this time a little more violently.

Fellowes seemed to sag in his chair, causing Koenig and Seddon to panic momentarily, then the man gave a cough, his eyes opened, and his hands moved up in an instinctive reaction to the overhead fluorescent lighting, rubbing them vigorously.

"Doctor Koenig? Is everything alright?" he asked, sleepily.

"Oh yes, John," replied a jubilant Koenig. "Everything is most definitely alright."

Turning to Seddon, Koenig smiled and said to his assistant:

"David, get on the telephone straight away. Phone the number on this piece of paper," he passed a sheet of foolscap to Seddon, "and tell the man who answers that we are about to begin production of the anti-virus for the people of Olney St. Mary. I think that Group Captain Forbes is about to feel much happier than he did yesterday morning,"

Seddon smiled back at Koenig, but the doctor was already on his way out of the office, rushing towards the lab where he had work to do, work which just couldn't wait!

CHAPTER 41

POLICE CONSTABLE KEITH GREAVES RESPONDED TO THE jangling ring of the telephone on the second ring. Tilly was sleeping peacefully beside him and he wanted to avoid waking her. A sixth sense had woken him mere seconds before the phone had begun ringing, and a quick glance at the bedside clock told him that it was not quite six a.m.

"Police," he replied, wearily rubbing the sleep from his eyes with his free hand.

The strange voice at the other end of the line expressed surprise at hearing Greaves answer the phone.

"Oh, I'm sorry. I was expecting to speak to a Group Captain Forbes. This is the number I was given."

"My name is Police Constable Greaves, and this *is* the number you require for the Group Captain, but he won't be here for some time yet. Do you have any idea what time of the morning it is, whoever you are?"

"Oh, I see, well, yes, as it happens, I do know the time, and my name is David Seddon. I have an urgent message for Group Captain Forbes from Doctor Wilhelm Koenig."

Greaves had been briefed by Forbes the previous evening on the latest news regarding hopes for the antidote, and at the mention of Koenig's name, the last of his sleepiness vanished and the policeman snapped into full waking consciousness.

"Right, I see. Exactly how urgent is the message, Mr Seddon? If it's really that important I can go and wake the Group Captain and get him to call you back if you give me your number."

"It really *is* that urgent and *especially important* Constable. I would appreciate if you would bring the Group Captain to the phone as soon as you possibly can."

Greaves wasted no more time. He took a note of the number from which Seddon was calling and immediately went to fetch Forbes. Within ten minutes the Group Captain was in Greave's front parlour, and engaged in conversation with Seddon, who assured him that the anti-toxin was being synthesized by Koenig even as they spoke. He explained that they'd tested it on a volunteer from within Koenig's own staff, and that it had produced no harmful effects.

"But do we know if it will work against the plague?" asked Forbes when Seddon paused for breath.

"The doctor has used every scrap of memory in reproducing the antidote, and he says that the only way to find out if it works is to administer it to your patients. There are no other options Group Captain. Whatever the outcome, it will do them no further harm, that much is certain."

"How soon can it be ready for use, Mr Seddon? Has he told you that?"

"He hopes to have it ready in sufficient quantities for your use sometime this afternoon."

"As soon as it's ready, please have Doctor Koenig call me and I'll arrange to have him, and it airlifted to Olney St. Mary."

"I'm sure he won't need telling Group Captain, but I'll do it anyway."

"Thank you, Mr Seddon, all of you for working through the night to try and help with the situation."

"I'll pass your thanks on to the doctor and to Mr Fellowes; they are the ones you should be grateful to. I did little but assist the doctor in his first attempts to produce the vaccine."

"Fellowes?" asked a quizzical Forbes.

"The volunteer, Group Captain. He was the one who allowed Dr Koenig to test it on him. He could have died if things had gone wrong."

"Then we are all massively in debt to your Mr Fellowes. I hope I get the chance to thank him in person one day."

"I'm sure you will, Group Captain. Now, if there's nothing more for the time being, I should get back to assisting Dr Koenig."

"Of course. Please do so, Mr Seddon, and thank you again."

The connection went dead, and Forbes turned to look at Greaves who stood waiting with a look of eager anticipation on his face.

"We have a chance PC Greaves. Koenig is producing a vaccine at this very moment. If it works, we can definitely cure those afflicted and prevent anyone else from contracting the disease."

"Yes!" was the single one-word expletive almost shouted by Keith Greaves, so loud in fact that the parlour door opened a few seconds later and a bleary eyed-sleepy Tilly Greaves peered around the door and asked:

"Is everything alright Keith? Oh, hello, Group Captain. What's happening?"

Greaves looked to Forbes for a sign of permission to talk to his wife and received a nod of assent.

"Well Tilly, my girl," he said, "It looks as if we might just be winning at last. Things are starting to go our way. Now, be a good girl and go and put the kettle on, will you? I'm sure the Group Captain would appreciate a nice hot cup of tea. I know I would."

"That would be very nice if it's no trouble Mrs Greaves," Forbes agreed, and Tilly disappeared into the kitchen where the gas was quickly lit, the kettle filled and within minutes the three of them sat comfortably around the policeman's kitchen table, cradling hot cups of tea. Knowing that the rest of the team were probably still asleep, apart from those on duty in the hospital marquee, Forbes spent an amiable half hour with the constable and his wife, before taking his leave and making his way across the road to where he knew he'd find McKay, Trent and the others.

As he walked into the space within the marquee that they'd all come to refer to as 'the office' Forbes could se that Angus McKay and Paul Trent were intently engaged in close conversation, so close in fact that the two men's heads were almost touching. Not wanting to be taken as interrupting what may have been a highly private dialogue he politely 'coughed' as he neared the men, who'd remained unaware of his approach, so intent were they on whatever they were discussing. Two heads turned as one and the men nodded in greeting. Forbes could almost feel a degree of tension in the air, not between the two men, but directed elsewhere.

"Gentlemen," he said, adding, "you appear to be agitated about something."

"Aye sir, you could say that. Doctor Trent has been voicing some concerns to me that I think you should be aware of, if you're not already, that is."

"I see, McKay. Which of you gentlemen is going to enlighten me as to these concerns?"

Forbes needed to know what had unsettled the two senior medical men in the village, apart from himself. For now he decided the news from Bristol could wait.

"I think it should be you, Paul," McKay said to Trent. Forbes raised an eyebrow in surprise, this being the first time he'd heard McKay use the other man's Christian name. "You were the one to bring it to me after all."

"Then please, tell me what's on your mind, Doctor Trent."

"Very well, Group Captain. I know our chief concern is quite rightly the patients in our care here in Olney, but you must admit that since this all began a lot's been happening that seems to have its roots elsewhere. So far, we've managed to find out a lot about the how and the why concerning this outbreak, but there's one thing, or rather one person, that hasn't been explained to my satisfaction."

"Go on," Forbes encouraged.

"Douglas Ryan," said Trent. "There's something that doesn't fit in what you've told us about him, both from your personal contact with the man and from what you've been told by Sir Robert Blake. His whole reasoning behind the motives he's given for trying to cover up the outbreak and virtually condemn everyone in the village to death, us included by the way, seems highly illogical. The business about not wanting to alarm the nation and needing to keep it quiet to prevent a loss of public morale are, quite frankly, a whole lot of hogwash! If everyone in Olney died of the plague together with a medical team sent to assist them, I'd have thought that would lead to an even bigger loss of morale amongst the British public, wouldn't you? Also, everyone in this village, well, most of them I would imagine, have friends and relatives scattered all over the county, if not the country! What did Ryan think they'd do? Just keep quiet about the affair because a man in Whitehall tells them to? No, if you ask me Group Captain, Douglas Ryan not only tried to cover up the initial outbreak, but I believe that once it began, he actually wanted it to run unchecked through the village. That's why he limited the help available, why he only gave you greater powers when your own boss intervened, and he never expected that anyone would find out about the biological bombs used by the Germans in the war. He could have told us about them in the beginning and we might have saved more lives than we've been able to, simply by evacuating the village and isolating the residents in a proper hospital."

"Just what are you suggesting, Doctor Trent?"

"I'm really not sure, but, if Ryan did want the disease to run its course through the village, then he must have been possessed by a motive that we haven't as yet been able to discover."

"And do either of you suspect what that motive might be?" asked Forbes, intrigued by the direction Trent's thoughts had taken. Forbes himself had of course been trying to work out why Ryan had acted as he did, without success. Perhaps Trent and McKay had a new slant on things.

"Well," said Angus McKay, "before you got here, we'd just had a thought or two on the subject, hadn't we Paul?"

"We had indeed. You see, Group Captain, the only reason we could work out that Ryan was happy for the plague to go unchecked would be if he *wanted* to see what would happen if it did so. When forced to provide medical help, he kept it to a bare minimum, and continued to wait and watch the situation as we struggled to cope with the altered plague bacillus. We asked ourselves what kind of man could do that, and we don't like the answers we've come up with."

"Which are?"

"Ryan is either mad, a theory we don't subscribe to, or, he was in the pay of someone else who wanted to find out what would happen if the German plague bomb were unleashed upon an unsuspecting population."

"Good God, Trent. That's a hell of a conclusion to come to. It's tantamount to accusing Ryan of murder."

"Aye, well, maybe that's just what it is sir. You know, if the cap fits and all that."

Forbes looked carefully at Angus McKay. The diminutive Scotsman had worked under him for the last two years, and Forbes had never seen him quite so vehement on any subject. The normal calm and reserved demeanour had been replaced by one that had its roots seated in deep anger and a feeling of betrayal.

"D'you know, gentlemen? There may just be a point of truth in your argument, I must admit. If Ryan was in the pay of an outsider, then we must do what we can to find out who that outsider is or was. That, however, is not our job. We're doctors not policemen. The people best suited to this kind of task are probably one of the less public branches of the police force, Special Branch perhaps, and I think that Sir Robert Blake will be just the man to set those particular wheels in motion. I thank you for bringing this to my attention In the midst of all that's been happening, I suspect that Ryan has been let off the hook a little too soon, and it's time we made the man dangle all over again."

Trent and McKay professed themselves satisfied with Forbes suggestion and he made his way back to the home of Keith Greaves, from where he called Blake, who instantly agreed with Forbes that the theory of an outside connection made sense where Ryan was concerned. The peer would immediately contact Special Branch and insist on a very fast and thorough inquiry into the affairs of Douglas Ryan. Discretion would be applied, he assured Forbes, as the last thing they wanted was for Ryan to disappear because he thought the hounds were closing in for the kill.

After speaking with Blake, Forbes returned to the hospital where he informed Trent and McKay of the result of his conversation with Blake. They were pleased that the peer had agreed to act. Both men had decided that someone had to be held responsible for what had happened in Olney, and both agreed that that man had to be Douglas Ryan.

Forbes next spent a good half hour filling the two men in on the events in Bristol, and by the time he'd finished and looked at his watch, he realised that the morning was rushing by quickly. In just a few short hours they should have Koenig's vaccine in their hands, and the litmus test of the last two days work would truly begin. In the meantime, a tour of the ward showed that several patients remained extremely ill, though maybe a third of those in bed were showing some signs of being able to hold their own against the ravages of the plague. Timothy Grafton and Billy Wragg were both sitting in wooden school chairs at the side of their respective beds for example, and Guy Dearborn stated that he hoped they might be well enough to be discharged perhaps as early as the following day.

As he completed the round of the ward with Trent and McKay, Donald Forbes thought that perhaps a corner had been turned, that the end was at last in sight, but even he had no crystal ball with which to view the future. If he had, perhaps he wouldn't have been quite so confident.

CHAPTER 42

DONALD FORBES HAD REASON TO FEEL REASONABLY OPTIMISTIC after speaking to Sir Robert Blake. The fact that Blake had agreed to involve Special Branch in the investigation into Douglas Ryan's activities mean that the peer agreed to some extent with Forbes and Trent. Special Branch, after all, was the division of the Metropolitan Police tasked with the protection of national security, offences against the Official Secrets Act, and close protection of public figures such as the Royal Family and the Prime Minister of the United Kingdom. Bringing them on board was a sure fire confirmation that Blake also realised that Ryan may not have been entirely honest at their last meeting, and that the man may be working under instructions from someone as yet unidentified, someone who may not have the best interests of the country at heart.

That dealt with, he now had just a few hours to wait until he received what he hoped would be the cure to the hybridized plague that had struck the villagers of Olney. If, as he strongly suspected, Wilhelm Koenig had memorised every step that his previous Nazi master took in developing the bacillus and had followed the formula detailed in the file named 'Katya' precisely in producing the antidote, then the patients currently languishing in the camp beds that made up the ward in the Marquee would soon begin a full recovery.

Now, all they had to do was find the remains of the bomb that had presumably been disturbed and had released its toxic payload into the air, infecting so many. That, unfortunately, was when the first of the day's setbacks reared up to place a dent in the Group Captain's new-found optimism.

As Forbes was leaving the police house and began to make his way across the green towards the field hospital, Flight Sergeant Eric Taylor, the man in charge of the small RAF Regiment team of searchers presented himself before the Group Captain, stood to attention and saluted. Forbes was surprised to see the man. He'd had McKay send the three-man team out to search for the bomb in the areas highlighted by Greaves and Sweeney over an hour previously.

"Hello Flight Sergeant," said Forbes. "Something I can do for you? I thought you'd be well into your search for the bomb by now."

"That's just it Sir, we are, or rather we were, and then..."

"Then what? Make sense man, what are you trying to tell me?"

"Well Sir, to save time I gave each of the men and myself a small search grid to comb, thinking it would make the job that much more efficient, rather than us all congregate together in one place. This way I thought we cover the whole area in a third of the time."

"That was good thinking Flight, but I presume you're going to tell me that something's gone wrong along the way."

"You can say that again Sir. Both LACs Grove and Bennet have disappeared!"

"Disappeared? This is a small village, Flight. Where could they go? What d'you mean by disappeared, exactly?"

"Leading Aircraftman Grove was supposed to be searching the area behind the playground, Sir, not where the rubble is piled, the bit where the old field would have sloped down into the drainage ditch, you know where I mean?"

"Yes, I've seen the plans. Go on."

"I sent LAC Bennet to search the other drainage ditch, around the crevice where we found one of the rat graveyards earlier. There are so many holes and small nooks along the side of the ditch, I thought it possible that a rat had found the remnants of the bomb and maybe dragged it into its nest and gnawed at it, which might have led to the release of the plague."

"That was very good thinking, Flight. Now, tell me why you think they've disappeared."

"Right, Sir. I set myself the task of searching where the rubble was at its heaviest concentration. Mr Sweeney has been driving and working the tractor. It's fairly hit and miss using the forks instead of a proper excavator, but we seemed to be doing ok. We stopped for a break after half an hour and while Sweeney went to the police house to fetch us a thermos of tea, I went to see how the boys were doing. There was no sign of Bennet anywhere around the ditch, so, thinking he might have gone to see Grove for some reason I went to the far side of the field, and Grove was gone too. There were footprints around to show they'd been at both sites, but I looked all over for them, Sir. Even Mr Sweeney helped when he came back with the tea, and I promise you, they're gone!"

Forbes was worried, though he refused to let the Flight Sergeant see it.

"Could they just have sloped off for a cigarette or something?"

"Not for this long Sir, and anyway, they're good reliable men. They knew I wouldn't mind them having a fag 'on the job' so to speak, and there was no need for either of them to be absent from his post when I went to look for them."

Forbes was silent for a few seconds, as he tried to make sense from what the Flight Sergeant had just reported to him. Taylor felt the need to remind his superior officer that he was still there.

"Sir?"

"Yes, it's alright, I was just thinking. This is a real mystery, Flight. Why on earth should two men just disappear when in the middle of an important search? I want you ask Mr Sweeney to continue to help you in your search around the rubble pile. I still think it's the most likely place for any bomb fragments to be located. You are wearing those NBC suits while you're working, aren't you?"

"Yes Sir, as you instructed, though it's bloody hot in them I can tell you that, and Mr Sweeney says he feels like an alien from outer space."

"Better an alien than a plague victim, Flight Sergeant, don't you think?"

"You'll get no argument from me on that score, Sir, but what about Grove and Bennet?"

"You leave that to me. I'll go and get the constable. He can organise a search party, though there aren't many people fit and able to join him. I might have to use some of our people from the hospital, but that's my problem now. You go and find me that bomb, Flight!"

"Yes, Sir," said Taylor, pulling himself up to attention and saluting once more, before turning away and running back towards the far end of the village, where Sweeney waited, sitting astride the seat of the tractor, still wearing his 'alien' suit.

As he walked towards the police house, Group Captain Donald Forbes had the distinct feeling that something strange was taking place in the village, something that had to be connected to the German biological bomb, but what that something was, and what it had to do with the disappearance of two of his men, he had no idea. All he knew at that point was that his day had just turned sour. A feeling of mild trepidation suddenly swept over him, and he felt as though he was being watched from afar. It was just a feeling, he told himself, but a cold shiver ran down his spine. Donald Forbes was a logical man, a highly qualified doctor and a virologist of the highest qualifications and experience, but suddenly he felt exposed and vulnerable. Someone somewhere was pulling strings that he knew nothing about, and he hated the thought that he and everyone else in the village could be being used as nothing more than pawns in some game over which he and they had no control whatsoever. He was pleased to see the smiling face of Tilly Greaves as the policeman's wife answered his knock at the door of the police house.

Greaves asked few questions, accepting the urgency of the situation without debate, and within minutes a search was launched for the missing airmen. Donald Forbes made his way to the field hospital, where he intended to recruit a few more searchers from amongst the medical personnel. He knew that the missing men, depending on what had happened to them, could be a key to what was going on in the village. Had they found something they shouldn't have, and been subsequently silenced by an unknown assailant? That seemed unlikely to the Group Captain as the men were employed in searching different areas. Could they have been lured away and attacked and immobilised to prevent them finding something incriminating, but incriminating to whom? Where could they have been taken if they had been abducted? Olney was such a small place. There weren't too many places to hide two grown men. Their disappearance was as illogical as it was worrying, and though he dared not admit it to anyone else, after his earlier thoughts of an end being in sight to the situation in Olney; at that moment, Forbes was himself becoming a very worried man.

CHAPTER 43

AT AROUND THREE P.M. THAT AFTERNOON TWO THINGS happened. First, the helicopter carrying Wilhelm Koenig and his newly distilled plague vaccine touched down on the village green, and within seconds of the German scientist setting foot on the green grass of Olney for the second time, a lumbering yellow beast in the form of a full size JCB excavator trundled along Olney's main street escorted by two black police cars, one in front and one behind, blue lights flashing to announce their arrival.

So far, there had been no reported sightings of either of the two RAF Regiment men who had disappeared that morning, and the search for them was continuing, led by Keith Greaves and a small team of willing volunteers, but for now Forbes had to prioritise his time, and the patients in the hospital had to assume the highest of those priorities. Flight Sergeant Taylor and Michael Sweeney were left in charge of the next priority, that of 'suiting up' and guiding the driver of the excavator to the precise location of the rubble from the playground. The two men had done their best, working without breaks all day, but in truth they had moved only a small amount of the mountain of brick, concrete and hardcore that had been left in the wake of the playground rebuilding, and they'd found nothing as yet.

"Doctor Koenig," said Forbes, shaking the German's hand warmly, "I'm pleased to see you again. I presume that you have achieved some success?"

Koenig held a small black leather case in his hand, no bigger than a camera case, which he lightly tapped with his free hand.

"I have what I hope you will require here in the case, Group Captain. There is enough anti-toxin here to treat everyone in Olney, including you and your co-workers. If I have done my job correctly it will not only cure those who are already afflicted but will serve as a preventative vaccine for those who so far remain untouched by the pestilence."

"Then I propose placing you in the care of my second-in-command, Doctor Angus McKay, and allow him to work with you on administering the antidote to the patients and then perhaps the two of you can organise immunisation of the staff and the remaining villagers."

"You do not want to join me yourself in the procedure?"

"I'm afraid that one or two pressing problems have arisen in the village today, Herr Doctor, and they require my attention at the present time. Nothing I can say or do will affect the outcome of what you are about to do. I will be here however to see how the patients respond. How long will it be before you know if the antidote is working?"

"I should know within four hours or so, Group Captain. If the anti-toxin is working the patients should begin to breathe more easily and there should be marked lowering of their fever symptoms."

"Then let's all pray that you have been successful in your overnight endeavours."

Forbes quickly led Koenig to the marquee, where he and McKay soon began administering the anti-toxin to everyone in the ward, patients first, followed by the medics themselves.

Meanwhile the yellow excavator had made its way to the designated area for its work to begin. Though owned by the local county council, the machine was being driven by a member of the RAF's Mechanical Transport team. Forbes hadn't been about to put another civilian's life in danger, and this way he could also ensure greater security, avoiding the possibility of a loose tongue letting the secret of Olney out. Unlike Ryan, he had no desire to evade the public scrutiny that disclosure would entail, but for now, he needed to avoid instigating a possible public panic. Thoughts of the future seemed irrelevant to Forbes at present. How they were going to clear up this mess both publicly and politically was anyone's guess, and Forbes was more than relieved that at least those decisions wouldn't rest on his shoulders. Back at the rubble mountain, Flight Sergeant Taylor was directing the driver of the excavator to begin his work by removing the largest of the remaining rocks in the pile, the ones that the tractor he and Sweeney had been using just simply couldn't move due to their bulk and weight. Michael Sweeney had just gone to fetch the three of them a supply of tea and biscuits from the kitchen of Tilly Greaves when the next catastrophe to hit Olney that day occurred.

The explosion that destroyed the excavator and ended the lives of Flight Sergeant Taylor and the unfortunate driver Corporal Bob Styles, could be heard from ten miles away, across the open fields of the Kent countryside. Luckily, there were no villages close by, and apart from those in the village, the farms in the local vicinity and the troops on duty enforcing the cordon around Olney, only the sheep and cattle grazing in the fields and the birds that sprang into the air in surprise and terror were witness to the awful sound as men, metal, rubble were blasted into oblivion!

Residents of the village, medics, nurses and even a few ambulatory patients from within the marquee appeared from their homes, beds, or places of work in the aftermath of the blast. At first, no-one appeared to know what had happened, though it soon became apparent that something terrible had occurred. Bewildered men and women stared in the direction of the rising pall that hung over what had been the children's playground. The smoke, thick and dense, hung like a black cloud over the blast site. Of the yellow excavator, nothing remained apart from the remains of one its caterpillar tracks, hanging like a dead crocodile over a piece of green metal fencing that had somehow remained upright, while all around the rest of the fence had collapsed under the weight of the detonation. Small dust particles, formed when the explosion destroyed the large mound of rubble, mingled with the smoking pyre, and fell as ash on those who'd gathered to witness the scene.

When the sound of the explosion first reached the ears of those in the village, and the concussion from the blast rocked every structure in Olney to its foundations, the first to react, perhaps predictably, were the medical staff employed within the field hospital. Guy Dearborn and Paul Trent had emerged from the marquee first, hastily followed by Hilary Newton, two of McKay's team of doctors, Spence and Fielding, and five nurses, including Christine Rigby and Edith Kinnaird. They were followed by Angus McKay, who'd been at his desk. Group Captain Forbes and Wilhelm Koenig, who had been at the far end of the marquee, furthest from the entrance, brought up the rear, and the whole party now stood aghast at the sight that met their eyes.

"Mein Gott!" exclaimed Koenig, reverting to his native language.

"What the hell?" was Trent's expression.

"What happened?" asked Edith.

"It sounded like a bomb," Hilary Newton volunteered.

"I think we'll find it was a bomb," said the Group Captain, "and it probably destroyed our last chance of finding whatever remained of the original German biological weapon."

"You mean, you think someone did this on purpose?" came the question from Guy Dearborn.

"I'm certain they did. There was nothing in that rubble that could have produced an explosion of that magnitude. Someone planted the bomb to prevent us finding what we were looking for. First two of my men disappear; now two more are killed by whatever maniac is loose in the village. Someone is afraid that we'll discover something they don't want us to unearth."

In seconds, the whole team raced across the field to the smoking pyre that marked the scene of the explosion. Of Flight Sergeant Taylor and Corporal Styles, there was no trace whatsoever. It was as if the two men had simply been vaporised by the blast that had rocked the village. Obviously, medical care was neither warranted nor possible in the aftermath of the explosion, but professionalism had dictated that the medics check for survivors, or at least for identifiable remains. With neither present, the talk returned to the bomb itself, and who might have placed it there, ready to wipe out anyone who encroached upon the secret that it now appeared must have lain hidden below the rubble, left over from the modernisation of the playground. Trent's eyes focussed on a cypress tree to the rear of the seat of the explosion. It hung crazily tilted to one side, its roots still clinging to the ravaged earth in a death grip, refusing to finally topple and die. Hilary couldn't take her eyes away from the vast crater that had opened up where the rubble had been piled. Smoke and dust hung over the entrance to the hole in a miasma of death. This was where Taylor and Styles would have been when the explosion occurred. She felt that at least, death had come swiftly and relatively painlessly for them, one quick searing moment of pain and then, oblivion! Edith Kinnaird just stood quietly weeping, Christine Rigby's arm around her shoulder. Rigby was simply too shocked to cry or react in any visible fashion at all. Her face was a mask of shock and horror.

Donald Forbes and Wilhelm Koenig moved as close to the epicentre of the explosion as they could, and the pair stood on the edge of the crater that now resembled the smoking caldera of a small volcano.

"Who could have done such a thing?" asked a shocked Koenig.

"Someone who didn't want us to find what was left of your bomb, Herr Doctor."

"Not *my* bomb, Group Captain. I may have helped to produce the infernal device, but it was never mine, it was Dreschler's."

"Of course, I'm sorry. This wasn't your fault Koenig. It was mine."

"Yours, but how could it be?"

"Because I should have anticipated any and every eventuality, Herr Doctor, that's why. If I'd had my wits about me, I'd have given some thought to the possibility that someone might try to stop us finding the remains."

"But why? What could anyone hope to gain by preventing us from discovering a few remnants of an old device that has already released its cargo of death?"

"That's the bit I can't quite work out," said Forbes. "If it was a simple case of stopping us from finding the bomb intact and discovering its secrets then I'd suspect that someone from the original team that made it might be attempting to sabotage our work here."

"I hope you don't think that I..."

"No, I don't, and unless you tell me that anyone else from the Straub biological warfare research team might still be trying to cover up for what Dreschler did during the war then none of this makes any sense at all."

"I just can't see that being the case Group Captain. No-one from back then could possibly be so stupid as to come to England and do such a thing. Anyway, how would they know where the bomb was? As far as I know from what you've told me, the bombs came down in an airplane that was shot down, and therefore Olney was not the intended target. That being the case, no-one in Germany could possibly have known where to find it."

"You're right, Koenig, and that means that if it's not the Germans, then it has to be either our own people, or some other outside agency that's responsible for what's just happened."

"Not your own people, surely?"

"Then who, Herr Doctor Koenig, tell me, who?"

Koenig never got around to answering Forbes's question. A second explosion now rocked Olney St. Mary, this time from the direction they'd just come from. Whatever degree of shock and horror the people around the bomb crater and sprinkled around the streets of Olney had felt at the first explosion now magnified a hundred fold as they turned their eyes to the flaming conflagration that had until a few seconds ago been the field hospital containing over seventy patients and medical staff!

CHAPTER 44

AS THE PERCUSSIVE DISCHARGE OF THE EXPLOSION ROCKED THE marquee the Reverend Timothy Grafton found himself flung to the ground by the force of the blast. As flames licked all around him, and dense choking smoke filled the enclosed space, Grafton raised his head to take in the scene of carnage. Patients had been literally thrown from their beds by the force of the blast, and many lay dead or dying, bleeding their lives away on the duck-boarded floor of the ward. Most of the dead had been close to the epicentre of the explosion, which Grafton assumed to have been the heating stove which had stood in the centre of the ward. Of the stove, nothing remained, and the beds where the patients had lain burned with a fierce intensity. He was horrified to see one man, barely recognisable, staggering, screaming through the smoke and flames with a surgical scalpel embedded in the space where his right eye should have been, his clothes on fire. There was nothing he could do but watch in horrified fascination as the man blindly, in his pain, pitched forward into the flames that quickly engulfed him. Grafton would remember the man's screams of agony for the rest of his life.

A movement to his left caught the vicar's eye and he turned to see an arm protruding from underneath a bed quite close to his position. The arm was moving, the hand trying to claw a way out from beneath the bed. Grafton swiftly moved across and took the man's hand, pulling gently to help the victim out from under the bed. In seconds, the shocked face of Billy Wragg was looking up at him.

"Bloody Hell, Vicar, what the heck was that?"

"I don't know Billy, but we have to get out of here, *now*!

Wragg looked around him at the scene of horror and fell silent. His vocal chords froze into inertia, and his legs turned to jelly as he saw so many of his friends and neighbours lying dead all around him.

"Can you stand?" asked Grafton, as he eased Billy to an upright position.

"I don't know. I'll try. My left leg hurts. It might be broken. Aargh!"

There was no doubt from his scream of pain that the poacher's leg was indeed broken. The action of trying to put his left foot on the ground had caused him intense pain. Grafton knew that they hadn't much time. The main body of the flames was creeping closer to their position. They had only seconds to try to escape the searing pain of burning flesh and lung searing agony as the superheated air scorched their internal organs and brought them the inevitable release of death.

"Lean on me," said Grafton as he placed Wragg's arm around his own shoulder and took the man's weight as best he could.

For what seemed like an hour, but was in fact no more than twenty seconds, the Reverend Timothy Grafton stumbled, staggered and choked his way through the dense smoke and heat of the conflagration as he fought his battle with the flames. Never once did he consider releasing his burden and saving himself. As the flames licked ever closer his tear-filled eyes at last recognised the exit from the ward. The light of salvation awaited him if he could keep going for just a few more seconds. At that moment, a horrific sound from above made the vicar raise his head for a second. The roof of the marquee, burning fiercely and with tongues of flame licking both across and down from its surface was falling onto what remained of the ward below. Grafton screamed, Wragg said 'Bloody Hell" and the vicar made one last superhuman effort to reach the elusive exit.

———

"All those people," Hilary Newton screamed. "We have to do something to help them!"

"How can we? No-one could possibly get in there with the flames and the smoke. It would be suicide to even attempt it," came the coldly logical but equally accurate assessment of Guy Dearborn."

"Did you hear it?" asked Trent. "There were two separate explosions, I'm sure there were, one after the other, but definitely two distinct detonations, I'm convinced of it."

"I think you're right, Doctor Trent," said Forbes. "Someone seems bloody determined to wipe out any trace of the original biological bomb and those infected by whatever it carried. That someone is trying to bury the secret of Dreschler's weapon for ever, Doctor Koenig."

"I just do not understand all of this, Group Captain. There is no logic to it. All those people are innocent. We just treated them all with the antidote. They would have recovered, I'm sure of it. Why kill them, what is the reason for this?"

"I don't know doctor. Maybe someone didn't want them to recover. Good God, is there no bloody fire brigade anywhere around here?"

His answer came from Keith Greaves. The policeman had come running at the sound of the second explosion(s).

"The nearest fire station is in the village of East Lewington, about twenty miles away, and they're part-timers, retained firemen they're called."

"Yes, I know what retained fire-fighters are thank you, Constable. They'd never get here in time to be of any use. Isn't there anything we can do?"

The marquee began its final collapse as Forbes spoke, the roof falling in on itself, flames and sparks shooting up towards the sky. A low roar accompanied the collapse and within seconds, the whole edifice simply crumpled to the ground, and a pall of black smoke rose to mingle with the flames and create a vision straight out of Dante's inferno. Yet, from within the inferno, as though delivered by a miracle, two figures suddenly appeared, stumbling through the flames and smoke. Willing onlookers ran to assist them as Timothy Grafton and Billy Wragg emerged from the smoke, Grafton hobbling and straining under the weight of the other man, who hopped on one leg, his arm clinging tightly to the vicar for support. As Guy Dearborn got closer to the two men, he could see that Grafton was struggling terribly to keep going. His chest and feet were bare, he'd obviously been in bed when the bomb went off, and the flesh was burned and blackened. Every step must have been agony for the man, who kept walking, like a man in a dream, supporting the injured Wragg. Grafton's eyebrows were gone, singed by the flames, and his hair was equally singed, and smouldering from the heat. Wragg looked just as bad, his feet also naked and burned, his head, hands and pyjamas black from the effects of the smoke, and his leg hanging at an angle that spoke of perhaps more than one break.

Dearborn, Edith Kinnaird, and Doctor Roger Spence gently pried the injured Wragg from his human crutch and laid the severely injured man on the ground. Paul Trent, Hilary Newton and Christine Rigby attended to the immediate needs of the Reverend Grafton. All of the medical equipment in the marquee had been destroyed in the explosion and Hilary threw the keys to her surgery to Doctor Norman Fielding, who ran as fast as his legs would carry him to procure whatever might be of use in aiding the two injured men. Keith Greaves, needing to feel of use, ran beside him all the way. He might not know what to pick up, but he could help to carry whatever the doctor needed.

"A bomb, it was...a" Grafton weakly gasped as Trent gently cushioned the vicar's head in the crook of his left arm.

"We know, Vicar. Please, stay quiet, and we'll soon have you fixed up."

"Will you? Will you really?" asked the vicar, and his eyes promptly clouded over, and he passed into the oblivion of unconsciousness.

"He saved my life," said Billy Wragg from where he lay a mere two yards from where the vicar's unconscious figure. "Pulled me through the flames and the smoke, he did. He's got to be the bravest man I ever knew. He'll be okay won't he, Doc?"

"I think so, Mr. Wragg," Trent replied. "I think he's just passed out from the pain and shock."

As Fielding arrived back on the scene, accompanied by Keith Greaves, the two of them laden with all the medical supplies they could carry from the surgery, the small band of medics began the task of treating the wounds and the burns of the two men who had emerged miraculously from the flames and the smoke of the burning marquee. Grateful as they were that Grafton and Wragg had made it out of the burning field hospital, every one of those attending to their injuries, and those who wore the shocked masks of the onlookers to the scenes of devastation around them were only too aware of the fact that no-one else had escaped from the flames. From a total of seventy-two patients and five medical staff, Grafton and Wragg were the only survivors.

Forbes and Koenig looked on as the medical team began their work. The German had the gaze of a man in deep shock, as indeed he was. Forbes's eyes appeared sunken into his face and his lips were set in a rictus of grim determination. Someone was going to pay for what had happened in the last hour in Olney St. Mary, and he was going to find out who was responsible if it was the last thing he did, and ensure that the price for the lives lost today was paid in full!

CHAPTER 45

LIEUTENANT JAMES ROSE LED HIS CONTINGENT OF TROOPS into Olney with a look of total disbelief on his face. The scene that greeted him and his men resembled something from a war zone, straight from a battlefield. A heavy pall of smoke continued to rise from the site of the first explosion, and both smoke and flames still issued from the remains of the field hospital. What horrified the new arrivals most, however, was the unmistakeable smell of burned flesh. The stench hung in the air, and the sight of stunned villagers standing looking on in trance-like horror as harried medical staff worked in the open gave the whole place a surreal appearance. It didn't take a genius to work out that a number of people had met their deaths by the most terrible of means imaginable.

Rose and his party had been despatched to the village by his commander Captain Leo Martin as soon as the senior man had heard the explosion that heralded the beginning of the devastation in the village. Acting on his own initiative, Martin had immediately realised that some tragedy had struck that surely overrode his orders to maintain the security cordon around the surrounding countryside, and Rose and his men were sent to investigate the cause of the explosions and provide whatever support they could if it were needed.

Rose walked straight up to the nearest person he saw as he approached the centre of the village. It was the constable, Keith Greaves who'd seen the small contingent of troops marching along the road into the village and had walked to meet them.

"What the hell happened here?" asked Rose, without pausing to indulge in any pleasantries. At a time like this such touches were unnecessary.

"Some bastard has laid bombs around the village. We've had one over there," Greaves pointed to the site of the first explosion, "and then the bloody field hospital went up! Nearly everyone inside was killed, only two got out."

"How many have you lost?"

"Over seventy people as far as we can make out."

Rose's face hardened as the thought that someone had deliberately murdered so many people hit home.

"What can we do to help?" he asked.

"You'd better report to the man in charge. Group Captain Forbes is over at the surgery, making a telephone call I believe," said Greaves, pointing to the home of Hilary Newton.

"Corporal, stand the men at ease, and wait here until I get back," Rose ordered his NCO, leaving his men standing watching the scene of devastation as he marched across to the surgery.

Half an hour later, Rose and his men were hard at work helping to find the bodies, or what remained of them, of those who'd perished in the flames within the hospital. Forbes had been glad of the arrival of the troops. The people in the village, residents and surviving medics, were all in a state of profound shock, and the newcomers would at least carry out their grim task without the terrible mental pictures of what the others had seen clouding their minds as they worked. The Group Captain had made a series of telephone calls, and had been astonished, when speaking to Sir Robert Blake, to discover that Special Branch had already made a startling discovery as a result of their initial inquiries into the background of Douglas Ryan. Blake wasn't prepared to talk about it over the phone however and promised to visit Olney himself in the wake of the bombings, to enlighten Forbes. As for the bombings themselves, Blake was horrified and expressed genuine sorrow at the news. As for the perpetrators, he could only share Forbes's belief that someone as yet unknown was responsible for the horrors of the day, and that the reasons for the indiscriminate murders and the destruction wrought in the village would remain unknown until they could be identified and apprehended.

"Surely we can't keep all of this a secret any longer," Forbes had said, thinking that Blake would order a full-scale relief operation for the village.

"For now, Donald, I'm afraid we have to try to maintain full security I'm afraid. Too much has happened already in Olney that can't be easily explained to the public. If we try to go public now, there'll be too many questions asked that we can't answer. The Press would have a field day at the expense of the government and the military, seeing 'reds under the bed' at every opportunity. They'd think we are all involved in a massive cover up of something highly illegal or suspicious and..."

Forbes suddenly interrupted the Peer of the Realm.

"Hang on, Sir Robert!"

"What is it Donald?"

"Something you just said, about 'reds under the bed' has given me an idea."

Blake fell silent at the end of the line.

"Sir, did you hear me?" Forbes asked.

The voice of Sir Robert Blake dropped almost to a whisper as he eventually replied to the RAF officer.

"Group Captain Forbes, I don't want you to say one more word until I arrive in Olney St. Mary. I'm calling for my car right now and should be with you within two hours. Do what you can for the people there until I arrive, but do not, I repeat do not discuss any of your theories, whatever they may be, with anyone at all in the village. Is that clear?"

Wondering just what he'd said to cause such an instantaneous reaction from Sir Robert, Forbes could only say a hurried "Yes, Sir, if you say so," into the phone before the line went dead.

Donald Forbes had been standing holding the receiver in his hand when Rose had knocked on the door and, for the time being, he'd had to put his conversation with Sir Robert to one side. Now, as he watched the remaining members of the medical team working side by side with the newly arrived troops in an attempt to locate and identify those who'd perished in the explosion, Forbes allowed his mind to drift back to the conversation with Blake. He'd cut Forbes off at the very mention of 'reds under the bed'. Did that mean that Sir Robert believed the soviets were somehow involved in what had taken place? After all the term was used quite liberally in the west to indicate the possibility of Russian Communist infiltration into the democratic nations, but if it was the Russians, then how had they planted the bombs in Olney, and for what purpose? It was after all, a German wartime experimental weapon that had caused the outbreak in Olney, not some secret Russian weapon. The implication suddenly hit Forbes like a sledgehammer. What if wasn't the German bomb that had caused the plague in the village? What if the Russians themselves were somehow responsible? But how could they have done it? How could they have ensured they placed a device in exactly the spot where a German aircraft carrying just such a weapon had crashed all those years before? They would have had to know about the Messerschmitt crash, which implied inside knowledge. A spy, perhaps? It would explain certain things, especially why the remains of the German bomb, if it existed had been destroyed, or was it the Russian's own delivery system for the plague bacillus that had been hidden under the rubble? Once again, Forbes found his mind filled with more questions than he could possibly provide answers to. And again, why the hospital? There could be no logical reason to destroy so many lives just to ensure a cover-up, surely. Try as he might, Forbes couldn't answer his own questions. He'd have to wait for the arrival of Sir Robert, who seemed to know something that Forbes didn't, something so secret that he'd felt unable to divulge it over the telephone.

His sadness with the current situation grew as he watched Guy Dearborn gently carrying a torn and battered human torso from the remains of what had been the filed hospital. The chances of identification seemed remote, there was so little left that was recognisable. Dearborn laid the grisly find down on a green tarpaulin, where Hilary Newton and Christine Rigby did their best to clean the cadaver so that someone might at least try to put a name to the deceased. Nearby, other finds had been placed, an arm, a leg, a pile of clothing, even a child's teddy bear, a poignant reminder that many of those who'd died came from Olney's younger generation. Even as he watched the sad collection of remains grow as more and more pieces of charred and barely recognisable flesh were added to those already on the tarpaulin, a voice from behind caused Forbes to wheel round in surprise.

"Look what I've found, Group Captain," said the voice of Michael Sweeney, as he pushed a dishevelled figure in RAF uniform towards Forbes. To the Group Captain's surprise, the dirt encrusted figure was none other than Leading Aircraftman Grove, one of the two airmen to go missing that morning.

"Mr Sweeney, LAC Grove, what on earth is the meaning of this performance? Explain yourselves!"

"Oh, this particular rat's got a lot of explaining to do," Sweeney said, his voice full of vehemence. "I found him trying to get well away from the village. He put up a bit of a fight, but I can handle myself quite well, thank you very much. He took a bit of 'persuading' to return with me, which is how he got a bit muddy as you can see, but in the end I convinced him that he wasn't going anywhere but right back here with me. Group Captain Forbes, allow me to introduce you to the murderer of Leading Aircraftman Bennet, and quite possibly the bomber responsible for the deaths of all the people in the marquee!"

Forbes stared open mouthed at the man who now stood trembling with fear in front of him. This was one of his own men, one of those charged with serving Queen and country, wearing the same uniform Forbes wore. The look in the eyes of LAC Grove however, told Forbes that Sweeney was correct. He'd never seen such a look of hatred in a man's eyes before. Along with that hatred he saw a realisation that Grove knew his time had run out. He'd been caught, and the man had nowhere to run any more. Whether he'd talk and explain his actions was another matter of course.

"Well, Group Captain, what d'you want me to do with the rat-faced little lizard?" asked Sweeney, prodding Grove viciously in the back as he spoke.

"I think before you do anything with him, we'd better have a little chat with Grove, don't you? And how do you know that he killed LAC Bennet if I may ask, Mr Sweeney?"

"Oh, that's quite easy. I found him burying the body, with its head all bashed in, Group Captain. That's hardly the sort of thing you'd do if one of your mates has just been killed accidentally, now, would you?"

With that, Grove suddenly turned and lunged at Sweeney, his face a mask of hatred and violent emotion. He might actually have done some damage to the village undertaker if Sweeney hadn't simply taken one step back, wound up his right arm in an instant and struck the traitorous airman with the finest roundhouse punch that Forbes had seen in a long time. Grove teetered on his feet for a second or two, then his eyes glazed over, and he sank to the floor, unconscious before his head bounced off the turf of the village green.

"That was some punch Mr Sweeney. If you don't mind me asking, where did you learn to fight like that?"

"Oh that, well I did a bit of time in the army in the war, Group Captain. It's amazing what a man picks up when he's fighting for his life against the enemy."

It was the first reference Sweeney had made to his wartime service to anyone in a long time. Forbes was impressed.

"Well, I dare say you took LAC Grove by surprise. He certainly wasn't expecting to come up against someone like you Mr Sweeney, that's for sure. Now, while he's out for the count, I suggest we get the constable to come and take him away and lock him up somewhere and you can tell me what you've discovered about what's taken place here today. I have a feeling you know much more than I do at the moment, and that just won't do now, will it?"

"I'll tell you all I know, but it doesn't make for a happy story, that's for sure."

Sweeney disappeared for les than two minutes, returning with Keith Greaves. The two men half carried, half dragged the unconscious airman to the police house, where Greaves had a small lock-up at the rear, usually used as a holding cell for the occasional drunk or minor felon who might fall into his hands. It wasn't as secure as Wormwood Scrubs, but it would do as a temporary prison for Grove.

Sweeney soon returned to the Group Captain, with Greaves at his side. Obviously, the constable wanted to know what had taken place and how LAC Bennet had met his death. Forbes was quite happy for Sweeney to share the information with the policeman, and together the three men walked slowly across the road to Hilary Newton's surgery, where they could talk in private.

"Now Mr Sweeney, I believe you have quite a story to tell," said Forbes, as they sat round the kitchen table.

"You might say that, Group Captain," Sweeney replied, and he began to relate the events leading up to the capture of LAC Grove to the two men who sat listening intently to his every word.

CHAPTER 46

THE STORY THAT MICHAEL SWEENEY RELATED TO THE
assembled gathering was in fact quite simple. When the first
bomb had exploded, killing Flight Sergeant Taylor and the
excavator driver, he'd gone to fetch refreshments for himself and
the two men. When the explosion occurred, Sweeney had
instantly run from the home of Graves intending to help in
whatever way he could in the aftermath. As he exited the police
house however, he'd seen something that made him stop in his
tracks.

"I saw someone coming out of the back door of Mavis
Thorndyke's cottage. She had no relatives so there was no reason
why anyone should be in there at all. Then I saw that whoever it
was, he was in RAF uniform. He bent down and then I saw him
hoist an inert body onto his shoulders. I knew something was
badly amiss, so I followed him as he lugged the body along the
little alley that runs behind the row of cottages on that side of
the street. I hid behind the side wall of Mrs Elder's cottage and
waited to see what he'd do next. He didn't go far, and when he
reached the end of the alley, he kind of tossed the body over the
hedge and into the copse on the other side. I waited to see what

he'd do next, and he ran back to the cottage and emerged again a few minutes later with a spade. He climbed the fence into the copse, and I heard him start to drag the body deeper into the trees. I daren't come out too soon or he might have seen me, and I wanted to be sure of what he was up to before I made a move. If I'd shown myself too soon, he might have made a run for it and I could have lost him in the trees.

I crept as quietly as I could up to the fence and looked into the copse. I couldn't see him, though I could still hear the sound of him dragging the body along the ground. He'd just begun digging when I heard the explosion that wiped out the field hospital. God, how I wanted to just turn and run back to help you all, but I knew I had to stay there and try and take this little creep down. I knew he must have something to do with the bomb, and I steeled myself against the sounds in the distance and began to make my way into the copse as quietly as I could. After I'd gone about thirty yards, I saw the bastard, digging what had to be a grave. I thought then that the poor sod that lay on the ground must be dead already, and that I wouldn't be jeopardising his life if I made a move, so I used my old army training and tried to creep up on him as silently as I could. I had to dodge from tree to tree to keep myself concealed. I didn't know of course who it was I was stalking until I got closer. Then I saw that it was Grove, and I had to assume that the body was that of the other missing airman. To cut a long story short, when I was close enough, I jumped him, and we sort of tumbled to the ground in a tangle and fought until I overpowered him. I admit I might have thumped him a few more times than was actually necessary, but I didn't want to take a chance on him having the strength to try and make a run for it when I brought him in. I dragged the little sod back here and met you all out on the green, and that's about it."

"All I can say Mr Sweeney, is thank you. You've done a great job, and possibly saved people's lives. There's no telling how many more he might have killed if you hadn't laid your hands on him," said the Group Captain.

"I'd thought it strange when you didn't show up after the first bomb went off," said Trent. "For an awful minute or two I thought that maybe you'd been caught in the blast as well. Then someone said they'd seen you heading for the police house before the explosion, so I assumed you were safe, but hadn't a clue where you'd gone. In the aftermath of everything else that then took place I suppose I forgot about you. I'm glad you didn't forget about us though, Mr Sweeney. As the Group Captain says, we all owe you a debt of thanks. But do you know why he killed LAC Bennet? Has he said anything to you?"

"He never said a word after I collared him. I asked him why he'd killed Bennet, and he just sort of growled at me and called me an interfering bastard, which is as good as an admission in my book. I presume that Bennet saw something he oughtn't to have done, or caught Grove in the act of doing something, and Grove killed him to keep him quiet. I just hope you *can* find out why the bastard did it. All those people, my friends and my neighbours, dead because of him! It doesn't make any sense to me. There's hardly anyone left alive in the whole damn village thanks to him and his bloody bomb!"

"We'll find out why he did it. You can rest assured on that point," Forbes guaranteed. "In fact, I want to begin questioning LAC Grove as soon as we've finished here."

Before any more could be discussed however, there was a knock at the surgery door, and Trent answered to find a chauffeur, resplendent in the full livery of the trade standing before him, a gleaming black Bentley on the road a few yards away.

"I'm looking for Group Captain Forbes. We were told he'd be here," said the man, his face set as though in stone.

"I presume that's Sir Robert Blake in the car, is it?" asked Trent by way of a reply.

"You're correct. I'm Sir Robert's driver. Now, is the Group Captain here or not?"

"Yes, of course he is," said Trent, at which the man turned on his heel without another word to Trent, and walked back to the car, opened the rear passenger door and held it open as the man inside the car made his exit. The driver touched his cap in deference to his passenger. Dressed in a blue pin-striped suit, his gleaming black shoes reflecting the afternoon sunshine, Sir Robert Blake walked up to Trent, introduced himself with a firm handshake and walked straight into the surgery without being invited. The chauffeur walked back round to the driver's side of the Bentley, placed himself behind the wheel and assumed the posture of a statue. Trent assumed he'd stay like that until his employer emerged from the surgery, so he turned inwards, closed the door and followed the knight of the realm into the kitchen where Blake had already found the others and introduced himself.

Sir Robert had been informed of the cause of the devastation that met him on his approach to Olney by two soldiers who'd met his car as he entered the village, having been pre-warned that something terrible had happened by the troops manning the cordon about ten miles away. Though horrified at the sight that had met his eyes on arrival, he could do no more than express his sympathies in a series of what he knew to be meaningless words. Nothing could compensate for the shock and the horror of what the people he now sat with had endured, and he was painfully aware of the fact. Forbes quickly filled him in with the events surrounding the bombings and the capture of Grove, though he admitted they were short on detail for the time being. Blake could do no more now than to do what he'd come to Olney for, and so he asked that those present in the room listen carefully to what he was about to relate to them, adding that what he was about to say was of a highly sensitive and secret nature, and that everyone, Sweeny included, would be bound by the Official Secrets Act not to reveal what he was about to tell them to a single living soul.

So, having heard the account of Michael Sweeney's capture of the errant LAC Grove the assembled group were about to hear another story, this time of even greater surprise value, and even greater magnitude in respect of recent happenings in the village.

———

"I'm sorry to have cut you off so abruptly earlier, Donald," Blake began, "but I didn't want to take any chances that a conversation over an open telephone line might be overheard in the wrong quarters. Your last comment about 'reds under the bed' came a little too close to what I'd recently learned, and I knew I'd need to come here and explain to you all the latest information that I've been made privy to."

Following that opening, Sir Robert paused for breath, cleared his throat, and, as every eye in the room fixed itself unerringly upon him, he continued:

"As soon as a shadow of suspicion fell on our friend Douglas Ryan, I instigated a full inquiry into his background and recent activities, which was to be carried out by Special Branch at the Met. As you all know I'm sure, the Metropolitan Police work closely with various government agencies from time to time, and within hours of Chief Superintendent Arthur Garside launching his inquiry, he was able to get back to me with some rather disturbing news regarding our chief virologist. It would appear that this is not the first time Douglas Ryan has appeared on

Special Branch's 'radar' so to speak. It transpires that they were contacted by MI5 some months ago regarding a suspected communist cell, with links to Moscow, that had its beginnings at Cambridge University long before the war. Among the names on that list was none other than Douglas Ryan, who studied at Cambridge in the twenties. Special Branch had run a cursory check on Ryan when they were first alerted by MI5 but found nothing to connect him to any current 'subversive' elements as they're known in intelligence circles. They did however leave a red flag beside his name with instructions that he be closely monitored in the light of any future developments. When I contacted Special Branch, Garside immediately found the file containing Ryan's name, and the Chief Super straight away gave orders for Ryan to be brought in for questioning. He suspected that Ryan might be a 'sleeper', in other words a communist sympathiser with long term allegiance to the Soviet cause, but who is left to build a career and live a normal life in his own country until activated by his contact, probably someone in the Russian embassy.

Well, it seems that our friend Ryan might be a clever chap and an expert in his own field of medicine, but when it came to interrogation by the police, and by Special Branch in particular, the man caved in within minutes. Like a lot of traitors the man is an abject coward underneath, and even now he's spilling his guts to his interrogators at Scotland Yard. Garside tells me that as soon as he mentioned the possibility that Ryan could be hung for treason the man became instantly co-operative."

"Ha, typical," sneered Sweeney.

"I'm afraid there's more to come," Blake went on. "It seems the man you have in custody, LAC Grove was connected to Ryan, and was probably his 'foot soldier', the man who carried out his dirty work for him."

"But Grove wears the uniform of the Royal Air Force," Forbes protested. "How and why would he become involved with a communist plot?"

"According to Ryan, Grove is a National Serviceman, not a volunteer. Once he's been fully checked out, I think you'll find that his true allegiance lies much further east than the Ministry of Defence. Before being called up for his military service, Ryan says Grove was training to become a demolition contractor, so Grove would know just where to place an explosive device in order to cause maximum damage."

"But, how did Grove get the explosives into Olney in the first place Sir Robert?" asked Trent.

"Now, that's the saddest part of the whole tale," Blake said, his voice trailing to a low whisper so that everyone had to strain to hear the next part of his statement.

"Ryan admitted to Garside that he had a second operative in Olney, sort of his lieutenant in the communist cell. He was the only man who had the means and opportunity to bring the high explosives and incendiary devices into the village before you got here group Captain. Tell me, who organised the supplies and the packing of the boxes that came with the relief party from Porton Down?"

"McKay!" Forbes spluttered, incredulously, as the awareness of his assistant's treachery struck home.

"Exactly, Group Captain. Angus McKay has been in league with Ryan and his cell all along. He was recruited by the Soviets years ago and has been steadily passing them information from Porton Down, through Ryan, for a long time."

"My God," said Forbes. "Is there no end to the damned Russians infiltration of our secrets? McKay even talked of suspected communist plots a day or two ago, I'm sure he did. He then came to me with Doctor Trent to voice suspicions about Ryan. He spoke as though he had his own suspicions about Ryan."

"A smokescreen to cover himself," said Blake. "He must have known we were getting close to discovering their plot, and he had to make it sound as though he was innocent of any involvement. What better way than to decry his own communist cell leader, without giving anything away that would incriminate Ryan, of course?"

"But, hang on," Sweeney now interrupted. "If the original bomb from the war was a German device, then why are the Russians so keen to stop us finding it, so keen that they blew it up to prevent us locating it, and how did they know about it?"

"Well done, Mr Sweeney," Blake responded. "You've now brought me to the real meat of the situation. The Russians knew about the German biological bomb from the beginning of course. Ryan would have reported its existence to them when he was called to Olney at the end of the war. The Russians have their own biological weapons programme as we know but the prospect of getting their hands on a working example of a plague bomb would have been so very tempting for them. So, when Ryan heard that an outbreak of plague had begun right here in Olney, where he knew the original bombs had dropped, it was too good a chance for him to pass up. He must have realised right away that he'd missed a bomb when he did the original work here after the war. He then did everything he could to seal the place off, and then sent in his own people with instructions to get their hands on the remains of the original bomb at all costs, so that it could be sent to Moscow."

"But the bomb was destroyed when Grove blew it up," said Hilary Newton.

"I think not, Doctor," Blake replied. "If we search the personal effects of Angus McKay, we will probably find that his briefcase contains whatever remains of the original device. He would hope to smuggle it out of Olney when he leaves and then pass it on to his Russian paymasters, through Ryan of course. Blowing up the site of the bomb's supposed hiding place was just a blind, a means of convincing you that there was nothing left to find."

"But he doesn't know about Ryan being exposed as a traitor, yet, does he? So he'll go on with his plan unless we stop him," Trent added.

"Oh, we'll stop him alright," said Blake. "That very efficient young army officer out there and his men have sufficient rifles with them to put the wind-up Mr Angus McKay, I've no doubt. We'll soon find out where he's hiding what's left of Dreschler's device."

Hilary Newton had to ask one more question.

"But, Sir Robert, why did they kill all those people in the hospital? That was just wanton and indiscriminate murder, surely?"

"Yes, it was I'm afraid, Doctor. They had to do something to focus all attention on the hospital so that Grove could dispose of the other poor RAF man, and give McKay the chance to squirrel away the Dreschler bomb's remains without being discovered. I doubt they planned quite such a large and destructive detonation, but time was against them and they probably panicked and laid the lot in one go. Even so, the deaths of over seventy people were of no consequence to them."

"Hang on," said Dearborn. "That would explain the second explosion we heard in the ward. It was probably the rest of the explosives going up by accident, touched off by the first explosion. McKay was one of the last to leave the marquee after the first explosion. He had something under his arm."

"A brown leather holdall, with the red cross symbol on it," Hilary added. "He's hoping to get the German bomb out of the village in his medical bag."

"I can assure you that Angus McKay is going nowhere young lady," Sir Robert Blake said, very firmly. "Now, let's go and find that young army officer, shall we?"

CHAPTER 47

BEFORE LEAVING THE SURGERY, HILARY CHECKED ON THE condition of the Reverend Grafton and Billy Wragg. Doctor Fielding and Christine Rigby were attending to the two men in the upstairs bedrooms, which Hilary had offered as temporary treatment rooms until the ambulances arrived. Her phone call to Ashford had stressed the urgency of the situation, and she'd requested a specialist burns team be despatched with the emergency vehicle. Satisfied that the two men were as comfortable and stable as they could be under the circumstances, she rejoined the men downstairs.

On the way out of the surgery Blake nodded to the impassive-faced man who sat behind the wheel of his Bentley. The man nodded in return and got out of the car, walking up to Blake, who proceeded to introduce him to the others.

"This is Detective Sergeant Lennard of Special Branch. He accompanied me in place of my own driver. I thought he might be useful in performing the task we now have ahead of us."

Trent immediately realised why the man had been so stony-faced with him on his arrival. The policeman wouldn't have known who he was addressing when Trent opened the door. He might have been McKay for all Lennard knew so Trent was prepared to forgive him his earlier brusque manner. Lennard nodded to the assembled group, still remaining silent. Trent wondered if the man could actually speak!

Blake now addressed the group before setting off for the police house, where he knew McKay would be, along with Greaves and the other surviving members of Forbes's team.

"When we get there, I would prefer it if only Sergeant Lennard, myself, group Captain Forbes and Doctor Trent entered the house at first. I'm sorry Doctor Newton, Doctor Dearborn, and you, Mr Sweeney, but I don't want everyone going in there like a posse from a Hollywood movie. Perhaps you could wait outside for a few minutes until we get McKay subdued."

The two doctors and Sweeney grumbled their disappointment at being left out of the showdown with McKay but had little option but to comply with Sir Robert's order. They did however accompany the others as they made their way to Constable Greaves's police house, where they dutifully remained at the front gate as the others walked up to the front door. Sergeant Lennard brought up the rear, assuming his role as Sir Robert's chauffeur again, for the time being at least. That way, anyone watching their approach from within would suspect nothing.

Blake allowed Group Captain Forbes to take the lead as they entered the house. McKay was Forbes's assistant after all, and, as he wouldn't be expecting trouble, the man would feel less threatened by the sight of his own boss walking into the house.

"Hello again, Constable," said Forbes, purposely ignoring McKay for the moment. "How's your prisoner?"

"Not a peep out of him Sir," Greaves replied. "I think he's got too much on his mind at present to be making a fuss in there."

"Quite so," said Forbes. "Allow me to introduce Sir Robert Blake. Sir Robert, this is Police Constable Greaves, and this is my assistant Angus McKay," he motioned towards the little Scotsman who stood up and moved to shake the hand of Sir Robert. As he did so, Sergeant Lennard moved forward with deceptive speed from the rear of the group and slapped a pair of handcuffs onto McKay wrist. The Scotsman reacted with total shock.

"What the...? What's the meaning of this Group Captain? Who is this man? Why have you...?

"I think you know exactly why, Mr McKay", Forbes replied grimly. "Your little game is up I'm pleased to say. Your boss, Douglas Ryan in already in custody, and he's singing like a canary. I thought you were a trusted and loyal member of my staff, and yet all the time you've been leaking secrets to the enemies of this country, you slimy reptile of a man."

If any of the group had expected denials and a struggle from McKay, they were disappointed in their expectations. The traitorous Scotsman simply stood where he was, a look of shock and incomprehension on his face. Clearly, the thought of exposure had never crossed his mind, and now that such an eventuality had come to pass, McKay had no idea whatsoever how to react.

"Well? Have you nothing to say, McKay? You were trusted to take care of the people here in Olney, and instead you've been responsible for the murders of over seventy innocent souls. At least try to deny it, or make some excuse for your traitorous behaviour, why don't you?"

"I have nothing to say to you, Group Captain Forbes. What I did, I did based on my own personal and political beliefs. I wouldn't expect you or any of your decadent friends here to understand my motives. I will say however, that my conscience is clear."

"Clear? You miserable little man!" This was Sir Robert. "You're nothing but a communist spy, an infiltrator and a murderer. D'you think that killing all these people is going to lead to your Russian paymasters handing you a medal of some sort. No, let me tell you McKay, they're going to deny your existence, or ever having heard of you, that's what they're going to do. As for the bomb fragments you've worked so hard to get hold of, they'll never leave this room. Sergeant Lennard, would you be so good as to bring McKay's briefcase to me please?"

Lennard walked around the table in the centre of the room and took the briefcase from the hand of Constable Greaves who'd picked it up as soon as Sir Robert asked for it. Lennard placed it on the table, and Blake asked Forbes to inspect the contents, carefully.

"It's locked, Sir," said Forbes. "Where's the key, McKay?"

McKay simply shrugged in defiance.

"Shall I search him sir?" asked Lennard.

"It's of no great matter, Sergeant. Have you a good strong knife, Constable?"

"I have indeed sir," Greaves replied, and he quickly made his way into the kitchen, returning a few seconds later with a vicious looking carving knife, which he passed into the waiting hand of Donald Forbes.

"Shouldn't you be wearing a mask?" asked Trent as Forbes began to work the knife in the flimsy briefcase lock.

"If there was anything lethal in here, I don't think McKay would be carrying it around without some form of protective wear, Doctor, don't you agree?"

"A good point, Group Captain," Trent agreed.

Despite Forbes's confidence, everyone in the room with the possible exception of McKay held their breath for the next few seconds, until, with an audible snap, the lock on the briefcase gave way under the urging of the knife. Forbes pried the case apart, the well-worn leather creaking as he did so, and the Group Captain leaned over the table to peer inside the cavernous interior. Slowly, his right hand disappeared into the bowels of the case and then, equally slowly it returned to the light, this time holding a piece of plastic sheeting from which he proceeded to pull a thin glass vial containing a small amount of an almost colourless liquid.

"This, gentlemen, is what McKay, Ryan and Grove were after all along," said Forbes triumphantly.

They all stared at the tiny vial. The thoughts of everyone in the room became focussed on the contents, knowing that so many people had died just so that the band of traitors could obtain it and send it to their Russian overlords. Sir Robert Blake was the first to break the silence.

"The Russians wanted that vial very badly," he said. "If they'd got their hands on it, they'd have been light years ahead of us, the Americans, and anyone else in perfecting a biological weapon that not only works, but dissipates in a set time period thus allowing the troops of the aggressor to move in and take control of a sick and dying population. They'd be able to invade and occupy any country of their choice and meet with minimum resistance once the disease got hold. Thanks to you gentlemen, we can be thankful that such a thing will now no longer happen."

"For the time being," said Trent, with a hint of scepticism in his voice. "Just because we've stopped them this time doesn't mean they'll give up trying to produce one of those awful contraptions, and neither will we or the Americans come to that. The world is going mad Sir Robert, and there's little we can do to prevent it. The Russians, the USA, and our own country are making atomic bombs and bigger and faster aircraft and missiles every day. They can even launch their nuclear missiles from submarines, I've heard. It would only take one madman to set the whole world on a course to Armageddon."

"You may be right Doctor Trent, but at least with good men and women on our side we can keep fighting to prevent the madmen from taking over completely, wouldn't you say so?"

Trent nodded, then fell silent as he looked with disgust at the face of Angus McKay, a man whose role in life had ostensibly been to save and promote lives, but whose political ideology had instead driven him to the murder of dozens of innocent people. Madness indeed, thought Paul Trent.

"Shall we be puttin' him in the lock-up with Grove? asked Keith Greaves, ever the policeman, and referring to McKay.

"No, Constable," Blake replied. "Sergeant Lennard and I will be taking Mr or should I say *Doctor* McKay directly back to London with us. Special Branch has a lot of questions waiting for our traitorous friend here. Grove can stay in your lock-up for a day or so, if that's okay with you. He's small fry, and probably can't tell us a lot, but we'll let him stew for a while. Then, the prospect of being hung for murder and treason if he doesn't co-operate should loosen his tongue and he'll at least tell us as much as he knows. I'll get Special Branch to send a car for him the day after tomorrow."

"I'll see to it that he doesn't get too comfortable in there," said Greaves, with a knowing wink.

"And what of the rest of us?" asked Trent.

"Ah, yes," said Blake. "Well, I would ask that you carry on doing what you can for the survivors here in the village for a day or two, until arrangements can be made to provide alternative accommodation for the residents. We'll also have to hold a full debriefing session with all of your medical and military personnel, and of course, I would remind you all that the Official Secrets Act applies to everything you've seen and heard here in Olney St. Mary."

"In other words, we're to keep quiet," said Trent.

"Absolutely, Doctor Trent. Apart from those who already know the truth, I don't want the other residents being given any information that might compromise the security either of the situation in the village, or in regards the greater picture of international diplomacy. Now, Sergeant Lennard, we should be going."

With that, Sir Robert Blake turned and made for the door, Lennard pushing McKay firmly in the back to propel the traitor on his way, behind Sir Robert. As they left the house, Michael Sweeney, and Doctors Newton and Dearborn, who'd waited patiently in the garden, now stepped toward the emerging group. Wilhelm Koenig followed the party from the house at a respectful distance. The German had watched with detached fascination as Forbes had removed the vial from McKay's briefcase. He'd said nothing but had instead allowed his thoughts to stray back to the days when he had been involved in perfecting the viscous liquid containing the altered plague bacillus that Forbes had held aloft for all to see. He'd also recollected his own family, destroyed by the Nazis, and perhaps just as much victims of the plague as those who'd perished in Olney. Now, he wondered what would become of the last, undamaged vial, which he knew to have miraculously survived the crash of the aircraft that had carried its deadly load so far, only to be shot down before it could deliver the plague to its intended target. Strange to think that after over ten years the bacillus had at last been released to perform its deadly work, with more than tragic consequences. Koenig was snatched back to reality and the present by the sound of a raised voice.

"You bastard!" shouted Michael Sweeney, and he stepped forward so quickly that no-one had time to stop him as he landed a heavy punch right on the chin of Angus McKay who crumpled to the floor instantly. "That's for my friends and neighbours, you fucking murdering swine," he screamed at the prone figure of McKay. Only when he pulled his right foot back and prepared to kick the man on the ground did Guy Dearborn suddenly step forward and restrain him by placing both arms around him in a bear hug.

"Leave him Michael, he's not worth it," said Dearborn, and his words at least had the effect of stalling Sweeney in mid-kick, giving time for Sergeant Lennard to pull McKay back and help him up and onto his feet.

Rather than offer Sweeney the verbal reprimand he might have expected for his attack on the prisoner, neither Blake nor Lennard uttered a word of condemnation. Instead Group Captain Forbes smiled at Sweeney before giving the man a short round of applause.

"I think you've just done what was in all our minds, Mr Sweeney. I have to say that you did it rather well. I hope you won't forget that in a hurry, McKay."

Angus McKay simply glared at Forbes. He might have been caught in the act, so to speak, but the man was determined not to betray his emotions or to give his captors the satisfaction of seeing him broken into submission.

"I think you'd better take him away now Sir Robert, if you don't mind," Forbes went on, "before one or two more of us are tempted to repeat Mr Sweeney's actions."

"Yes, I think you're right Group Captain. Let's go, Sergeant."

With that, Lennard bustled the unhappy but defiant Angus McKay into the back of the Bentley, still handcuffed. Sir Robert climbed into the front passenger seat beside the Special Branch detective, and within seconds the car pulled almost silently away from the kerbside. As the sleek black Bentley disappeared from view, a silence hung over the small group of people who'd so recently been involved in so many life and death situations. It was as if, with the departure of the man whose actions had led to such grief and tragedy, there was nothing left for them to do. The field hospital was gone, the patients within it murdered in the flaming conflagration caused by McKay and Grove. Grafton and Wragg would live, but, as with the plague, the survival rate from the explosions had been appallingly low.

There was no further need to search for a source of a plague that had flared up and was now gone, along with those who'd engineered it. All that was left was the still smouldering pyre where the marquee had stood, and the separate, smaller one where the first bomb had destroyed the excavator and taken two more lives.

A small number of survivors from the residents of the village now began to gather on the street, looking towards the pitiful remains of the place where their friends, relatives and neighbours had perished just a short time ago.

Seeing them, Donald Forbes drew himself to his full height, assuming the role of a senior officer of the Royal Air force in all his grandeur and turned and spoke to those who stood beside him.

"I think we still have work to do, Doctors," he pointed at the stunned villagers. "If nothing else, we have a great deal of shock and mental trauma to contend with. I suggest we do what we can for these people, until other help is at hand."

Without a word, Trent, Dearborn, Hilary Newton, and Edith Kinnaird, who had appeared at Dearborn's side walked slowly towards the stunned people of Olney St. Mary. The process of mental and physical healing, of repairing the hearts and minds of Olney St. Mary, began at that very moment, and they all knew it would take a long, long time.

EPILOGUE

WHEN COMPARED WITH THE INTERNET-CONNECTED, FREEDOM of information age in which we now live, it can be hard to imagine the England of a mere sixty-five years ago. In the days before mobile phones and instant television news, the people of the time had a far greater respect for authority and for the edicts of government than they perhaps do today. So it was that in the aftermath of the plague that struck down so many in Olney St. Mary, and the subsequent actions of the soviet agents who did their best to destroy that small part of England in their greed for an advanced weapon technology, many strange events occurred.

Two days after Sir Robert Blake's departure, a police car arrived, with two Special Branch officers aboard to take Leading Aircraftman Grove back to London for questioning. Grove was subsequently incarcerated in Wormwood Scrubs prison to await his trial on charges of espionage. None of the medics looked back as they drove away from the village.

An hour after the car carrying Grove left the village a convoy of Army trucks rolled into Olney St. Mary. The surviving residents, Hilary Newton plus sixteen adults and five children were taken from their homes and transported to a disused army base near

Dover, where they were informed that they would be temporarily housed until they could return to their homes. They were surprised the following day, to receive a personal visit from the Prime Minister himself, who assured them that they would be looked after by the authorities, but that a return to their village was impossible for the foreseeable future. They were even more surprised when he informed them that they would each be given the magnificent sum of five thousand pounds each, a fortune in 1958, with which to help rebuild their lives and businesses. The only condition attached, they were informed, was that they must each sign the Official Secrets Act and agree never to divulge the truth of what had taken place in Olney St. Mary. The official story would be that a gas main had exploded in the centre of the village, setting off an unexploded German incendiary bomb that had lain undiscovered from the war years, and that the village had been all but destroyed in the ensuing firestorm, which had claimed the lives of most of the residents of the village. When some expressed the belief that the story would be sneered at in some quarters, the Prime Minister assured them that no-one would doubt the story as a news blackout had been imposed on the subject and a 'D' notice issued to the press, which effectively prevented them from reporting on the case. In short there would be no-one to question the official version of events. Faced with a request from the Prime Minister for their silence and co-operation, the people of Olney felt it their patriotic duty to do as they were asked and agreed to go along with the official version of events. Personal belongings were collected by the army and sent to the families at the transit camp. None of them saw their homes again.

The government arranged for a very private requiem service to be held in remembrance of those who'd died, in a small church on the outskirts of Ashford, and the service was carried out by Timothy Grafton upon his recovery, attended by the surviving residents and medical staff, plus invited family and friends from around the country, none of whom of course, ever learned the true cause of the deaths of those who'd perished. Grafton studiously avoided all allusions to the plague and the Soviet spies in his service.

Sam Bradley soon built a new business, and eventually his car showroom in Folkestone became a chain of six dealerships, and he prospered until his death in nineteen ninety-nine, dying quietly in his bed with his wife by his side. Emily still lives in the house they shared in the seaside town, and their daughter Carol runs the family business. Keith Greaves was surprised to be promoted to the rank of sergeant soon after the events in Olney, and he and Tilly soon moved into their new home in the village of Ashburnham. Tilly remarked that it was very much like Olney St. Mary.

"I bloody well hope not!" joked Greaves, and the pair collapsed into nervous laughter. It was the first time either of them had laughed since Olney had burned, and they felt guilty for doing so. In truth, the new village was much larger, and with two constables working under his instructions, Greaves found a new lease of life, eventually retiring and living to a ripe old age. He died on the eve of the millennium at the age of eighty-eight. Tilly Greaves still lives in the village, in a cottage not unlike that once lived in by Mabel Thorndyke in Olney St. Mary many years before.

Simon and Ellen Parkes left Britain altogether, heading for the open spaces of New Zealand, where he became a successful sheep farmer. As for the Reverend Timothy Grafton, he was appointed to a new ministry soon afterwards, and was last heard of working as a Christian missionary in the Amazon rainforest, working with the local tribespeople. Perhaps most surprisingly, he was joined on his departure from England by his friend Billy Wragg, who had found God after his experiences in Olney, and subsequently followed the man who'd pulled him from the flames to help him in his work.

Of the medical staff who'd been involved in the events in Olney, Paul Trent returned to Ashford, where he eventually took over the role of his retiring boss, Malcolm Davidson. Hilary Newton found a new post as a general practitioner with a joint practice in the East End of London, where she married one of her partners and now lives in retirement.

Perhaps predictably, Guy Dearborn married his beautiful Edith, and became a senior consultant at the appropriately named Guys hospital in London. Edith gave up nursing to look after the three children their marriage produced. They are now proud grandparents.

Group Captain Donald Forbes left Porton Down two years later and rose to the rank of Air Commodore before retiring and living out the remainder of his life in the United States with his sister and her husband in Utah. Wilhelm Koenig was rewarded for his efforts in Olney by being appointed to the role vacated by Douglas Ryan, and despite his German nationality he became as English as it was possible to be, eventually becoming a naturalised citizen of the UK. Charles Macklin continued as his deputy until his death in a car accident five years later.

As for the traitorous trio, at a trial held in camera, behind closed doors with no public or press presence, Douglas Ryan and Angus McKay were both sentenced to life imprisonment for the crimes of murder, treason and conspiracy to cause explosions. The death sentence wasn't considered as it would have been impossible to keep the executions secret, and the government wanted to avoid a scandal. Too much would have had to be revealed in order to justify such a sentence. Both men died behind bars, but not before Ryan identified his contact at the Russian embassy, code name 'Uncle' real name Boris Petrov. Petrov was subsequently 'invited' to leave the country by the security serves, and left immediately, though in the cold war years, the intelligence community knew that he would be instantly replaced by another KGB controller. No one fooled themselves that the war against soviet espionage was won, despite this one victory. Soon after the trial Ryan's wife was known to have boarded an Aeroflot flight to Moscow. She never set foot in the United Kingdom again.

Martin Grove, under 'intense' questioning by Special Branch interrogators, confessed to killing his fellow airman, LAC Bennet when the other man discovered the wires that led from Grove's detonation device to the bomb which he'd earlier placed strategically beneath the rubble beside the playground. Bennet had innocently called Grove over to investigate his find, and Grove had battered the man to death with a large rock which he'd picked up on his way to join his comrade. Grove then detonated the bomb, removed all traces of the detonator, and, with everyone's attention focussed on the aftermath of the first explosion, he'd dragged the body into the garden of old Mabel Thorndyke's cottage, broken in through the back door and left the body there for future disposal. When the field hospital bombs were set off, again by Grove, he returned to the cottage and was in the act of removing and burying the body when Sweeney discovered him in the act. In return for his co-operation in testifying against his communist confederates, he was spared the death sentence, and received a twenty year jail term, and, on his release he found it impossible to find work and ended his days as a vagrant on the streets of London, eventually being found dead one morning under the railway arches near Paddington station.

Olney St. Mary no longer exists. In a move that might have won the approval of Douglas Ryan, the Prime Minister ordered the village to be demolished in the wake of the events that had taken place there. He didn't want to take a chance that more vials of plague bacillus might lie somewhere beneath the ground and hurriedly approved plans for a new regional airport to be built on the site of the village. What was once a thriving village now lies under thousands of tons of concrete and modern-day travellers who arrive and depart from St Mary's airport have little or no clue as to the existence of the village which once stood there.

And what of the hero of Olney St. Mary? By popular consent it was agreed to award that title to Michael Sweeney. His efforts over the days from the first signs of the plague, to the apprehension of the murderous airman, Grove, and his subsequent punch to the face of McKay had become legend among the survivors. As always, Sweeney shunned the limelight, and despite receiving a citation for bravery from the Prime Minister, couched in terms applicable to the official version of events, the local undertaker and former war hero quickly vanished from sight. He was once spotted some years later, by Hilary Newton, working as a humble gravedigger at a London cemetery, and she spent a few minutes conversing with him, but when she next visited the place, Sweeney was gone. Months later, she learned that he'd died of lung cancer, and his grave now stands in the very graveyard where she last saw him alive. In memory of a brave man, and in remembrance of those he saved, Hilary Newton places fresh flowers on the grave every Sunday.

Though the village he called home is long gone and forgotten, Michael Sweeney, at least, is remembered.

———

POSTSCRIPT

The vial of the altered plague bacillus discovered in Angus McKay's briefcase was taken back to London by Sergeant Lennard of Special Branch in the Bentley along with Sir Robert Blake and the handcuffed McKay. From the headquarters of the Metropolitan Police, it was taken under guard to a waiting Royal

Air Force transport aircraft and flown under heavy guard to an airfield on the west coast of Scotland. From there it was flown by helicopter to the Research facility on the island of Magavin, where, even today, tests on the bacillus continue to be carried out by Ministry of Defence scientists...

Dear reader,

We hope you enjoyed reading *Pestilence*. Please take a moment to leave a review, even if it's a short one. Your opinion is important to us.

Discover more books by Brian L Porter at

https://www.nextchapter.pub/authors/brian-porter-mystery-author-liverpool-united-kingdom

Want to know when one of our books is free or discounted? Join the newsletter at

http://eepurl.com/bqqB3H

Best regards,

Brian L Porter and the Next Chapter Team

Brian L Porter is an award-winning author, and dog rescuer whose books have also regularly topped the Amazon Best Selling charts, twenty-two of which have to date been Amazon bestsellers. The third book in his Mersey Mystery series, *A Mersey Maiden* was voted The Best Book We've Read All Year, 2018, by the organisers and readers of Readfree.ly.

Last Train to Lime Street was voted Top Crime novel in the Top 50 Best Indie Books, 2018. *A Mersey Mariner* was voted the Top Crime Novel in the Top 50 Best Indie Books, 2017 awards, and *The Mersey Monastery Murders* was also the Top Crime Novel in the Top 50 Best Indie Books, 2019 Awards Meanwhile *Sasha, Sheba: From Hell to Happiness, Cassie's Tale* and *Remembering Dexter* have all won Best Nonfiction awards. Writing as Brian, he has won a Best Author Award, a Poet of the Year Award, and his thrillers have picked up Best Thriller and Best Mystery Awards.

His short story collection *After Armageddon* is an international bestseller and his moving collection of remembrance poetry, *Lest We Forget*, is also an Amazon best seller.

Writing as Harry Porter his three children's books *Wolf, Alistair the Alligator and Charlie the Caterpillar* are all Amazon bestsellers, as is his book of romantic poetry, *Of Aztecs and Conquistadors*, written under his pseudonym, Juan Pablo Jalisco.

Rescue Dogs are Bestsellers!

In a recent departure from his usual thriller writing, Brian has written six bestselling books about the family of rescued dogs who share his home, with more to follow.

Sasha, A Very Special Dog Tale of a Very Special Epi-Dog is now an international #1 bestseller and winner of the Preditors & Editors Best Nonfiction Book, 2016, and was placed 7th in The Best Indie Books of 2016, and *Sheba: From Hell to Happiness* is also now an international #1 bestseller, and award winner as detailed above. Released in 2018, *Cassie's Tale* instantly became the best-selling new release in its category on Amazon in the USA, and subsequently a #1 bestseller in the UK. Most recently the fourth book in the series, *Penny the Railway Pup*, has topped the bestseller charts in the UK and USA. The fifth book in the series, *Remembering Dexter* won the Readfree.ly Best Book of the Year 2019. The most recent addition to the series is *Dylan the Flying Bedlington*

If you love dogs, you'll love these six illustrated offerings which will soon be followed by book 7 in the series, *Muffin, Digby, and Petal, Together Forever*

Writing as Harry Porter his children's books have achieved three bestselling rankings on Amazon in the USA and UK.

In addition, his third incarnation as romantic poet Juan Pablo Jalisco has brought international recognition with his collected works, *Of Aztecs and Conquistadors* topping the bestselling charts in the USA, UK, and Canada.

Many of his books are now available in audio book editions and various translations are available.

Brian lives with his wife, children, and a wonderful pack of ten rescued dogs.

His blog is at https://sashaandharry.blogspot.co.uk/

FROM INTERNATIONAL BESTSELLING AUTHOR BRIAN L PORTER

The Mersey Mysteries
A Mersey Killing
All Saints, Murder on the Mersey
A Mersey Maiden
A Mersey Mariner
A Very Mersey Murder
Last Train to Lime Street
The Mersey Monastery Murders

Thrillers by Brian L Porter
A Study in Red - The Secret Journal of Jack the Ripper
Legacy of the Ripper
Requiem for the Ripper
Pestilence
Purple Death
Behind Closed Doors
Avenue of the Dead
The Nemesis Cell
Kiss of Life

Dog Rescue (Family of Rescue Dogs)
Sasha
Sheba: From Hell to Happiness
Cassie's Tale
Penny the Railway Pup
Remembering Dexter
Dylan the Flying Bedlington
Short Story Collection
After Armageddon

Remembrance Poetry
Lest We Forget

Children's books as Harry Porter
Wolf
Alistair the Alligator, (Illustrated by Sharon Lewis)
Charlie the Caterpillar (Illustrated by Bonnie Pelton)

As Juan Pablo Jalisco
Of Aztecs and Conquistadors

Many of Brian's books have also been released in translated versions, in Spanish, Italian and Portuguese editions.

Pestilence
ISBN: 978-4-86745-978-2

Published by
Next Chapter
1-60-20 Minami-Otsuka
170-0005 Toshima-Ku, Tokyo
+818035793528

24th April 2021

CPSIA information can be obtained
at www.ICGtesting.com
Printed in the USA
BVHW031128040521
606415BV00002B/289

9 784867 459782